A CRY FOR JUSTICE

A SOPHIE STAR SERIES BOOK FIVE

L. J. WEBB

A CRY FOR JUSTICE
A Sophie Star Series Book Five
BY L. J. WEBB

Copyright © 2023 by Linda J Webb
Published by L. J. Webb
Longview, WA

Cover by Adebayo S. Oluwatosin

eBook ISBN 979-8-9888416-0-9
Paperback ISBN 979-8-9888416-1-6
Library of Congress Control Number: 2023914422

TABLE OF CONTENTS

Let your light so shine before men, that they
may see your good works and glorify your
Father in heaven.

Matt. 5:16

CHAPTER ONE

Henderson, Nevada

My name is Teresa, and this is the worst day of my life. I thought the day mama left us was the worst, but now I know it was just a blip on the radar compared to this.

After mama delivered my little brother, Kato, she changed. The happy person I knew was gone. The one who hugged me at least ten times a day disappeared. Papa called it Postpartum Depression. I didn't care what they called it. I just wanted her back. The days of helping her make pancakes for breakfast, and tucking me in at night, were no more. At six years old, those things mattered. Now nothing matters.

I blamed my little brother for a while, but that was when I was six. As I got older, I realized mama was sick. Papa worked hard to keep the diner going without his wife and partner. I heard him on the phone borrowing money to hire a nurse/nanny to take care of us.

Papa took mama to the doctor, who gave her medication for depression. But the drug made her psychotic, so they added an antipsychotic medication. That medication made her sit in a chair, staring out the window like a zombie. Then they gave her another medicine to counter the side effects of the other one, and so on and so on. Six months later, she ended up hospitalized in a mental institution. I realize I'm no doctor and I know medicine helps lots of people. But I wondered if it would have been better to take her off all the medication and see if she could come out of it on her own.

Papa's only kitchen helper was a man hired to help him cook when mama got sick. His name was Bently. I always thought that name made him sound rich. He wasn't rich, not in money, but he was rich in character. His only other employee was a waitress who also bused the tables and washed the dishes.

Three months later, mama left the mental institution when no one was looking and disappeared. Kato was nine months old, and I would be seven in two months. Papa would get off work and search for her all night, then go to work and do the same thing again. If he got any sleep, it was only a few hours. Predictably, he had a breakdown. Papa, the strongest man I ever knew, went to bed one day and didn't get up again for a week. If Bently hadn't one-handedly run the kitchen, my papa would have lost the diner.

One Sunday morning, Bently walked into our house. The only day the diner was closed and went straight to papa's bedroom. He opened the blinds, pulled the covers off him, and insisted he shower. We were going to church.

I knew Papa believed in God. I heard my folks talk about starting us in Sunday School, but they were always too busy.

It was a small church. One you would see on 'Little House on the Prairie." White, with a steeple. We sat on a pew not far from the platform. The music was great, and Kato stood on the bench, clapped his hands, and moved his feet. It made papa laugh. The first time he'd laughed in months.

The music ended, and the preacher told the story of a man named Jesus. Jesus came from a place called heaven to die for our sins. I had no idea what he was talking about, but papa seemed to get it. The preacher asked if there was anyone who wanted to

2

make Jesus their Savior to come forward. Papa stood, and Bently walked down to the altar with him. Papa got down on his knees and wept. Other men from the church moved around him and prayed with him.

Papa was different after that. He was happy again, and he did his best to do the things for us mama used to do, like read to us at night and tuck us in. I remember waking up one night to go to the bathroom and heard papa talking to someone. His bedroom door wasn't shut all the way, and I saw him on his knees praying for mama and us. But it didn't sound like a prayer. It sounded like he was talking to his papa.

All of that, we survived, and when I turned twelve, papa let me work in the diner. I bused tables and worked the commercial dishwasher. Last year when I turned fourteen, he let me wait on tables during the summer so I could earn tips. I liked working the tables and enjoyed talking to the customers; it was fun.

All that is gone now, as I kneel beside my father, lying on the diner's floor. His blood pouring out of a hole in his chest, saturating my jeans, Kato next to me wailing. With his last breaths, papa told me to take the money and the metal box with his important papers and run. I told him I was going to call 911. But he said it again louder when I didn't move.

"Run!"

It was the last word he'd ever say. I kissed his forehead, and I did what he said, dragging Kato, screaming behind me. I almost slipped on papa's blood, but I caught myself.

I took the money out of the till and then headed to papa's office to get the cash he kept to pay the suppliers who preferred cash. I saw papa's wallet and took out the ATM card, then unhooked his laptop and took it with me. His laptop stored the security footage from the cameras around the diner. It had proof on it of who killed papa. One day I will come back to get justice for my father. But not today. Today I will do what my papa told me to do; *run*. I ran out the back door to our double-wide trailer behind the diner.

"Kato, please stop crying. I need you to change out of those clothes and put on three layers of everything. Hurry."

"But papa..." Kato whispered.

I knelt down and hugged him. "I know, Kato, but papa is gone, and he told us to run. We have to do what papa said."

I quickly changed, took my long, thick, black hair, put it in a pigtail, and stuffed it under my hat. Then I layered my clothes too. I took the duffle papa gave me for my overnight stays with my friends and stuffed in more clothes, the money, the laptop, one of my jackets, and one of Kato's. I ran to papa's room, grabbed the small metal box, and stuffed it in the duffle too.

I went into Kato's room; he was sitting on his bed. "Did you take everything you wanted?"

Kato nodded, "but this won't fit." He lifted the mitt and ball he used to play catch with papa.

"I'll put it in my bag." As we headed out of the house, I looked around for anything else we might want. I spotted some framed pictures of the family, one with mama and one without her. I shoved it in the bag and headed to the refrigerator. I grabbed a plastic shopping bag and took all the juice boxes and three bottles of water. Then I went to the cupboard to get bread, peanut butter, jelly, a knife, and napkins.

"Cookies, Teresa," Kato said. I grabbed them and papa's flashlight that was on the counter and put them in my backpack.

Grabbing the duffle in one hand and Kato's hand in the other, we headed for the door.

I couldn't help looking around one more time, knowing I would likely never see my home again. I turned out the lights and locked the door as we stepped onto the porch.

I tried to hurry Kato, but he walked like the Michelin Man. The layers of clothes were hindering him from walking right. I had no idea where to go. I watched enough crime dramas with papa after Kato went to sleep to know we couldn't take a bus or a train. When papa told us to run, he knew the man who killed him would be coming back for us. We couldn't leave a trail. There was an ATM by the 24-hour truck stop a mile down the road. I pulled Kato's ballcap down low, did the same to mine, and kept my eyes on the ground. We walked the alleys instead of the sidewalk to avoid the cameras. I noticed a public phone near the ATM, the only one left in town as far as I knew. I decided to disguise my voice as best I could and call the police.

"911. What is your emergency?"

"I heard shots at Rio's Diner on Clementine, the freeway access road."

"You heard shots?"

"Yes."

"How many?"

"Three."

"Your name?"

I hung up, hoping they were required to respond to all emergency calls.

I didn't want the ATM camera to get a good shot of me. I pulled my cap down lower. I checked the balance first. There was $3823 in there to cover the diner's bills. I tried to withdraw two thousand, but it denied the request saying the limit was one thousand. I took the thousand, and we walked to a truck stop around the corner.

"Where are we going, Teresa?" Kato asked.

"I don't know yet. But we need a ride." I looked around and saw a nice pickup with a canopy on the back. An older man was backing it into a parking space between two eighteen-wheelers. The older gentlemen got out and headed to the restaurant. I took Kato's hand, and we walked behind the large rigs stopping at the pickup.

Please be unlocked. I turned the handle on the canopy, and it opened.

"Ok, we will ride back here until he finds us, or we decide to get out. We'll have to be quiet. Ok?"

"Ok, but I have to go to the bathroom."

I told him he'd have to go in the bushes behind the truck, but he had too many layers to undo. I opened the tailgate and lifted him onto it. I took off his shoes first and two of the three pairs of blue jeans and put his shoes back on. I stuffed his pants in my backpack while he went to the bathroom. When he finished, we got in the back of the pickup and settled in, closing the tailgate and canopy.

The back of the pickup was clean and empty except for a small suitcase, a suit, and three dress shirts hanging on a hook covered in plastic. The sun had heated the bed of the pickup. There was a push out window on each side of the canopy. I opened the one on the passenger's side so the man wouldn't notice when he got in. I only pushed it out a half inch, but it helped. I told Kato to remove the extra shirts and did the same with my extra shirts and pants. I rearranged Kato's duffle and was able to roll up the extra clothes and put them in there.

I heard the car beep; the man was coming back to the pickup.

"Lay flat, Kato, and be quiet until we get on the road, ok?" Kato nodded and laid his head on my lap. I laid my head on the duffle.

We sat in his blind spot, right behind the driver's seat. He was listening to music, so we were able to whisper. Kato started to cry again.

"Why would someone kill papa?" he asked. I pulled him closer and held him.

"I don't know, Kato. But don't worry; I will take good care of you." I was glad Kato hadn't seen what happened. He was in the office watching cartoons when he heard the shots. The man was gone by the time he came out. I stayed strong until Kato fell asleep, then I covered my mouth with my forearm and screamed into it. I screamed for my loss and the injustice of it. But I knew one day I would return and settle up. Once Kato was safe and stable. I would be back.

Burly Blackrock left the Coleville Indian Reservation in Okanogan County, Washington State. He moved to Issaquah, where he bought five acres outside of town. He used the money he saved from the stipend the government gave each registered Indian each year.

Burly hired on as an independent contractor falling timber, earning a good living. He lived in a small travel trailer on the property. The first thing he did was have a well drilled. Then he put in the septic system himself, one big enough to support the home he planned on building.

After a long run of no injuries on the job, Burly's 36" chain on his Husqvarna kicked back when it hit a knot in an old-growth tree. The chain hit his thigh and gave him a severe injury taking out a huge chunk of his muscle. The other fellers called for a Life Flight, and he was taken to the Seattle University Hospital.

A beautiful young nurse named Lisa Miranda was taking his vitals. She cut the pant leg to expose the wound and was preparing things for the ER doctor who would come to examine him. She saw he was in a great deal of pain and asked the doctor if she could put pain medication in his IV.

The doctor took off the bandage the EMTs applied to try to stop the bleeding. He cleaned up the wound first, then bandaged it and asked the nurse to call for a surgeon and an X-ray to see the full extent of the damage.

The nurse made the call and sat with Burly until an orderly came and took him to an operating room. The surgeon had come in an told him he needed to try to repair as much of the damage as he could but that the chunk of muscle the men sent with the EMTs was not salvageable. He would have a dent in his leg.

The next three weeks, Lisa drove to Issaquah to bring Burly food and change his bandage. Six months later, they married in a private church ceremony, and one year later, their only child, a son, was born.

After the accident, Burly quit the woods and went to college. He paid for it with the money he received from a settlement from the Employment Security Division and his private contractor's insurance settlement. With Lisa's input, he decided to become a lawyer.

For forty-five years, they lived happily. When Burly turned sixty-five, he thought it was time to retire. Lisa continued to work at the hospital until she got ill.

Ten years earlier, a chemical spill caused by a train derailment had the city call out all available nurses and doctors to come to the scene. The ones not working the train wreckage, were sent door to door to evacuate the residents in the surrounding area. They needed to be examined to be sure they had no symptoms from the chemicals, before leaving the site. They wore full body protection as they went door to door to evacuate the houses.

Lisa came to a home not far from the spill. She knocked on the door, but no one answered. Lisa looked through the window and saw a mother and child lying on the floor. She forced her way into the house and called for an ambulance.

Lisa put the one extra respirator she had brought with her on the young boy. But the mother was gasping like she couldn't get enough air. She didn't think the woman would make it until the ambulance came, so she removed her oxygen face mask and put it on the woman.

Over the next ten years, the chemicals Lisa inhaled that day caused lung damage, giving her life-threatening asthma. The northwest's damp weather, pollen, and moss became deadly. The doctor suggested they move to a warmer climate.

Lisa retired, eligible for her full pension. They had enough money to live comfortably somewhere in dry weather.

After a lot of research, they decided on Henderson, Nevada. They said goodbye to their son, who didn't want to leave his good-paying job at Boeing and rented a U-Haul. They loaded the things they didn't want to leave behind and hooked it up to their new F150.

Five years later, the love of Burly's life died. He had no reason to live except to keep his promise to Lisa. For months he grieved; he barely left his home, though his friends encouraged him to. Finally, Burly's pastor came to see him and reminded him that this wasn't what Lisa wanted for him.

Burly decided to go back to work to have something to do. He opened a small practice and only took the cases he wanted. He didn't need the money, but it would keep his mind off his loss.

Burly only took on criminal cases when he felt the defendant was innocent, cases other attorneys said were unwinnable. His acquittal rate gained him national attention and recognition. Law schools started calling, asking him to speak about his cases.

Burly decided to accept the invitations to speak. He accepted six engagements a year and arranged them so that he did them all in ten days. For the past three years, Burly would get into his F150 and traipsed across the southwest. He was doing just that when Teresa and Kato snuck into the back of his truck.

Burly only stopped for gas once on the way to his first stop in Albuquerque, New Mexico. It was 11:30 pm when he parked in a shopping mall's parking lot. He laid his seat back, choosing not to pay for a hotel room, and closed his eyes.

Albuquerque, New Mexico

Kato and I had fallen asleep long before the truck stopped, exhausted from crying. I was startled awake when the latch on the canopy popped open, and the sun blinded me. I wasn't the only one with a shocked expression. The older man jumped back when he saw two hitchhikers under his canopy.

"Mister, please, we didn't hurt anything. We just needed a ride." The words rushed out of my mouth before the man could say anything. My eyes adjusted to the sun, but I couldn't see his face, only his silhouette. The sun was behind him. Kato woke up, hearing a man's voice. Thinking they were in trouble; he began to cry.

"Hey, it's all right. You just startled me," Burly said. "What are you doing here?"

"We needed a ride. But we'll get out now. You don't have to call the police or anything," I said as we gathered our things.

"Where are you heading?" He asked. I knew the man could tell we didn't have a destination when I hesitated. He knew we were running from something or someone.

"Look, if you're running away from home. You need to call your folks. They must be worried sick."

"We don't got no folks," Kato blurted between sobs.

"Hey, kid, it's all right. Calm down," the man watched as I wrapped my arms around Kato.

"Look, I need to change and clean up in the public bathroom there," the man pointed to the mall. "I'm giving a lecture at the University down the road. You guys can come with me and wait in the truck. When I'm finished, I'll buy you breakfast. Then we can decide what to do from there."

"You won't call the police on us?" I asked.

"No. You have my word on it. But you can't ride in the back. You need to sit up front. By the way, my name is Burly Blackstone."

"I'm Teresa, and this is my brother Kato."

"No last names?" Burly asked. I just shrugged my shoulders. "Can we bring our stuff up front with us?"

"It's safe back here."

"I know. I just want it close," I said.

Burly helped us carry our things to the cab.

Two hours later, Burly pulled the truck into a parking space at Denny's Restaurant.

After the waitress took our order, Kato said he needed to use the bathroom. Burly pointed to the sign, and Kato walked off.

"Teresa, what's going on? Why are you running?"

"It was the last thing my papa said before he died," I tried to hold back the tears.

"Your father is dead? Are you illegals?"

"No. My mama and papa were citizens."

"Where is your mother?"

"She disappeared years ago."

"I'm sorry to hear that, but you can't just take off with a little brother. How will you live?"

"I don't know, but when papa said run, we ran."

"You said he died. How?

"Someone shot him," my voice trembled, remembering seeing the man shoot my papa.

The conversation ended when Kato returned, and the waitress brought our food.

After we ate, we returned to the pickup, and Burly said, "look, you can travel with me to Austin, Texas. That is my last stop; then, I head back to Henderson. We can talk about how to handle this while on the road."

CHAPTER TWO

The F150 drove through Arizona, New Mexico, and Texas, as Mr. Burly made five more stops. We stayed in motels while Mr. Burly did his lectures. Kato swam in the pools while I watched him. When we were fifty miles from Austin, he started questioning me.

"What are your plans, Teresa? I can't just let you out on the streets of Austin and drive away."

"I have a plan," I lied.

"What plan? If you don't have your social security cards, you can't get work, and Kato can't go to school. Where will you live? You can tell people you're eighteen, but no one will believe you."

"I have enough money to get a small apartment. I'll get a job. Kato can homeschool."

"Teresa, who is going to rent to you?"

"I don't have any other choice."

"You do. Why don't you come back to Henderson and live with me? I won't turn you in. I can say you are my brother's children. That way, you can go to school."

Kato heard the conversation and scooted up on the bench seat behind them, poking his head between their seats. "Please, sis, I like my school back home. I have friends there."

"Let me think about it." I knew we couldn't go back. I know the man who shot my papa and saw him do it. Eventually, he will come looking for me. The man panicked after he shot papa and ran out, but when he gets his wits about him again, he will realize I saw him.

They arrived in Austin just before it was time for him to speak. I waited for him to get out of sight and opened the door.

"Come on, Kato, we have to get out of here before he returns."

Kato looked at me, "what? Why? Mr. Burly said we could live with him. I want to go back home. He is a nice man."

"He is, Kato, but papa told us to run because he knew the man who killed him would come back and look for us."

Kato started crying, so I opened the back door and slid beside him. I wrapped my arms around him and kissed his cheek like mama used to do to me before she got sick.

"Please, sis. Can we go back?"

"I'm sorry, we can't. Now come on. Get your stuff."

Austin, Texas.

We wandered. I had no idea where to go or what to do. I saw a park with play equipment. I needed time to think, so I let Kato play until it got dark. The first thing I needed to do was find someplace to stay the night. I picked a direction and started walking like I knew where I was going, so Kato wouldn't be afraid.

It was getting darker and darker, and the traffic and people on the street started to thin out. We were in the downtown commercial area. I didn't see any houses. We went down an alley and I spotted a bench, next to a commercial metal garbage container. There were two floodlights on the building. The one over the bench was out.

"I'm tired. I want to go to sleep," Kato stopped in his tracks. I pulled his arm and pointed to the bench.

"Look, we'll sleep there for the night, then in the morning, we'll find a place to live."

"You want us to sleep out here?"

"Use your backpack as a pillow and lie down. I'll sit up and watch out for you." I decided to keep my backpack on and lean against it and put my duffle under my thigh. That way, if I fell asleep and someone tried to steal our stuff, it would wake me up.

Kato fell asleep right away. I tried to stay awake, but I must have dozed off because I was startled awake by someone trying to take my duffle. I stood up and pushed him away, yelling, "get away from me, or I'll scream."

"Hey, I don't want to hurt you. I just want your money, kid." The big man reached for my duffle again. Kato was awake now and yelling at the man to get away from us.

This time I screamed at him, "get away from me!!!" and pushed him again. I could smell the alcohol on him and knew he was drunk and probably homeless. He wanted my money for another bottle, but there was no way I was giving up our stuff.

Sienna had to get up early in the morning; it was her turn to start the bakery's ovens downstairs. She and her partner took turns starting the ovens and getting the morning's baked goods started. Even after a year, waking up at three o'clock was hard.

Sienna looked at the clock and counted the hours until she had to get up. *Lord, please let me fall asleep right away.*

Sienna sat straight up in her bed, thinking she had a bad dream, but she heard the scream again. She ran to the bedroom window that opened to the alley. She saw a young girl fighting off the homeless man who lived in an abandoned building not far from her store.

Sienna grabbed a robe and slipped on shoes as she ran down the stairs. She slammed through the back emergency exit door downstairs.

As I kept trying to push the drunk man away from us, a woman came charging out of the building.

"German, get away from her," the woman yelled.

German twirled around, almost falling. "I just wanted enough money for a bottle. I wasn't going to hurt her."

"German, you will never get another meal from me if you don't get out of here. And don't you ever bother someone sitting on my bench again."

The man stumbled away out of sight. The woman turned to see us staring at her.

"What are you doing out here alone?"

"We'll go. We didn't mean to cause you any trouble," I said.

"No, you're coming upstairs with me. You can't be out here alone at night." The woman punched in the security code that opened the door and held it for us, not allowing for an argument.

Henderson, Nevada. Afternoon of the murder.

Captain Christian Desmond, head of the Internal Affairs Division of the Henderson Police Department, stood in the doorway of Deputy Chief Anthony Edwards. Because a police officer was shot, Internal Affairs was involved.

A CRY FOR JUSTICE

Deputy Chief Edwards was a severe-looking man with dark skin and a bald head. The captain wondered if he ever smiled. He was on the phone listening to someone on the other end. When he saw the captain, he ended the call, leaned back on his office chair, tilted it back, and looked at him.

"Come in and close the door, Captain. Please tell me we didn't get one of our own killed on this undercover."

The captain closed the door and sat down. The Deputy Chief's office was large. The only office at headquarters bigger was occupied by the Chief of Police. Edwards remodeled the office, removing the old wood paneling and installing drywall. The pale green color he chose accentuated the color of the new carpet. One wall was covered in walnut bookcases. The wall across from it had an original painting of a stormy sea. He had no idea who the artist was, but it fit the deputy chief's personality.

"We don't know yet, sir. Dispatch got a call that shots were fired at Rio's Diner on Clementine; officers were dispatched. When they arrived, Detective third class Morry Cox and the owner, Rio Nuñez, were dead."

Deputy Chief Edwards ran his hand down his face. "What do we know? Is Detective Gilbert involved?"

"The information Cox gave me at our last meeting was that Gilbert and Cox went to Rio's Diner every day at closing time. The owner would let them in, lock up, and feed them while he did his closing routine."

"A gratuity?" Edwards asked.

"No, they paid."

"Good. Go on."

"Detective Gilbert was nowhere to be found when the officers showed up. He was asked where he was. He said he got a text from a CI that he needed to see him immediately, so he left his partner at the diner.

"Convenient. We need the name of the CI. You have someone you trust on it?" The deputy chief asked.

"I do. But why do you suspect Gilbert, sir?"

"I don't believe in coincidence. His partner gets shot, and he was nowhere to be found?" Edwards responded.

The captain's phone rang. "Detective Willis, what new information do you have?"

"Two missing children, sir," Willis said. The captain put his phone on speaker.

"What kids?"

"When we searched the house, we discovered that Nuñez has two children. A girl fourteen and a boy seven, sir. We've been searching for them."

"Maybe they're with their mother."

"Should I put out an amber alert? Willis asked. Deputy Chief Edwards shook his head. Desmond furrowed his eyebrows, questioning the decision.

"No, look for the mother."

"Yes, sir," Detective Wills responded and hung up.

Desmond questioned Edwards' order. "Sir, we need to put out an Amber Alert."

"No, if they saw the shooting, they probably ran. They are better off in hiding. If Gilbert finds them, he might kill them."

"Sir, that's a leap. I have never heard anyone say that Gilbert is the type of man who would shoot children."

"Did you think he was the kind of man to kill his partner?"

"No, sir. But we have no proof that he did."

"Not yet."

"Then how do we know Gilbert didn't kidnap them?" Desmond asked.

"Maybe he did, or maybe he's already killed them. If we put out an Amber Alert, the FBI would get involved. We need to clean up this mess on our own. If the children ran, they would be better off for the time being. No, we look for the kids quietly. If

Gilbert did kill Cox and the owner of Rio's Diner, then he will figure out that one or both of the children saw him. We have to get to them first."

The captain never understood why the deputy chief had put a man undercover on Gilbert. Edwards never gave him an explanation.

Christian stood to go back to work. He had been to the Deputy Chief's office before, so he didn't do a double take this time when the man stood up. Edwards was a formidable man, and no one questioned his authority or reputation as a man who saw everything as black or white. But when he stood, he was barely five feet five inches, a good eight inches shorter than the captain. Though short, he was muscular and fit.

The chief came around, walked him to the door, and told him he needed to get surveillance on Gilbert immediately.

Austin, Texas.

"My name is Siena Pierce; I own the bakery downstairs. I'd like to know your names."

"My name is Teresa, and this is my brother Kato."

"Please sit and explain why two minor children are sleeping on the street?" Sienna directed the question to Teresa.

"We arrived in Austin this afternoon and were supposed to go to our aunt's home, but we got lost. I don't have a cell, so I couldn't call her. We figured we would sleep on the bench and then go to a store in the morning and ask to use the phone."

I knew the woman didn't buy it for a second but played along. "Alright, for tonight, why don't you sleep here, and in the morning, you can use my phone to call your aunt. But you are not to leave until she arrives to pick you up. Understood?"

I nodded.

"There is a queen bed in one bedroom and a Murphy bed in my office. You are welcome to use one or both."

Kato looked at me, unsure. "I think we'll stay together if that's alright."

"Of course. I have to start baking in," she looked at the clock in the kitchen, "a half hour. Sleep as long as you like. You can come down for breakfast or make your own up here. But before you leave, I want to speak with your aunt."

"Ok, no problem," I said.

Sienna led us to the bedroom and said goodnight.

Sienna's night was over; she needed to shower, get downstairs, and turn on the ovens. After locking the doors and setting the alarm, Sienna headed to her master bath. As she passed the second bedroom, she heard Kato crying.

"I want papa to come back," he sobbed.

"I do too, Kato, but he's gone. We'll be ok. I'll take care of you."

"But we just left papa on the floor; maybe he wasn't dead."

"He was, I know for sure. He's in heaven. You remember the preacher talking about heaven, right?"

"Yeah, he said when you die, you go there, and it's a beautiful place."

"That's right, and papa is waiting there for us. We will see him again someday," I held Kato close until he stopped crying. "Now you need to get some sleep."

Jean-Paul met Sienna in Paris at the Culinary Arts school. They both specialized in the pastry chef program and became friends. It was a two-year, year-round program. When she graduated, a famous pastry chef offered her a mentorship in his bakery. She worked under him for a year, then they offered her a position.

Jean-Paul got hired right out of school at one of the elite Restaurants in Paris as the assistant to the head Pastry Chef. The hours were long, and he worked six days a week. But the compensation was good. So, he stayed.

Sienna and Jean-Paul's friendship waned as they spent most of their time working.

When Sienna got tired of working under ego-driven chefs at fancy restaurants, she quit. She went home to live with her folks in Austin, Texas, while she decided what she wanted to do.

Sienna's father, former Governor of Texas, and her mother were happy she was home. She knew she could stay with them as long as she wanted.

Sienna was walking downtown with her best friend, Lizzy. They were heading toward their favorite coffee shop when a big for-sale sign caught their eye. They peeked in the window. It was an abandoned bakery storefront. The two friends stood there speculating about how Sienna could open her own bakery. They decided how it would look and what she would serve, then they laughed and moved on.

Sienna couldn't get the idea out of her head. That night she talked to her mom and dad about it, and they said they would support her decision. Sienna didn't need their money; she had been paid well over the last four years and saved most of it. But having their support meant everything. The more she thought about it, the more she knew she needed a partner. The only person in the world she would ever partner in a bakery with was Jean-Paul.

Two weeks later, he was in Austin. He was sick of working himself to death for someone else's benefit. He jumped at the chance of opening his own business.

Jean-Paul and Sienna went to CJ, Lizzy's architect husband, to redesign the old building. To their surprise, the building had four apartments upstairs. Sienna and Jean-Paul decided to live up there, so they had CJ redesign it into two larger apartments.

Their dream shop opened a year later.

"Jean-Paul, what did you say to German when you took food out to him today?"

"I told him if he ever bothered anyone in the alley again, I would call the police, and he would be taken to the homeless camp. I'm sorry I didn't hear anything last night in my apartment."

"It's all right, Jean-Paul; I handled it. I knew German wouldn't hurt me."

"His friend, Squeaky, said he's been acting strange lately. He wonders if he might be getting dementia or something," Jean-Paul said.

"Oh, I hope not. We should call a cab and send him to the clinic to be checked out."

"We can offer, but I don't think he'll go."

"Are you ok here on your own for a while? I want to take this bread," she lifted one of the warm loaves their bread maker just took out of the oven, "up to the kids and make them breakfast.

And I want to talk to their aunt before they leave here," Sienna said.

"Do you believe there is an aunt?"

"No, but I could be wrong."

Sienna wrapped the warm bread in a clean kitchen towel and headed to the stairs. When she opened the door from the bakery to the stairs, she saw Teresa and Kato heading down with their belongings.

"Where are you going?" Sienna asked.

"My Aunt wants us to meet her at her job. She said she can't leave right now," I lied.

"Oh, I'll drive you. I want to meet your aunt before I let you off."

Kato's eyes got as big a saucer, "Teresa..."

"No, I don't want to take up any more of your time."

"It's no problem," Sienna insisted.

The three of us stood on the stairs looking at each other for a long time.

"There is no aunt. Is there?" Sienna asked.

I shook my head, "no."

"Come on, let's go upstairs and talk about this."

Sienna directed us to the kitchen table, and we sat down. "I want you to tell me what you can about your situation. I know you didn't just come over the southern border. You are obviously running from something. Is it your parents?"

"No. Our mother disappeared from a mental institution years ago. And our father...died recently."

"Do you have family you are trying to get to? She asked.

"No, we have no family."

"Then what is your plan? Where were you going just now?" her eyebrows furrowed.

"We needed to go before you called Child Services on us. I won't let them take us. I'll take care of Kato myself," I said with more snark than I intended.

"Do you even have identification? How will you get Kato in school? And no one is going to believe you are eighteen. You won't be able to get an apartment."

"I'll figure it out."

"Do you have your birth certificates and social security cards?"

"Yeah," Kato chimed in. I shushed him.

"No..."

"But Teresa..." Kato tried to interrupt.

"No. We don't."

"Look, I don't know what has happened to you or your family. But I can't let you leave here and live on the streets. It's too dangerous," Sienna paused, looking back and forth between us. "Stay here with me. It's summer, so Kato won't miss school, and maybe, in time, you will trust me enough to tell me the truth."

"You swear you won't call the authorities?"

"I'm telling you I won't do anything until we agree on a course of action. No matter how long it takes."

"Teresa, please, I don't want to live on the streets; it's scary," Kato looked over at me, pleading.

"Ok, but I want to pay for our keep."

"We'll discuss it later. Right now, let's get you both breakfast.

CHAPTER THREE
THREE YEARS LATER

Henderson, Nevada

Captain Desmond was called to the office of the Deputy Chief. *I know what he wants, but I have nothing to give him. The chief knows more than he's telling me about Detective Gilbert. I'm going to insist he tells me. It's been three years, and we are no further than when Detective Cox was murdered.*

The Deputy Chief's door was open, and he waved Captain Desmond in and motioned for him to sit.

"Christian, tell me you have something on Detective Gilbert."

"Sir, the wiretap and the surveillance team were on him for three months; they have nothing. Again. Same as three years ago. No suspicious meetings, no phone calls talking about money. Nothing," Christian hesitated before speaking his mind. "Sir, you know more than you're telling me. If you want me to weed out corrupt officers, I can't do it on a wing and a prayer. I need to know what convinced you Gilbert is dirty."

Edwards stared at him for a long time, then refocused on the picture of his police academy graduation class.

"What I tell you can never leave this room. I'm not sure it will help you to know, but you are right. I gave you a puzzle without all the pieces."

Deputy Edwards went on to tell his story. "The men I was in the academy with, twenty-five years ago were close. A group of us signed up together, the others were like-minded, and we all got along. No one works for the police department for the paycheck, but the pay was even worse then. We were on a mission to make Henderson a safe place to live. Criminals from Las Vegas were leaching into our city and bringing their illegal activities. They were paying off police officers and literally getting away with murder. After graduating, we split into small groups and signed on to different precincts. We felt we could impact the entire city that way." The chief was reminiscing rather than speaking to the detective. "It took us eight years of tediously working our plan to make a dent in the crime. On the way, we all went up in rank and stature. We spent our off time together, and eventually, most of us got married and started having families.

"Detective Mason was my best friend; his wife and mine were best friends too. Mason's wife had gotten ill, and the police department's insurance didn't cover the treatment she needed because it wasn't FDA approved. He was desperate; he loved his wife. He came over to my house, and we sat drinking coffee as he poured out his frustration at being unable to care for her. He was angry. Angry that the criminals we caught did little or no time and were right back on the streets. They raked in tons of money on their illegal enterprises, and he couldn't even pay for medication.

"I'd never seen him like that," Edwards paused. "Mason went through his savings account and all of us emptied ours too, to help. I don't know what he did to get the money, but eight months later, he paid us all back and he had his wife's medication and sent her to a specialist. She recovered, but Mason quit hanging around with us, and some of our other friends seemed to drop off too.

"Fifteen years later an old college buddy called and asked if I would meet him at a restaurant out of town. I was captain of the East precinct at the time, and he was an attorney. I met him, and he told me his client said the police had been extorting protection money from him. I was shocked. I'm not naive; I know most police departments have some corruption. But I never saw any indication of it in Henderson. This man claimed it was an organized group doing it in every precinct in the city. I didn't want to believe him. He gave me one name, Detective Gilbert.

"As I thought about it, Mason's name came to mind. He had retired from the police department after twenty years of service and moved to Florida. I figured if anyone would know about it, it would be Mason. He'd never talk about it over the phone, so I took vacation time and went to see him.

"He was surprised to see me and asked how I found him. I told him the accounting department had his address for pension purposes. His wife was out, so he invited me in.

"Asking him about the corruption was the hardest thing I have ever done. I wasn't sure he would answer me. But after asking me if I was wired, he said, 'what I'm telling you now, I will deny it if you ever take it to court, but I owe it to you.'

"He told me that when he couldn't buy medication for his wife, he was contacted by a car thief that ran a chop shop. The man had heard his wife was ill and made him an offer. The thief would pay for her monthly treatment if Mason protected his shop.

"As time passed, other small and midsize criminal enterprises asked for the same protection. Gilbert began making large sums of money that he hid in a safe deposit box. His wife had no idea. When he heard other officers discuss their financial woes, he carefully invited others into his scheme. They organized and took great precautions with the money. They would give it to Mason, Mason took it to Vegas, turned it into casino chips, and then put it in a safe deposit box. Four times a year, they would split it up. They took their chips and cashed them in small increments, even turning in a portion of it as winnings to the IRS. It helped to explain the influx of cash. They limited their small group to one from each precinct and only provided protection.

"It worked as long as no one got greedy. When Mason retired, he left, separating himself from the crew. He didn't know if the operation was still running; most of his team had retired.

"If he knew anything else, he wouldn't tell me. That's when I first approached Detective Cox and told him what I suspected. I couldn't bring anyone else in because I had no idea who these men were. Morry Cox agreed to go in as Gilbert's partner. He was so new that I didn't think anyone would suspect he was working undercover. He'd only been in the department for three years and had just become a third-grade detective. My instructions to him were to be on the lookout. He came to me three months later and told me he was certain I was wrong about Gilbert. He saw nothing to indicate he was taking payoffs. I told him to start complaining about being able to pay his bills, to see if Gilbert would take the bait," Edwards looked at the captain then looked down at his desk. "Now you know everything I know."

"And now Cox is dead," the captain said.

Edwards' head jerked back to him, his face stern, "yes, and three months later, he was dead. But we need to weed out the entire clique, not just Detective Gilbert."

"You sent him in without backup, sir."

"And I won't make that mistake again. Nothing in Gilbert's file gave me concern that he would kill a fellow officer. I was wrong. Dead wrong. I need you to assemble a small group of men you can trust to work this. But you can't tell them what I told you."

"I have a handful of men under me in Internal Affairs I can trust," Desmond said.

"You better. You'll be betting their lives on it. And they must keep this completely off-book," Edwards warned. "I want Gilbert and the others in jail. We'll have to be able to prove this in court." Captain Desmond got up, "yes, sir. I'll keep you in the loop."

Austin, Texas.

Sophie and Houston were staying in Emmett's cottage. It was quiet for the first time since Sophie left the hospital two weeks ago. Most of the families had left to go back to their lives four days ago. Katsumi, the former Kumicho of the Akuza, who Sophie called uncle, stayed with Emmett until yesterday. He hated leaving her.

It was a miracle Sophie survived. The task force was commissioned to capture the most wanted terrorist in the world. They were successful, but not without paying a heavy price. Sophie was one of the costs. She was knocked out and tossed over the side of the yacht into the ocean. She was unconscious for days, and their unborn baby's life was at risk too. Prayers were going up 24/7 for her recovery. God answered the prayers.

"I can't believe I got to meet Blaze Cornish," Houston said, lying in bed. He rubbed Sophie's back as she threw up into a small garbage can, she had set by her bed.

The morning sickness started when she got out of the hospital and was literally in the morning as soon as she woke up. Houston would clean out the can and bring it back in time for her to throw up again. When it subsided, she would get up to shower, and Houston would start breakfast. Feeding her seemed to help. Bully would put his paws on the bed and whine, worried about her. Today was no exception.

"I'm throwing up, and all you can think about is Blaze. Bully is more concerned than you." Sophie patted Bully's head between dry heaves and said, "you are such a good boy, Bully." She was teasing Houston; he had been very attentive to all her needs since this started.

"I never considered myself a sycophant, but he is the coolest guy I have ever met."

"He is great. I know he wanted to stay, but..." she dry heaved a few more times, "his contract requires him to go on the PR tours with his teammates. I think most of the fans come out to see him. He signs anything put before him. He knows some people sell what he signs, but he's happy to do it."

When Sophie felt better, she ate Saltine Crackers and hurried to shower. Bully lay at the bathroom door waiting for her.

"I'll start breakfast," Houston hollered after her through the bathroom door.

Sophie's morning sickness had been relatively mild compared to horror stories she'd heard. Even though these episodes lasted hours, it could have been worse. The only food that made her nauseous was mayonnaise. Houston made sure to keep it out of sight and out of her food.

After breakfast, Houston and Sophie walked over to Lizzy's, it wasn't summer yet, but by mid-day, it was hot out. Houston was becoming friends with all of the families, but he and CJ immediately hit it off. Since it was Saturday, he would be home. Houston had been invited to the Saturday excursions with the guys and had taken them up on it, until Sophie started with the morning sickness. He didn't want to leave her to fend for herself.

As they walked through the undeveloped section of desert between Emmett's house and the subdivision, Bully kept an eye out for anything that moved. He froze, waited for another movement, and tore out after some critter. The way it was zigzagging, it must have been a lizard. The critter must have found a hole to hide because Bully stopped cold and started digging. Houston hollered at him.

"Bully, you've chased that poor critter enough; leave him alone." Bully ignored him. "Bully, come." Bully looked up, looked down again at his nemesis, barked, letting him know he'd be back, then obeyed.

"Sophie, I have to go back to DC. Director Cosby wanted me back weeks ago to complete my resignation papers. He was willing to accept my after-action report by email, but I have to be there in person to finalize my resignation."

. "I know, sweetheart. Do I need to do something to end my contract with them?"

"No, I set it up so you could refuse to work any mission at your discretion. Since the task force is in limbo right now, there is no mission to reject, and your contract is up in a month anyway."

"We can go whenever you want."

"You'll go with me?" Houston said, surprised.

"Of course, why wouldn't I?"

"I didn't know if you would be willing to leave your family. You're so happy here."

Sophie stopped and turned to him. "Houston, you are my family. Where you go, I go."

"We haven't talked about where we will live yet."

She got on her tiptoes and kissed him. "We have time. Knowing we don't have to take on another task force operation has given me room to breathe." They started walking again.

When Bully realized, they were going to Jett's house, he ran up the porch and looked through the window. He must have seen Jett because he started barking, and his whole body wagged.

Jett came to the window patting it with his little hand, trying to touch Bully.

Houston and Sophie walked up the same steps she had walked up a million times growing up in Austin. Before Sophie left nine years ago, she asked Uncle David Scott to rent it to Lizzy and CJ. He was one of her father's partners in the law firm. He managed her estate when her father died.

Lizzy opened the door, and Jett charged at Bully, wrapping his hands around his neck. Coco, Lizzy's miniature poodle, came over to see what all the commotion was. When he saw it was just Bully, he returned to what he was doing. Coco often snubbed Bully. A lot of small dog breeds feel superior to other dogs. Sophie wasn't worried, Bully would win him over.

Houston reached down and grabbed Jett. He tossed him in the air. Jett giggled, then Houston gave him a hug. Jett leaned over to wrap his arm around Sophie's neck to hug her. She laughed and rubbed her nose against his.

"Still having morning sickness, Soph?" Lizzy asked, coming to greet her from the kitchen.

"Same as yesterday morning, like clockwork."

"Well then, it is time to put more food in that tummy. When I had morning sickness, I found eating routinely through the day helped me."

"What do you have in mind?

"How about cream cheese and avocado on rye toast?"

"That sounds delightful," Sophie laughed. They headed to the kitchen. When Jett saw them going into the kitchen, he followed. Bully padded behind him, hoping to catch whatever Jett might drop for him.

"Houston, I bought a new edger; let me show it to you," the men headed to the shed outback. CJ had all the equipment one would ever need to keep up the lawn. "Houston, I don't know if Sophie told you much about her life here, but this house is hers.

32

If you want to live here in Austin, we will happily vacate so you can live here."

"CJ, thanks for the offer, but no way would Sophie ever want you to do that, and neither would I. We are still trying to figure out what to do. We have a good life in DC and in Manhattan. But I see how much she loves you all and told her if she wants to move here, I will make it happen. If we do, though, we will build a house."

"It would be hard on all of us if she left again. Especially Lizzy. You can't imagine how close they were. But I know she has had a whole life outside of Austin the last nine years, and I know your work is important."

"I resigned my commission from the President's Task Force after the last operation. We might open up a Detective Agency. That way, we can pick the cases we want to take."

"Whatever you do, I hope you both spend a good deal of time in Austin," CJ said, slapping Houston on the back.

"I have no doubt," Houston said.

"Would you like to play handball at the country club?"

"I thought you guys already did your outing today?"

"We did. We played basketball. But Sienna called and wants Lizzy and Sophie to have lunch with her at the bakery. I thought I'd drop Jett off with mom for a few hours, and we could go."

"I'm in."

Teresa was taking empty trays out of the display case. It was only an hour from closing, and the case was almost empty.

"Hello, Aunt Lizzy, Miss Sophie. Aunt Sienna told me to get her when you arrived."

"Thank you, Teresa. We'll find a place to sit."

"I'm so impressed with this place every time I come here. It's perfect. I'm so proud of Sienna," Sophie smiled.

"Sienna likes to give Jean-Paul credit for it, but she designed the place. Let's sit over here by the fireplace," Lizzy directed.

Sienna came from behind the counter and gave them each a hug. "I've made us finger sandwiches and a fruit salad. Do you want tea, coffee, lemonade, or soda?"

"Strawberry Lemonade sounds good, but we don't want you waiting on us; let me get it," Sophie said.

"No way. You are my guests."

"Strawberry lemonade sounds good to me too," Lizzy said. "I'll be right back."

Having lunch with Lizzy and Sienna was always a blast. Sophie's sides were aching from laughing so hard.

"Can you all come to dinner next Saturday at my house? I'll invite Xander and Piper too."

"Oh, Lizzy, I can't. Houston and I have to go back to DC."

"You're leaving?" Lizzy looked stricken.

"For a while. Houston has to fill out paperwork to finalize his resignation."

"Do you know what you plan on doing yet?" Sienna asked.

"We talked about opening a private investigation agency of our own."

"In Manhattan?" Lizzy asked. Sophie reached out and took Lizzy's hand.

"I would move here in a second, Lizzy. But Houston's family and friends are up there. I can't ask him to leave everything and everyone he loves. But I intend to spend a lot of time down here."

"You'll be here for my wedding, won't you?" Sienna asked. "I want you to be a bridesmaid."

"I'd love to be in your wedding. I wouldn't miss it for the world."

Before they left, Sophie headed to the lady's room. Teresa stopped her in the hall. "Miss Sophie, do you think I could speak to you and your husband privately sometime?"

"Of course, Teresa, just call me."

"Thank you. Will tonight work at six?"

"Yes. That will be fine."

A knock came on the cottage door at six that evening. Houston opened the door. Bully by his side, his tail wagging.

"Teresa, come in, please."

"Thank you, Mr. Houston." She bent down to pet Bully.

Sophie came out of the kitchen and gave her a hug. "Please sit down. I have sweet tea, soda, or juice. Which would you prefer?"

"Nothing, thank you, Miss Sophie. I just had dinner."

Teresa sat in an overstuffed chair, and Houston and Sophie sat on the loveseat arranged close to it.

"Is there something we can help you with, Teresa?" Sophie could see Teresa was having trouble addressing the reason she came over.

"No one knows the real story of how Kato and I came to live with Aunt Sienna," she paused and looked at them. "Aunt Sienna took us in and never pushed us about how we ended up on the street. I couldn't tell her because we were hiding."

When Teresa looked down again and paused, Sophie encouraged her to continue. "Our father was murdered by a police detective in Henderson, Nevada." Teresa had rushed the words out as if she were afraid, she would talk herself out of it.

Houston leaned forward, putting his forearms on his thighs. "I think you better start from the beginning."

Teresa told them everything about how her mother left. Then went on to tell them she saw the detective get shot, then the

35

gun turned on her father, and watched as the man shot him too. She told them how they got a ride to Austin and ended up on the bench behind Sienna's bakery. Teresa broke down and covered her face with her hands. Sophie moved to the arm of the chair and sat, rubbing Teresa's back. Houston got a box of tissues and handed them to Sophie, who pulled a couple out and put them in Teresa's hand.

They waited for Teresa to calm down. Sophie moved back to the couch. Houston spoke first.

"I'm sorry, Teresa. No one should have to go through that. You said you took the computer off your father's desk. It held the security camera footage?"

Teresa sniffed one more time and wiped her nose. "Yes, I never looked at it because...I just couldn't."

"Do you still have the computer?" Houston asked.

"I do," Teresa opened the backpack she had laid on the floor next to her.

"Teresa, why are you coming to us with this. Why not tell Sienna?" Sophie asked.

Teresa handed the laptop to Houston before she answered. "I didn't want to put them in danger. I knew she would try to do something. But you are like spies, right? I figured you could help me get justice for my father."

"Theresa, we are not spies," Sophie corrected.

"But you were on a mission for the government when you ended up in the hospital. Right?"

"Yes. We were part of a task force," Sophie said.

"Yeah, so you can investigate?"

"Yes, Teresa, that is what we do, investigate."

CHAPTER FOUR

Houston found the security footage and got Sophie's attention. He turned it so Teresa couldn't see. There was no volume, just black and white footage.

"What time did this happen?" He asked.

"I don't know exactly; it was after closing at three," Teresa said. Houston fast-forwarded to three o'clock.

He and Sophie watched as Teresa's father let in two men. He smiled, greeted them, locked the door behind them, and served them coffee. He acknowledged their order with a head nod and went back to the kitchen.

The two men sat there talking. Soon, you could see one of them getting animated. Teresa's father brought out the food, and the men stopped talking. Her dad left the frame, and the men began to eat.

One man was a few years older and had light hair; he said something that startled the younger man with black hair. The young man pointed at him and said something, then tossed a twenty on the table and got up. The other man blocked his way. His face was distorted in anger as he yelled at the younger man and shoved him. The young man pushed him back and said something. He headed for the door, and the older one pulled out his weapon and shot the younger one in the back. The shooter had a look of shock on his face, like he couldn't believe what happened. He looked at the gun in his hand in disbelief. Then he noticed someone else in the room, turned, and shot again. The man he shot was out of the frame, but they knew it was Teresa's father. The shooter panicked and ran out of the building.

Sophie had a hand to her mouth. Houston closed the laptop. He looked up, "Teresa, why didn't you show this to the police?"

"My papa told us to run. He knew they were detectives, and I didn't know who we could trust."

Houston nodded. "What's changed? Why are you telling us this now?"

"I graduated last week. You were there. By the way, thank you for the gift," Teresa looked up at them. Sophie nodded in acknowledgment.

"I want to go to college. I need to use my real name and ID. I also need to settle my dad's business. I know he left the diner to Kato and me. If we sell it, the money will pay for our college and help support Kato. Aunt Sienna has paid for everything and offered to pay for our college, but I can't let her do that." Teresa scooted up in the chair and looked at them. "Miss Sophie, my papa worked his whole life in Rio's Diner. When my mom disappeared, it broke him, but he came out of it. He wanted to leave something for us. I want to claim. I have no idea what's happened to it. Can you help me?"

"Teresa, what do you have in mind?" Sophie asked.

"I would like you and Mr. Houston to go with me back to Henderson. I want to see what happened to the diner and find out if anyone figured out who killed my father."

"I see. And what happens if the murderer is still free?"

"Then we will go to the authorities and show them the video," Teresa said.

Houston stood, "Teresa, give us a minute to discuss this. Get something to drink from the kitchen if you like."

"Mr. Houston, if it's money, I have saved most of my paychecks from the bakery. You can have it all."

Sophie stood next to Houston, "Teresa, you are family. We would never take your money. But Houston and I need to discuss this for a moment."

After Houston shut the door to the bedroom, he walked over to where Sophie was sitting on the bed.

"The video proves that what she is telling us is true. But you barely survived the last mission we were on. We quit the task force to avoid this kind of danger."

"I know, sweetheart, but I'm not sure how much danger we'd be in. We can turn over the evidence if the detective hasn't already been arrested.

"I think it's moral support she needs to face the place where she saw her father murdered. And I know she will need help getting the Will executed."

"Ok, but we need to go to DC first and finish the paperwork to get Cosby off my back. When we return, we'll take her."

"I'm uncomfortable doing this behind Sienna's back," Sophie said. "Teresa has never told her where she came from. I don't think it would be right."

"I agree. If Teresa wants us to help her, she needs to tell Sienna."

They headed back out to the living room. Theresa hadn't moved from the chair. She was petting Bully, who had put his head in her lap.

After they sat, Houston told her their decision. "Teresa, Sophie and I have to go to DC for a week. When we return, we will take you back to Henderson and try to get your affairs in order. However, we won't do this behind Sienna's back. You need to tell her everything. We can be with you when you do if that helps."

Teresa nodded. "I know I need to tell Aunt Sienna; she saved us from a life on the streets. I'll tell her while you are in DC."

Washington DC.

On the flight back to DC, Houston started questioning Sophie. "Sweetheart, we need to decide what to do with the house in DC. I know we want to keep the Manhattan penthouse."

"I don't want to push Fons and Carol out, and I know it would stretch their budget to get a loan if they wanted to buy it. Have you asked Fons if he will go into business with us if we open a detective agency?" Sophie asked.

"Not yet, but that goes back to where would we open it. And I can't ask Fons to leave a good paying job until I have another good paying job for him to go to."

"Houston, we don't have to live in Austin to make me happy. I told you. I won't take you from your family."

"We can share our time between the two. But we still have to plant our business in one or the other," Houston said.

"Can we get private investigator licenses in both states?"

"I don't see why not. We have to apply and pass each state's exam. With our law enforcement experience, I don't think we will have to take any classes except for the state's rules and regulations."

"I don't want to encroach on Uncle Manny's business. He investigates civil and criminal cases for Uncle David and Uncle Jonathan's law firm. He also investigates for other law firms in town that don't have their own in-house investigators."

"That brings up another question. What kind of investigating do we want to do?" Houston asked.

"Well, I don't want to do divorces, for sure."

"I agree."

"Looking for Dajao Taru was very rewarding. I read that 800,000 minors are missing every year. That includes runaways, lost, and parental abductions; a lot of children are never found."

"I like the idea of specializing. And that doesn't preclude us from taking other clients if we want to," Houston agreed.

"Good, we know we want to specialize in missing person cases. But we still have to decide on a home base. How long will it take us to be up and running?"

Houston looked up the requirements for applying for private investigators licenses in New York and Texas. He mentally clicked off the requirements.

"We are over 25, check. We have three years of experience, check. We need to take an exam. That means we will have to study, but I think we could be licensed in three or four months. It will take longer to find an office and fix it up," Houston said.

"Fons is your partner, Houston. I don't want you to lose that."

"I know, me either. I'll mention it while we're here and see how he feels about it."

"As to where, I guess the question comes down to where we want our children to consider home," Sophie said.

"I don't like the idea of raising him or her in a big city."

"We could open the business in Trenton," Sophie suggested.

"Yeah, that would be a good place to raise a child. But so is Austin."

Sophie laid her head on his shoulder and closed her eyes. Houston thought she was sleeping.

She lifted her head and said. "I hope Bully isn't too much work for Lizzy."

"Are you kidding, Bully and Coco will keep Jett out of her hair all day. Bully loves him."

"Yeah, remind me to call Marci when we get off the plane," Sophie put her head back on his shoulder and went to sleep.

Marci Beauchene married Sophie's father when she was in high school. She retired as a flight attendant but remained a handler for the CIA. She handled only one man, Roman De Carlo, the CIAs most valuable asset. Marci eventually married Roman. Marci was with Sophie on the last mission that captured the most wanted terrorist in the world. That mission put them both in the hospital.

No one was home when the town car dropped them off at their house. Houston carried the luggage in, and Sophie checked the refrigerator to see what groceries they needed. To her surprise, a lasagna was in there, ready to bake with a note on it. 'WELCOME HOME!'

Sophie preheated the oven as Houston checked out the house.

Carol pulled into the driveway to see that the lights were on downstairs. She hurried to grab her grocery bags and ran them upstairs. Carol was calling, to see if she could come down when she heard a knock on the inside door of her apartment.

Carol ran to open the door and threw her arms around Sophie, who was waiting with a smile.

"Sophie, I'm so glad you're home. Come in," Carol stepped out of the way. "Where's Bully?" Bully always came up to get one of her homemade dog biscuits.

"He's still in Austin."

"Oh, so you've decided to move there."

"We haven't decided but we do intend to spend time there."

"Fons is having a tough time adjusting. He misses Houston as his partner," Carol said.

"I know. Houston says the same thing. When he gets home, will you come down?"

"Of course." Sophie hugged Carol again and said she needed to get the lasagna out of the oven.

"Thank you for the meal. It's my favorite," Sophie said.

"Sophie, everything is your favorite if you don't have to cook it," Carol laughed.

"Now you know my secret," Sophie chuckled.

Sophie went back downstairs and saw Houston in the kitchen, cutting up vegetables for a salad to go with the lasagna. She leaned her back on the counter next to him.

"Houston, how do we choose. Fons is your best friend, and I love Carol, but I don't want to live in DC."

"And I don't want to raise our child in New York, either," Houston said.

Sophie turned her face to him. He stopped chopping and pulled her close.

"I don't know the answer yet. We need to pray about it. But whatever we decide, we will make a way to spend time with everyone we care about."

Sophie nodded into his chest, then asked, "are you still going to ask him to partner up with us?"

"Yes."

It was seven o'clock before they heard the upstairs door open and heard Fons and Carol come down the stairs.

"We're in the kitchen. Come in," Houston hollered. They were going over the loan papers on the house. There was only a small balance because they put a considerable sum down.

"Houston stood up and gave Fons a hug and gave a quick hug to Carol too, before asking them to sit.

"How are things at work, Fons."

"Cosby called us to Quantico today to update us on what's happening. Since we still don't have a command center, Cosby has been passing our missions to other agencies. The money is on us ending up in Quantico."

"That was a great facility," Houston approved.

"Yeah, we hear they might build us a new command center in their annex. They want to keep theirs for training. But the team is unsettled about how the task force will manage without you and Sophie," Fons said.

"Fons, you know as well as I do it was the team that made us successful, not Houston and me," Sophie said.

"I don't think that's how they see it," Fons said, moving the coffee cup Houston set in front of him around in a circle.

"You'll want to sell this property. How soon do you need us to move?" Carol asked.

"No, Carol, there is no need to worry about moving. We don't have plans of selling this place any time soon," Sophie said.

"You said you wanted to open a private investigation firm," Carol said. She knew her husband wanted to partner up with them.

"That's true. We want to specialize in missing-person cases. We thought we would get licenses in several states. Finding Dajao Taru was rewarding," Sophie looked at Houston and nodded.

"Fons, it might take a while for us to get set up, but I would like you to be a partner in our business," Houston said.

Fons' eyes shot up. "Really? You want me to be your partner?"

"Who else. There is no one I trust more than you. You're more than a partner; you are a brother."

Fons looked over at Carol. "Where would you open the shop?"

"We haven't decided. But I do not want to raise my family in DC or New York. Either Trenton or Austin. Would you consider it if we decided on Austin? Your family is in New York," Houston asked.

"I love my family, I spend time on the phone with them several times a week, but I can do that from anywhere. We only see each other on holidays. If I lived further away, I would stay longer when we visited and spend more time with them than we do now. And Carols' family doesn't live here, so it wouldn't change things for her."

"So does that mean you would consider it?" Houston asked. Fons looked over to Carol. She had a big smile on her face and nodded.

"Yes, I would love to partner up with you and Sophie. How would it work, and how soon?"

"I don't expect you to move until we have a shop up and running. But you'd have to apply for your licenses. I don't know how long it will be before we have enough cases to support us. So, if you want to keep your job here until we get money coming in, I'd understand."

"We would want to come as soon as you need us," Fons said. "When it's time we'll sell my home in New York, so we can put a down payment on something else. And I'll make sure there is enough money left to pay my portion of the partnership."

"Don't worry about us. We've been talking about this for a while, hoping you would invite us to join you," Carol added.

"Not having you two around was our biggest concern. Houston hated the idea of working without Fons," Sophie smiled.

Houston and Fons stood and shook hands ending in a hug.

"It's settled then," Houston said. The four of them sat and made plans for their future until after midnight.

Fons drove Houston to the FBI headquarters to meet with Director Cosby and fill out his resignation papers. Ms. Deasun stood when they walked in to greet them.

"SAC Townsend and SAC Rodriguez, good to see you again," she turned to Houston. "I hope the rumor that you and your wife are resigning from the President's Task Force aren't true."

"I'm afraid they are, Patsy. Is Director Cosby in?"

"Yes, he is expecting you. I'll let him know you are here."

Ms. Deasun stepped into Cosby's office, closing the door behind her. She opened it again a moment later and ushered them in, offering them coffee, tea, or water.

"Coffee would be great, Ms. Deasun," Houston said. Fons agreed.

"Have a seat SAC Townsend, SAC Rodriguez."

"Thank you, sir," they echoed.

Director Cosby leaned back in his leather office chair and waited for Ms. Deasun to finish serving the coffee. She brought the carafe to refill her boss' cup again, then set it down on the counter by the coffee maker. When she left, he turned to Houston.

"Houston, is there any way we can change your mind? I know these last few years have been exhausting, but you know it isn't always like this," Cosby said.

"Sir, you know you can't guarantee that, and it wouldn't matter. My wife never wanted this life; she was pulled into it. And I don't want my children raised here."

"Where will you go?"

"Either Trenton, New Jersey, or Austin, Texas."

Director Cosby rocked his chair for a moment, still looking at Houston. The President and First Lady were disappointed to hear you would be leaving us."

"I'm sorry to disappoint them, sir. But our team is more than capable of continuing the good work this task force has done."

"Yes, I'm sure they are," he turned to Fons. "SAC Rodriguez, are you resigning too?"

"Not at this time, sir."

"That was an ambiguous statement. Does that mean you have plans to quit in the future?"

"I plan on staying for now, sir."

"It seems that's the only answer I'm going to get from you at this point."

"Yes, sir."

"Alright, SAC Townsend," Cosby stood up. "Ms. Deasun has your papers ready to sign. Then you will have to go to accounting to sign papers there. They need to know where to deposit yours and Ms. Star's final checks."

Houston stood and stretched out his hand. "Director Cosby, working with you has been a great honor. My wife feels the same way. Our team's work makes me proud, and I will keep the memories with me forever."

Director Cosby nodded and shook his hand. "I would like to see Ms. Star again before you leave. Will you bring her by?"

"Yes, she would like that. Thank you, sir."

Houston and Fons left his office.

The following day after Sophie recovered from her morning sickness, they went through the house and started packing what they wanted to take with them. They decided to leave the furniture with the house. When they finally decided to sell it, it could be a selling point to the buyer.

"Houston," Sophie hollered. She was in the room they used as an office. Houston walked in. "I like my office furniture. Let's keep it and have it sent to the penthouse. When we find a building, I'll use it in my office."

"The whole room?" Houston asked.

"Yes, the whole room."

"Ok, pack up the drawers and the small things. I went to U-Haul and bought a bunch of boxes while you were in the shower. But don't lift anything."

"All right. Before we leave, I'd like to have a BBQ for the team so we can say goodbye," Sophie said.

"We'll need to do it before we pack up the kitchen."

"Check the weather online; see if this clear sky will last a few days," Sophie said.

Wednesday is clear. I'll call the team and see if they are available."

"Good," Sophie walked to him and kissed his cheek. "I'll get with Carol to see what we'll need."

"Director Cosby asked if you would go by and say goodbye before we leave."

"I'd like that."

Wednesday

By the time their first guests showed up on Wednesday, the lights on the back porch were on, and the bug-killing tiki torches were lit. Just off the patio, were outdoor heaters that Houston had rented for later in the evening. Yard games were out for the kids and adults who wanted to play, and a table was loaded with covered containers filled with food. Chairs were scattered around, and Houston had the grill warming up.

Sophie answered the door; it was Matt and Sissy. They had gotten married before the last mission. Sophie hugged them both and escorted them to the back.

After that, everyone came at once. Houston and Fons worked the grill, and Carol helped serve. When they all had food and something to drink, they sat and spoke with their friends.

"Sophie, I'm not sure I'm going to stay on the task force now that you and Houston are leaving," Sissy said.

"Will Matt leave too?"

"I don't think so; he wants to stay to get his full pension at twenty years."

"What will you do?"

"You know that the requests for my services have increased threefold since I've been on the task force. I'll do what I do, on the private side."

"Houston and I plan to open a private investigation firm. We want to specialize in missing persons. If we need help, can we hire you?"

"Of course, I'll always put you at the top of the list," Sissy smiled. "So, you aren't getting out, just changing venues."

Sophie laughed, "I guess you're right."

Sophie enjoyed having Denny and his wife and kids and Ken and his wife and children. The two couples were close friends and spent a lot of time together. She would miss seeing them.

Sophie was glad to see that Major Flynn Murphy, the Navy drone pilot assigned to the task force, and Trindi Martin, the DOJ prosecutor, were still dating.

Lieutenant Troy Denison, head of the SRT team assigned to the task force, and his wife, Darla, came. Sophie had never met her before. She was a pretty blond with an engaging smile.

The other team members who had family brought them too. The group talked and laughed until one in the morning. The kids were sprawled out on the couches and floor inside, asleep. They all hated to end the night, but it was time to say goodbye.

There were tears all around, and Houston packed out more than one sleeping child. He and Sophie stayed on the porch until the last set of taillights were out of sight. Fons and Carol were already cleaning up inside.

"No, you are our guests; we will clean up," Sophie insisted.

"We aren't guests; we are family. I would never leave you with all this cleanup," Carol insisted.

CHAPTER FIVE

Thursday

After Thursday's morning routine and breakfast, Sophie was in the bedroom packing the closet and the drawers. Houston was packing up the kitchen. A knock came at the front door.

"Houston, the door," Sophie hollered.

"I have ears, Sophie," Houston chided her.

"Just trying to help," she chuckled.

Houston opened the door to find a messenger. He signed for the letter, gave the young man a tip, and headed for the bedroom.

"What is it, Houston?"

Houston sat on the edge of the bed and opened the envelope. Sophie came and sat next to him.

YOU ARE INVITED TO DINNER AT THE WHITE HOUSE RESIDENCE ON SATURDAY. PLEASE RSVP.

"Oh, Houston, I hoped we would be out of here by then. I still want to go to the penthouse and see the family in Trenton. But we promised Teresa we would be back in a week."

"I don't see how we decline an invitation from the president and first lady, Sophie."

Sophie let out her breath. "I know. I'll tell Teresa we won't be back when we anticipated." Houston kissed her forehead.

"I've made a decision, sweetheart," he turned to look at her. "I think we should make our base in Austin, at least until after the baby is born. Doctor Banerjee is there. He has been our baby doctor from the start. He knows the history."

"Grandpa Emmett will let us stay in the cottage."

"Temporarily. CJ said he plans to build a house in the gated area," Houston said.

"Houston, it would be hard for me to live in the house I grew up in. Too many memories of my father."

"No, I know. I want us to purchase one of those triple lots in the gated community too."

Sophie got excited, "really?"

"We can replace the cost of building when we sell this house."

"Are you sure, Houston?"

"I am."

"Houston, I can't ask you to do that. What about your family, Izumi, and Katsumi?"

"When CJ and Lizzy move out of your house. It will be available for our family to stay anytime, as long as they like. And we can come up here and stay for a month or two at a time, whenever we want."

Sophie wrapped her arms around him. "Houston, it's such a big sacrifice for you."

"No, I feel good about it." They sat there absorbing the decision that would substantially change their lives.

That evening they went over to Roman and Marci's for dinner. Ojala answered the door, Sophie hugged her and kissed her cheek.

"Ojala, you look wonderful. How are you?"

"I am well, Miss Sophie," Ojala, responded, her accent was slowly fading away.

Marci came to the door and hugged them both, kissing Sophie on both cheeks. A custom she embraced after marrying Roman. "Roman is in the kitchen; come in."

"Your house is beautiful, Marci."

"Thank you. We love it."

They saw Roman at the stove finishing the gravy." (Spaghetti sauce to the rest of us.) He hugged Sophie, kissing both cheeks. Then hugged Houston, air-kissing his cheeks.

"Please sit. Dinner is ready." Ojala placed plates of food on the long country-style table. Fresh bread and an olive oil dispenser were already on the table. Teresa added an antipasti platter, a bowl of dressed broccoli and tomatoes, and a large platter of spaghetti in gravy. Marci added a plate of sirloin medallions, a bowl of insalata, and a variety of Sparkling Ciders.

Typically, these dishes would be served as courses, one at a time. But Marci put her input in and said that in the US we like to eat all at once. Roman accommodated.

Ojala looked at all the food. "I thought meals at home were a spread until I ate one of Roman's dinners."

"Do you eat like this every night?" Sophie laughed.

"No. I told Roman we would have to go to the gym daily to work it off. So, we cut it down most nights."

"My dear wife worries too much," Roman said as he passed the extra virgin olive oil dispenser around. Sophie poured olive oil into her individual China dipping bowls.

After Roman said grace, everyone was quiet as they filled their plates.

"We plan on spending time during the summers, in Italy, now that Roman has his citizenship back," Marci said.

"My brother and his wife will meet us there and stay at our compound now that it has been returned to us," Roman added.

The De Carlo brothers brokered the sale of illegal contraband to anyone who could afford it. The Agenzia Informazioni had the brothers on the most wanted list. When the brothers escaped a compound raid to capture them, they confiscated the property.

As the conversation progressed, Sophie noticed that Ojala was strumming her fingers, and she kept looking at Roman and

Marci. It was apparent she had something she wanted to say but didn't want to interrupt.

When Houston finished speaking, Sophie jumped in and took the floor. "Ojala, why don't you tell me how all this is affecting you."

She quickly looked at Marci and Roman and blurted, "we are moving to Austin." Ojala could barely stay in her seat.

Sophie smiled, "you are? Tell me how that happened."

"Well, when you and Marci were in the hospital. China, Emily, Drew, Kato, Teresa, and I became good friends. And their parents were really nice to me. Marci and Roman live here, so we had to come to DC to do paperwork so I could stay with Marci and Roman. And the CIA wanted me to give than all the information I could about my father's followers and life in Afghanistan.

"But I stayed connected to my friends by Facebook, and we video chat and text," she paused and looked at Marci. "Marci knew it would be hard to make those kinds of friends in a new school in DC. Since they have retired, there was no reason to live in DC."

"That is wonderful news, Marci. So, you are both retired for sure?"

"Yes. Roman bought a parcel in the gated community by the subdivision," Marci said.

"You did," Ojala jumped from her seat and wrapped her hands around Roman's neck where he was sitting. "Thank you, Roman. We'll live next to Emily, China, and the family."

Marci continued. "The plan is to move down there before school starts. Director Perry still occasionally calls Ojala in to ask her questions or look at pictures. But I've told him he needs to be done by August because we are leaving. If he wants to put a SCIF in our new home, so he can talk to her, that's up to him. I've already enrolled her in Parkcrest Academy."

"Parkcrest is a wonderful school, but making friends in any new school is difficult. When Lizzy and I were new, we found the same thing. But we didn't try to be a part of a clique, like the popular kids. Instead, we would find anyone eating alone at lunch and invite them to eat with us. That's how we met Sienna, Xander, and many other students. We became very good friends."

"That's true, Ojala. They even named a table after Sophie. Many of the 'who's who' in Austin sat at that table," Marci said.

"Who's who?" Ojala asked.

"Famous or well known. Like Xander, Sienna. and Dr. Lawson," Marci said.

"Dr. Lawson had his own group of friends, but they came to join us. It's how we all became so close. Even to this day," Sophie said.

"What about you, Houston. Where do you and Sophie plan to make your home," Roman asked.

"We are going to make Austin our home, too. I better get on purchasing a spot in the gated community before they are all gone," he chuckled. "But once Sophie has the baby, we will spend time in Trenton with family. And I'm sure they will come down often."

"Oh, that is so awesome. Can I babysit for you, Miss Sophie?" Ojala asked.

"We would be blessed to have you," Sophie reached across the table to take her hand. "But you might have some competition from Drew, China, and Emily when they're in town."

Ojala laughed. "Yeah, I can see that happening."

The evening ended soon after the Tiramisu was consumed. Sophie helped Ojala clean the kitchen.

They were a day behind on having the movers load their personal things to go to the penthouse in Manhattan. Houston called the manager to see if storage space was available in the basement. Fortunately, there was. Houston had to pay overtime, but on Saturday morning, the movers came. Houston asked them to deliver their things on Monday before noon. He planned to leave DC Sunday morning. Besides the clothes in their suitcases, they kept dressier clothes to wear to the White House residence.

Saturday

The president sent a town car to pick them up. They were escorted to the residence by the secret service.

Emma and Michael met them in the entry hall. Emma hugged them both, and Michael shook their hands. Covering Sophie's hand with both of his.

"Please come in. We have other guests, but you know them well." Emma walked them into a formal dining room. The wallpaper depicting the revolutionary war that was once on the dining room walls was gone and stored away. Emma had chosen a textured pale-yellow silk wall covering.

The dining room had one long table for ten, which left room for a small conversation area. Sophie noticed the tablecloth on the dining room table matched the pale-yellow design of the Victorian sofa upholstered in silk with small cherry blossoms embroidered on it. It matched the pale-yellow loveseat sitting across from it. Two overstuffed Victorian chairs upholstered in red silk with subtle pinstripes running through accented the ensemble. An antique, heavily carved coffee table sat in the middle of the furniture.

Sophie wasn't surprised to see Director Cosby and his wife Trish sitting on the sofa. But she was surprised when she spotted former Governor Mitch Pierce and his wife, Aileen. She smiled and hurried over to hug them and kiss them on the cheek. Not meaning to be rude, she turned to Gram and Trish, kissing her cheek, and shaking his hand.

Houston made the rounds, and they found a place to sit. A White House Butler came with a tray of assorted drinks for them to choose from.

"Emma, this room is…beautiful," Sophie whispered as she waved her hand to encompass the room.

"Your girls made everything in this room. Including the wallpaper."

"My girls?" Sophie didn't understand.

"Some of the young women you rescued were offered training with a family-run company that makes furniture by hand. I hired them, but I insisted your girls did all the work so they could use it on their resumes in the future. The owner agreed. It paid well, and having the White House listed as a customer was good for business.

As the guests were visiting, the butler announced dinner was served. Staff working in the residence needed to sign a non-disclosure agreement in case they overheard sensitive conversations. The staff knew that before they applied and understood writing a memoir would be out of the question. The compensation was good; most felt it was an honor to work so close to the President and First Lady.

The intimate group stood and moved to the dining room table. President Madden stood at the head of the table; the First Lady stood to his right. The Governor stood to his left; his wife next to him. Director Cosby and his wife stood next to them. Sophie and Houston waited to be directed where to sit, not wanting to take liberties.

"Sophie, dear, come sit by me. No formality tonight, and please call us by our given names.

The butler pulled the chair out for the President first, then the First Lady. Once they had been seated, the Governor pulled out the chair for his wife, then sat down. Director Cosby did the same for his wife. The butler pulled out the chair for Sophie, and Houston sat once she was seated.

As the food was served, Sophie asked the former Governor, "Uncle Mitch, I had no idea you were friends with President Madden and the First Lady."

"Michael and I worked together when I was trying to get bills passed in the Texas legislature. It helps to have the president backing you up when trying to get action, even in your state legislator.

"Mitch and I have similar views on our country's direction. I have asked him to replace Wayne next month when he resigns as vice president. His health has declined rapidly. We are praying surgery will make a difference," Michael said.

"I heard rumors, but nothing was verified," Houston said.

"We kept it as quiet as possible, hoping the cancer could have been shrunk during Chemo and radiation. It hasn't helped, now his only option is surgery, and the outlook is not good."

"I'm so sorry, sir," Sophie said.

"Yes, losing Wayne as VP is going to be a great loss to me. But Mitch will be a great addition to our administration. If I could get him to commit. What do you say, Mitch?" Michael asked.

"Sir, we would be honored," Mitch smiled.

"I knew you would be good luck tonight, Sophie," Michael laughed.

Congratulations were said all around.

During the dessert, Emma turned to Sophie. "Is there no way we can convince you and Houston to stay? I understand you want a normal routine for your child, but many families are raised with parents in law enforcement."

Sophie put her spoon down. "Emma, I know what an honor it has been to be part of the President's Task Force. And the work we have done is rewarding. But it's time for us to move on."

"What will you do, Houston?" Michael asked.

"We want to open a detective agency specializing in finding missing persons."

"I see. What you did trying to locate Ms. Taru was nothing less than a miracle," Michael said.

"We had no idea about the tragedies that caused you to leave, Austin, Sophie. Aileen told us what happened to your father and your fiancé. You had a few rough years after that, but you were able to come back; that is a testament to who you are. And what you were able to do with the task force is exceptional," Emma took her hand. "You will both be missed. Please come see us on occasion."

"If we are privileged to have a second term. We would like you to come to the inauguration," Michael said.

"We will, and as for me, I will vote for you," Sophie smiled.

As the evening progressed, the conversation got lighter, and laughter filled the room.

Sophie and Houston said their goodbyes and were escorted to their car by the secret service.

Sunday

After a delicious breakfast spread up at Carol and Fons' apartment on Sunday morning, they said their goodbyes and headed to Manhattan.

"You told Fons you thought we could be up and running in three months. Do you think that is too optimistic?" Sophie asked.

"Maybe, but the hardest part will be finding a building to buy or lease. It will take time to remodel it, but we can get our PI licenses while we work on it."

"Oh, that reminds me, I need to call Teresa. It's Sunday, so she shouldn't be at work, and church should be over now."

"Hello?"

"Hello, Teresa."

"Miss Sophie, are you home already?"

"No. That is why I'm calling. It is taking us longer than we thought to get things done. Would it be all right if we postponed our trip for another week?"

"That's no problem. It's waited this long," Teresa replied.

"Did you talk to Sienna and Jean-Paul?"

"Yes, they were worried I might be putting myself in danger, but when I told them you are coming with me, they were supportive."

"What about Kato?"

"I haven't told him yet. He might panic, thinking I could get killed doing this. I'm the only family he has left. I couldn't do this if we didn't have our extended family. If something happens, I know Kato will be loved."

"We won't let anything happen to you. But you will need to be honest with Kato."

"I know. I'll see you when you get back. Have a nice trip," Teresa hung up after the goodbyes were said.

"It sounded like she was ok with our delay," Houston said.

"She was. I am a little concerned about doing this without backup. We always knew we had a task force behind us."

"If it gets too dicey, we can call in the FBI. Their jurisdiction includes corruption in law enforcement if their help is requested."

"Houston, we need to put Sissy on retainer for this. We are going to need information that no one is going to want to tell us."

"I agree. Call her and see if she is willing."

They were almost to the Manhattan penthouse when Sophie got ahold of Sissy.

"Hello, Sophie," Sissy still had her in her contact list.

"Good afternoon. Am I taking you away from something important?"

"Matt and I just came from a church BBQ. It was a beautiful day for it."

"Wonderful. If you have a moment, I would like to talk business."

"I do, Sophie. Go ahead," Sissy said as Matt said something to her in the background.

"Matt wants me to put you on speaker. Are you all right with that?"

"Yes, I'll get on speaker too, so Houston can hear."

"Great," Sissy said.

"Houston, that was a great get-together at your place. Thanks for inviting us," Matt said.

"You guys are what we will miss the most by leaving the task force," Houston responded.

"I heard through the grapevine that you were invited to a private dinner at the White House residence," Matt said.

"The DC rumor mill is on speed dial," Houston laughed.

"Were they trying to convince you to stay?" Matt asked.

"It came up, but it's not happening," Houston answered.

"Can I speak to Sophie? If you two are done gossiping, that is. You are worse than women," Sissy chuckled. "Go ahead, Sophie. Why did you call?"

"I'd like to put you on retainer for a job that involves corruption in the Henderson, Nevada, police department. I'm sure no one there will give us the information we need, and now that we don't have the task force backing us up, it will be more difficult."

Matt butted in, "Sophie, going after corruption in law enforcement is extremely dangerous. Are you sure this is something you guys want to get involved in?"

"We have to. A young girl came to us with a video of one detective shooting another detective and then her father. She saw her father die in a pool of blood. His dying words to her were *run*. She took her brother and the surveillance video on her father's laptop and ran. She ended up being taken in by a friend of mine. She never told anyone what happened or who they were. She wants to go back now and get justice for her father."

"She must be a smart girl if she had the presence of mind, after seeing her father murdered, to grab the laptop," Sissy said.

"She is. Her name is Teresa. Will you be available?"

"When is this happening?" Sissy asked.

"A week from now," Sophie told her.

"The task force is on hiatus, but I have been upgrading security for a private corporation. I managed to hack into every area of their system, including their proprietary patents, at their request, of course. They wanted to be sure they weren't open to ransomware. If I'm not done by next week, I should still be able to help you."

"Great, what do you charge private companies?" Sophie asked.

"That's not a fair question. Your husband increased my prices with the contract he negotiated with Cosby," she chuckled. "I now use that same contract with other clients. I'll give you the friends and family rate."

"Gee, thanks," Houston teased her.

"Ignore him, Sissy. You are worth ten times what you charge."

"A five-thousand-dollar retainer will work. If we go beyond that, I'll let you know."

"That's more than fair. I'll get it to you when we get back to Austin. You and Matt are always welcome to see us in Austin anytime."

"We'll take you up on that," Sissy said.

Before they said goodbye, Matt said he would be glad to help in any way he could.

Manhattan, Monday

The movers arrived on Monday. The concierge directed them to a ramp in the back that slanted down to the basement for deliveries. Then he contacted Houston, who met them and directed what items went to his storage unit and what went to the penthouse.

Sophie and Houston sorted the boxes of clothes, putting aside what they wanted to donate.

Houston carried the boxes to the concierge station, letting him know the Salvation Army would pick them up.

Sophie felt she couldn't leave without saying goodbye to Captain Cartwright. She looked for his number in her contacts and called.

"Hello?"

"Captain Cartwright," Sophie said as she smiled hearing his voice.

"Sophie? Is that you? It's been a while."

Houston walked in, "Don, I'm going to put you on speaker," Sophie whispered to Houston she was talking to Captain Cartwright. "Houston's here with me. We felt we couldn't leave without saying goodbye."

"Goodbye? That makes it sound permanent," Don said.

"Don, I just resigned from the task force. We are moving to Austin, Texas," Houston said.

"Austin? What's in Austin?"

"My family, Don. After our last mission, I ended up in the hospital there. I reconnected with my family."

"I never heard you speak about your family."

"I know. But Houston and I decided we wanted to raise our children there."

"Children?"

"Sophie's pregnant, Don," Houston said, with a smile.

"That's great news. I'm so happy for you. What will you do now?" Cartwright asked.

"We are going to open a detective agency and specialize in finding missing persons," Sophie said.

"Oh. Dajao Taru, right?"

"Yes. Finding her influenced our choice."

"How will I ever get promoted again," Don asked, laughing.

"I'm sure you'll manage," Sophie laughed with him.

"Sophie, I found someone."

"Oh. You mean a woman?"

"Yes."

"That's great news. I knew you could do it," Houston teased.

"How did you meet her?" Sophie asked.

"At church. She just moved here for a job with a law firm."

"She's a lawyer?" Houston asked.

"No, she is their investigator. They work criminal cases."

"I wish there was time to meet her, Don. But we are leaving in the morning," Sophie said.

"We were having dinner tonight. Would you come so I can introduce you? I'd really like her to meet you."

Sophie looked over to Houston, "it's up to you, sweetheart," he said.

"That would be wonderful. Where and what time?"

"Bamonte's at six."

"Are you sure she won't mind?"

"No. I'll see you there," he paused. "I'm going to miss you guys."

"We'll miss you too," they both echoed.

A CRY FOR JUSTICE

CHAPTER SIX

Houston and Sophie waited inside the front door for Don and stood when they saw him hold the door for a beautiful African American woman with flawless caramel skin. She wore heels that made her nearly as tall as Don. She had a fashion model's body and an engaging smile.

"Houston, Sophie, this is Melina Abebe," Don said looking at her with a big smile on his face. "Melina, these are my friends Houston and Sophie Star…sorry, Townsend."

Sophie moved to Melina and gave her a quick hug. "Thank you for letting us crash your date."

Before she could respond, the maître'd came up and escorted them to a table.

"Don speaks so highly of you both. He told me some of your story, Sophie. I hope you don't mind," Melina said after the waiter took our drink orders.

Sophie didn't feel any resentment in her tone. A lot of women would have been offended when their date spoke of another woman.

"No, of course not, it was his story to tell too. He saved my life."

"Oh, he never told me that. He told me how you always included him in your missions, giving him a lot of notoriety in the police department. He gives you credit for his quick rise to the top of the department."

"Not so, he deserved every promotion he received."

The group talked and enjoyed each other's company through dinner. As they were leaving, Sophie stepped over to hug Melina. She whispered, "I'm so happy Don found you. He's a good man."

"I know," she smiled.

Captain Cartwright gave Sophie a quick hug when they left the restaurant. "I will miss you, Sophie." He hugged Houston too and wished them both well.

Trenton, New Jersey

They made it in time for breakfast at Houston's family home. They hadn't called ahead, and Lily and Jack were excited to see them.

"Did you just fly up, Houston?" Jack asked.

"No, we arrived a week ago and went straight to DC. We gathered up everything we wanted and had it moved to the penthouse. We will keep the house in DC as long as Fons and Carol live there, then we'll sell it."

"So, you did resign your commission on the task force and the US Marshals?" Lily asked.

"I did, mom. I'm done. I don't want to raise my children in DC, and I don't want to worry whether my wife and I will make it home every night."

"I get it, Houston. So have you decided where you are going to put down roots?" Lilly got up to refill the plate of bacon. She didn't want him to see her disappointment if they didn't choose Trenton.

"We have, mom. Dr. Banerjee, Sophie's Obstetrician, is in Austin, and with the problems she had early on, we want to keep him. We plan to open our detective agency there too. But once Sophie has the baby, we will be coming here for long visits," Houston paused. "It was a hard decision, mom. But it is what I think is best for my family."

Lily placed the plate of bacon on the table, then put her hands on Houston's cheeks and turned his face to her. "Houston, your only job is to do what's best for your family. Of course, we will miss you, but I have no doubt your father and I will spend time down there with you when we can." Then she kissed his forehead.

"Thank you, Lily," Sophie said, getting up to kiss Lily's cheek.

Sophie and Houston spent every minute with their family and friends the next few days. It would be a while until they came this way again.

At dinner with Spring and Josh, Spring sat by Sophie. "Do you think you and my brother can come up when I deliver?"

"Spring, nothing would keep me away unless I can't fly when it happens. But regardless, Houston will want to be here," Sophie promised and hugged her.

Kim was sitting on her other side and heard the conversation. "It would mean the world to Izumi and me if you could be here for our delivery too."

"Kim being here for you and Spring is at the top of my list. Being in Lennox for Cade and Chantel may not be a possibility. But I'm hoping the timing will be on our side."

Houston told his dad he planned to drive back to Manhattan Tuesday night, leave their vehicle in the penthouse parking garage, and fly home from there. But Jack suggested they fly out of Trenton and leave the SUV here so he could turn over the engine periodically to keep the vehicle in running condition.

Sophie made it clear to everyone that the penthouse was available if they wanted to spend time in NYC. "You would be doing us a favor looking in on our condo occasionally."

They said their goodbyes at a BBQ at Lily and Jack's house Wednesday night. Jack took them to the airport the following day for their 10 am flight to Austin.

Austin, Texas. Thursday

Emmett was there to pick Houston and Sophie up late that afternoon. "How did things go in DC?"

"It was hard leaving Houston's family and our friends behind, Grandpa. But we made the decision to make our home here for now."

"I know it's hard, but I can't say I'm sorry you chose Austin," Emmett said.

"Emmett, could you walk us through the gated community tomorrow and show us what lots are still available. We want to build a home. I'd love to be in it before the baby comes, but I know that's not likely."

"There are still some triple lots on the cul-de-sac left and ten other triple lots still available. Liam and Ricky plan to buy lots now, so they will have them when they get married. They can afford them. The three-dimensional games they created have made millions for them. Well-known game conglomerates have made offers in the millions to buy them out, but they won't do it.

"David and Jonathan explained that they don't need to sell their patents. They can maintain their patents and license their games to one of the larger gaming companies. They would receive royalties in perpetuity. Or until the games stop selling. They are not ready to relinquish the business yet, but they liked that idea."

"Wow! They have always been enamored with video games. I guess it paid off. Good for them," Sophie chuckled.

"Emmett, you know everyone in town. Can you think of anyone with a commercial building for sale or lease downtown? Sophie and I want to open our detective agency."

"I'll check around," Emmett said.

"Thanks, Grandpa," Sophie leaned over the middle console and kissed his cheek. He smiled as they pulled into his driveway. Houston and Emmett grabbed the luggage and headed to the cottage.

After settling back into the cottage, Lizzy called and said she had dinner for them and would bring Bully home.

"Lizzy, you shouldn't have gone through all that trouble."

"Of course, I should. You are my best friend."

A few minutes later, Lizzy had the roast and Bully in her car and pulled into Emmett's driveway. Bully realized he was going home and started prancing and whining in the back seat, his wagging tail hitting the back of her seat.

When she let him out, he ran to the gate and started barking as Lizzy reached in to get the roast. By the time she was at the gate, Sophie had opened it and was loving on Bully, whose whole body was shaking in excitement.

Lizzy hugged Sophie as best she could with a roasting pan in her hand.

"That smells wonderful," Sophie tried to carry it to the house for her, but Lizzy insisted.

"Houston, Lizzy's here with a roast."

Houston came out of the kitchen. "Lizzy, this is very nice of you. Better than what we had in mind for dinner," he smiled and took it from her.

"Come sit down," Sophie said. They sat on the couch. Bully followed Houston. "I hope Bully wasn't too much work?"

"Are you kidding? He is an excellent babysitter. And watching Coco, Bully, and Jett play was entertaining," Lizzy paused. "How did everything go?"

"Houston formally resigned, so we got that done. We had a BBQ for our friends and teammates to say goodbye. That was hard. Then we packed everything we wanted to keep from the DC house and sent it to the condo in Manhattan.

"Marci invited us over. Roman knows how to put out a spread. His food is better than any restaurant. Ojala told me they are moving down here too."

"Yes, I heard that from Drew and Teresa; they're excited."

"We were invited to dine at the president's residence on Saturday night. That was really cool. Guess who else was there?'

"Who?"

"Uncle Mitch and Aunt Aileen."

"Really?"

"Yeah, the president wants him to take the vice president's job when he resigns for medical reasons," Sophie could see Lizzy already knew. "You knew and didn't tell me?"

"I was sworn to secrecy. Sienna told me."

"Maybe he'll be president someday, and we can take our kids to the big Easter Egg Hunt on the White House lawn," Sophie and Lizzy laughed.

Lizzy hesitated before asking, "do you know where you want to live?"

Sophie took her hand. "We are making Austin our home base, but we will travel to NYC and Trenton often to see Houston's family, Izumi, Lee, and Katsumi. In fact, we are looking at lots in the gated community tomorrow with grandpa."

"Oh, that's great. I was worried about who would move next to us," Lizzy said.

"Which lot is yours?"

"You know Xander's is right in the center of the cul-de-sac. There is an empty lot on each side of his. On the left after that is Blaze's house, and our lot is on the right of the street across from his. One more lot is on each side of those still in the cul-de-sac."

"We definitely want to be in the cul-de-sac. But I heard Ricky and Liam want to buy lots there two. I don't want to take spots from them."

"They don't care about where their lots are, as long as they are close to us."

"Grandpa told us about their business. I am so happy for them," Sophie said.

"Yeah, they have made a boatload of money but don't advertise it. They just like working together." Lizzy stood up, "I need to let you eat before your food gets cold."

Sophie hugged and thanked her, then walked her to the car.

After dinner, Sophie made a call to Teresa.

"Hello, Mis Sophie," Teresa had put her number in her contacts.

"Teresa, why don't you come over tomorrow afternoon after work? We can talk."

"I'll be there, Miss Sophie."

"Did you talk to Kato?"

"Not yet."

"You have to do it before we leave."

"I know."

"See you tomorrow."

They said goodbye and hung up.

Houston was working on transferring funds so they could buy a lot from Emmett. Sophie decided to do research into the Henderson area. She knew helping Teresa would take more than a few days. She looked up the restaurant Teresa's father owned on Clementine Road. Rio's Diner was on the freeway access road, but it wasn't deserted as she expected. Someone was operating it. At least it didn't look abandoned. She scrolled the satellite picture toward the back of the property. The manufactured home was occupied too. There was a car in the driveway.

I don't understand. If Teresa's father owned that place, no one could sell it without probate, and Teresa said her father's Will left it to her and Kato. I wonder who is the executor of the Will?

Sophie decided to check the tax records for a change of ownership, but it was still in the name of Rio Nuñez, Teresa's father.

Then Sophie checked for long-stay hotels near Clemintine Road. The Residence Inn by Marriott was not far from where they wanted to be. She made reservations for two weeks starting Monday.

Sophie showed Houston what she found when he came into the room.

"See, there are no tumbleweeds in the parking lot, and the foliage that lines the front of Rio's Diner has been trimmed back. Someone is running this establishment."

"Did you check the tax records?"

"Yeah, it's still in Rio Nuñez's name. I reserved a two-bedroom suite at the Residence Inn starting Monday. Henderson is only twenty minutes from the city limits of Las Vegas."

Friday

After the regular morning sickness and breakfast routine, Lizzy walked with them and Emmett to the gated community.

Jett was in a jogger stroller. Bully and Coco walked alongside him.

Emmett paid for the landscaping of the unsold lots. It made the gated community very appealing for those who lived there and for future buyers. He felt the cost was worth it, even though he knew the landscaping would be torn up when construction on each lot started.

Emmett used his remote fob to open the gate, and they walked through. Xander and Blaze's homes were approximately the same size, with three levels. A more appropriate name would be 'mansion'. Lizzy stopped at her lot and let Jett run on the grass. He took off running, and Bully and Coco chased after him. Lizzy threw a little ball for them to play with, and Jett picked it up, threw it, then ran to try to beat his friends to get it.

Their attention was drawn to Xander's house when the door opened, and he came out.

"Good morning," he hugged Sophie and Lizzy. Said hi to Grandpa and fist-bumped Houston.

Jett ran to him, colliding with his leg yelling, "Unk."

Xander picked him up and kissed his cheek, then Jett squirmed to get down and run on the grass again.

"Are you going to buy a lot here?" Xander directed the question to Houston and Sophie.

"Yes," Houston said.

"That's great. Wait until Piper finds out. She will be thrilled."

"Which lot?" Xander asked. "On the cul-de-sac, right?"

"Yes, Xan. On the cul-de-sac," Sophie smiled.

"How do you like living here, Xander?" Houston asked.

"Are you kidding me? It's great. "I have people I love close by," he pointed to Blaze's house. "And in the subdivision," he swiped his hand in that direction. Grandpa is trying to save these lots for family and friends, but he gets so many requests to purchase them that he convinced Jared to start construction on another gated community nearby."

"Sophie, which lot do you want?" Houston asked.

Sophie walked onto the lot on the edge of the cul-de-sac, right next to Lizzy's. "This one will have the sun in the morning. We can put our breakfast nook back here. And the Green Arborvitae that grandpa lined the fence with for privacy generally doesn't grow higher than fifteen feet, so it won't hinder the sun."

"I'm so happy you'll be my neighbor, Soph. We can build a gate between our back fences for easy access." Lizzy smiled.

"There is no one else in the world I would want to be neighbors with, Lizzy," Sophie hugged her.

Houston stepped over to Emmett and spoke softly. "Emmett, can we get a sales agreement done today. I have the cash; I know it takes a few days for a Title company to do their job, but I'd like this settled as soon as possible."

"I can call Jonathan to start the paperwork. But Houston, getting a house built in less than six months is not likely."

"I know, but knowing we have it started, will make me feel better."

Xander was talking to the ladies and said, "Why don't you all come in. Piper's not home, but the espresso machine is warmed up, and I brought cinnamon rolls from Sienna's Bakery just before you showed up."

Everyone but Emmett headed in. He needed to get home to get the legal description and call Jonathan.

After spending time with Xander and eating a cinnamon roll, she washed down with an expresso. Lizzy mentioned she had clients' hair to do this afternoon, so she needed to get Jett ready to go to CJ's office.

"We'll take him. We need to sign papers for the lot anyway. Jett can stay with us until then," Sophie said.

"Are you sure he won't be in your way?" Lizzy questioned.

"Never," Houston answered her. His phone rang. "Hello, Emmett."

"Hello. I spoke with Jonathan, and he said he could have the papers ready this afternoon. It's a standard form; one of his paralegals can fill it out. He'll look it over before you sign it."

Lizzy and Coco headed home.

After feeding and playing with Jett at the cottage, Houston and Sophie put him in the car seat Emmett had loaned them. Bully lay down beside him in the back seat. Jett was asleep the minute he was strapped in.

Jett was still sleeping when they got to the firm, so Houston lifted him out of the car seat while Sophie took out the stroller. They headed inside.

"It seems strange to come in this entrance. It used to be where Mr. Zolin had his architectural engineering firm. I wonder what Tasha and Tanya are doing," Sophie spoke aloud, mostly to herself.

"What did you say, sweetheart? I couldn't hear you."

Sophie smiled up at him, "nothing, really."

Inside, Sophie didn't recognize the receptionist. She stepped up and asked for Jonathan Young.

"Do you have an appointment?"

"No, but I believe he is expecting us," Sophie said.

"We don't take walk-ins anymore, but I would be...."

The door opened, and Rex came in. He stopped short. "Sophie?"

Sophie turned, "Rex," she smiled.

"I heard you were back. I'm so happy to see you."

Sophie turned to Houston, "Sweetheart, this is Rex; he worked here while getting his law degree. He took over dad's criminal practice."

Houston extended his hand, "Houston Townsend."

Rex reciprocated, "Rex Ford."

"Who are you here to see?"

"Uncle Jonathan…"

"They don't have an appointment, Mr. Ford," the receptionist interrupted.

"They're family," he said, then turned to Sophie, "I'll walk back with you."

"You stayed all these years, Rex."

"I'm happy here. You can't believe all the horror stories I hear from my friends in other law firms. They complain all the time. I never tell them how great the people are here to work with. I'm afraid they will try to get a job here," he chuckled. "You might not remember, but Casimir Calascione stepped in for your father when… He mentored me. He taught me more in those years than law school ever did. He passed away a few years ago. I miss him. Your dad too."

They stopped at Jonathan's open door. "Jon, look who showed up on our doorstep," Rex smiled. "I hope to see you again," he said as he walked off.

"Sophie, Houston, come in," He gave Sophie a quick hug and shook Houston's hand. Jett woke up and reached for his grandpa.

"Pa-Pa-Pa," he said.

Jonathan unclipped the stroller belt and picked him up. He put his lips to his neck and blew a strawberry, making him laugh. "Are you here to sign papers?"

"Yes, we told Lizzy we would drop Jett off with CJ."

"Good. The paralegal just brought me the papers. Could you give me ten minutes? I need to review it before you sign."

"Not at all. We'll go see CJ," Sophie said.

A CRY FOR JUSTICE

CHAPTER SEVEN

Jonathan had put Jett down, and he was running down the hall to his dad's office. Bully next to him. When Jett reached the door, he knocked, saying, "DaDa."

CJ opened his door and scooped Jett up. "Jett, did you walk here all by yourself?"

"Ya," Jett said. CJ smiled and saw Sophie and Houston coming. Jett squirmed down, and he and Bully ran into the office.

"Sophie," CJ hugged her and shook Houston's hand. "Come in. Thank you for bringing Jett. His grandmas would watch him anytime, but if I don't have clients coming in, I like having him here with me. I hate being away from him all day."

"No problem, we bought a lot in the gated community. We needed to sign papers," Houston said.

"Which lot?"

"The one next to yours. I hope that's not too close. I promise we won't be nosey neighbors," Sophie said.

"No, it's perfect. When we bought that lot, Lizzy asked Grandpa if he would hold the lot next to it in case you came home," CJ said.

"CJ. I'm sorry..."

"No, Sophie, we understood why you had to leave. It was a painful time for all of us. But Lizzy and I never gave up hope that you would come home one day. We prayed for you every day."

Sophie hugged him again. "Your prayers likely saved my life, CJ," Sophie stepped back.

"Does the fact that you bought property mean you plan on living here?"

"Austin will be our home base. But we will be spending time up north too."

"Do you want to come over for dinner?" CJ asked.

"Lizzy's at work; you can't expect her to cook for us when she gets home," Sophie said.

"No, I'll bring home Kentucky Fried Chicken. Lizzy made a potato salad yesterday. And we always have salad stuff in the refrigerator."

Sophie looked at Houston, and he smiled.

"Sure, but we have an appointment this afternoon. Would seven be too late?" Sophie asked.

"No. We'll see you then."

"We better get back to Uncle Jon."

Houston picked up Jett, kissed his cheek, and said goodbye. Sophie did the same. They closed the door behind them when they left. Bully stopped. Looked at the door and whined.

"Come on, Bully, we will see Jett later," Sophie said. Bully took a few more steps, looked back one more time, and followed.

After signing the papers, Jonathan said he would have the receptionist take the documents to the Title Company before they closed. It would take about a week before closing. "An all-cash deal tends to close pretty fast," Jonathan said.

"That's what I was hoping for," Houston responded.

"Where's Uncle David?" Sophie asked.

"He had court today."

"Ok, we're going up to see Uncle Manny. Do you know if he is in?"

"I saw him a little while ago. He should still be here."

They said goodbye and headed upstairs.

There was no receptionist on the second floor of the firm. Houston and Sophie looked around as they headed to Manny's office at the end of the long hall. Bully followed them.

"Mr. Zolin was the architect/structural engineer before CJ. He and his two girls lived up here when it was an apartment until they moved to Florida. Tanya and Tasha were great friends of ours.

"It looks like they have done some serious remodeling," Sophie explained.

"Uncle Gregori's kitchen was much larger." She saw that they turned it into a break room and rearranged the rest of the space and the living room into a command center with three workstations and two cubicles. "Uncle Manny must have a lot of investigators." Sophie said.

Two men were at the command workstation with a street map of Austin on one of the big screens.

So far, no one has noticed them. On the left were two medium-sized offices. One had a person talking on the phone. The other was empty. Adjacent to them was a glass enclosed conference room with a glass door.

"That looks like a Smart TV." The credenza underneath it held a laptop, a coffee maker, and a carafe. Houston stepped over to the glass and looked up. "This looks like it has the technology to turn dark for privacy," Houston commented.

Sophie could see the sliding glass door on the other side of the conference room that led to the balcony. The girls used to have sleepovers and spent a lot of time gossiping on that balcony. Sophie smiled at the memory.

They continued down the hall, and to the left was a full-size bathroom that was part of the original apartment. Across from it was a supply room. The wall to the left had shelves filled with supplies and what looked like surveillance equipment. Across from it were four long horizontal filing cabinets and, in the back, boxes were stacked up.

One more office was on each side before they reached Uncle Manny's door. It was open, but his back was turned to a credenza under a window with the view of downtown. On one side of the credenza were six short file cabinets. The room took up the entire far end of the second floor. Two comfortable chairs were facing his desk. A conference table and chairs filled up a corner of the room, along with bookshelves.

Manny turned and saw Sophie, Houston, and Bully standing at the door. He smiled, got up, and went to greet them.

"Come in," he hugged Sophie and shook Houston's hand, bending down to pet Bully. He directed them to the chairs and leaned against his desk. Bully lied down next to Sophie's chair.

"Uncle Manny, this place is awesome. It looks like you keep pretty busy."

"We do. Today most of the team is out in the field. We have several cases we are working on."

"For the firm?" Houston asked.

"Some. We are on retainer for larger law firms that don't have an in-house investigation unit. We usually have more work than we can handle."

"Wow, Uncle Manny, the success of this is on you. It's amazing."

"Thanks, Soph. I was so looking forward to you and…" Manny hesitated and looked away. "You joining the firm."

"That is one of the reasons I wanted to see you today, Uncle Manny. Houston and I decided to make Austin our home base…."

"Does Lizzy know?" Manny interrupted.

"Yes. We bought the lot next to hers in the gated community."

"I'll have my two girls back together," Manny reached out for her hand and covered it with both his. When he let go, he turned to Houston. "I heard you resigned your commission."

"I did. We want to open our own detective agency."

"Here?"

"Yes, Uncle Manny. But I wanted to talk to you first. We don't want to be in competition with you."

"Competition? No, Sophie. Parents always want their children to follow in their footsteps. I would love it if you wanted to work for me, but I understand if you want your own agency."

"Really?"

"Yes, of course. Is there anything I can do to help you get started?"

"Thank you, Uncle Manny. But we'll be all right. We wanted to make sure we weren't stepping on your toes. We want to specialize in missing persons, but I know we'll have to do more than that," Sophie commented.

"We often have more work than we can manage. I can send it your way once you get your licenses," Manny offered.

"Thank you, Uncle Manny. We did want to talk to you about one other thing," she paused. "It has to be kept confidential." Manny got up, closed the door, sat behind the desk, and waited for her to speak.

"Teresa came to us before we went north and told us who she was and where she was from." Sophie told Manny everything Teresa told them. Then Houston spoke up.

"Manny, we don't have a task force behind us anymore. But it would not be wise to go on a job if no one knew where or who we were after. So, we wanted you to know in case something happens."

"Does Sienna know?"

"We told Teresa she had to tell her and Jean-Paul. We wouldn't do this unless they knew, but they are sworn to secrecy too."

"When are you leaving for Henderson?"

"Monday if we can hire Jared to take us. We want to take Bully to help protect Teresa."

"Listen, if you need me to do any research or background work, I will do it myself. No one else will know." He lowered his head, "I feel awful for them, seeing their father murdered."

"It *was* awful. And thanks for the offer of help, but we have a researcher that works with us. However, we don't have access to surveillance equipment anymore. And we won't have time to purchase what we need before we leave," Houston said.

"You can take whatever you need from the supply closet, put down my initials beside each item you take," Manny said. "What is she hoping she'll accomplish by going back?"

"Teresa knows that Rio's Diner was left to her and Kato in her father's Will. She wants to sell it to take care of college for her and Kato and help support her brother. Teresa said Sienna won't let her help with their support. She feels if she had the inheritance, she could take the burden off Sienna. But it's more than that. She wants to make sure the man that killed her father was arrested."

"Inheritance or not, no way will Sienna or Jean-Paul take any money from her. They love those kids," Manny said.

"I know," Sophie agreed. Houston looked at his watch.

"We need to go. Teresa is meeting us at three," Houston said. Bully got up when Houston did. Manny came around and hugged Sophie again.

"We've missed you so much."

"I know, Uncle Manny. I'm glad to be home."

They stopped by the supply closet, and Houston filled a small duffle bag on the shelf with everything they might need. Sophie filled out the log.

"Sis, can you hurry, Liam is letting Drew and me test out the new game they're developing. He took it over to Drew's hours ago, he promised not to play it until I get there, but I need to hurry," Kato prodded her.

"Then you need to help me do my closing chores," Teresa said as she locked the front door to the bakery at 3 pm. "Wash your hands, put gloves on, carefully put the leftover pastries in boxes, and take them to German. He should be outside waiting to distribute them to his friends."

"Why aren't they at the homeless camp like the others?" Kato asked.

"He says there are too many fights. So, a small group of the homeless hang out on this block and live in the abandoned commercial building set to be demolished next year. The neighbors here agreed to feed them as long as they keep the alley clean and watch out for thieves. They also give them work now and again for cash."

"They just use it for alcohol."

"That is not our business, Kato. Where would we be if someone hadn't helped us."

Kato took the boxes to the back door and gave them to German. They chatted for a while, and when Kato returned, Teresa was mopping the floor.

"You ready, sis?"

"I need to change first. I'm going to see Miss Sophie and Mr. Houston after I drop you off."

They headed back through the kitchen, where Sienna and Jean-Paul were prepping for the morning. "I'm taking Kato to Drew's, Aunt Sienna. Then I'm going to Miss Sophie's."

"Alright, Teresa, Jean-Paul and I will be at my mom's. They got home last night, and she wants to work on wedding plans."

"Ok. Aunt Anna always feeds Kato when he's there, but I'll make sure he's eaten when I pick him up."

"Thanks, Teresa. We'll probably be home by nine."

After Teresa changed, she took her work clothes and other laundry to the washing machine. "Do you need any shirts washed? I'm doing a load."

"Yeah, I have T-shirts that are dirty."

"Go grab them, and I'll toss them in with my stuff."

Kato took her his shirts and sat on the couch, waiting for his sister. She came out of the laundry room and sat next to him.

"You ready?" He asked.

"I need to speak to you first," she said.

"Can't you do it in the car?"

"No, Kato. You need to hear this," she paused. "I'm going to be gone for a while. I'm going back to Henderson to settle pa's estate so we can have college money. And I want to get a used car and get one for you when you turn sixteen."

"No, Teresa, you can't go back there. That guy...he will kill you. Papa told us to run." The fear Kato felt that day came back.

"I'm not going alone. Miss Sophie and Mr. Houston are taking me. You know they are like spies. They can help."

"No, don't do it. If he gets you, I will be alone," Kato started crying.

Teresa wrapped her arms around him. "He won't get me. But you aren't alone. We may not have blood relations here, but we have family. You know that, right?"

"No, sis, you can't go. I'll tell Aunt Sienna. She will make you stay."

"I've already told her what I was doing. She said no until I told her Miss Sophie and Mr. Houston were taking me. She trusts them." Teresa hung onto Kato until he stopped crying. "I need to know that the man who killed pa is in jail, Kato."

"Why now?"

"I will turn eighteen in less than a week. I can claim pa's estate and take the evidence I have to the police. They can use it to arrest the man who murdered papa, if they haven't already. And now I'm old enough to be your guardian if we come forward using our real names. I don't have to worry about you being taken away."

It took another few minutes for Kato to calm down, then they headed to Drew's.

"Can I stay with Drew while your gone?" Kato asked.

"I'll let Aunt Sienna know."

When Houston pulled into the driveway at Emmett's, they saw Sienna's car. They knew it was likely, Teresa. Sienna seldom used that car. They headed to the backyard and could smell the BBQ grill. As they got closer, they heard Teresa and Emmett talking. Emmett noticed them round the corner. Bully ran to Emmett, knowing there was a bone in it for him. He waited patiently as Emmett took a ribeye bone, he had saved from one of the BBQs and warmed it for him.

Houston wasn't crazy about Bully getting people food, but how could you deny a dog a good bone.

"Hi, steak kebabs are on. There's plenty. Want to join us?"

"Of course, Grandpa. Where is Kato?" Sophie asked as she went over to kiss Emmett on the cheek.

"He's at Drew's, Liam brought over a game prototype, and they are testing it out."

"I bet they love that," Houston said.

"Kato couldn't wait."

They chatted and ate kebabs, corn on the cob, and a mixed salad. It was delicious, as always. Emmett brought out the makings for 'smores and got a small flame up on the grill to roast the marshmallows.

After melting her marshmallow, Teresa squished it between two gram crackers and chocolate, then smiled. "Perfect."

Emmett noticed and asked. "What are you smiling about, Teresa?"

"I was thinking of how lucky Kato and I were to have been taken in by Sienna and the family, Grandpa. I know we aren't the only children with tragedy in their lives. But we could have ended up fending for ourselves without family or friends.

"I thank the Lord for what He's done for us. I look at Kato; he has good grades, good friends, and even a brother in Drew. He's happy, likes attending church, and has all the makings for a good life."

"We didn't *take you in*, Teresa. You became part of our family and always will be. God blessed us when he sent you, our way."

Teresa's eyes misted. She nodded, then ate her 'smore in five messy bites.

After cleaning up from dinner, Teresa walked with Houston and Sophie to the cottage. Bully was still gnawing on the bone. He looked up to see his family leaving, grabbed the bone, and took it with him.

"Please have a seat, Teresa," Houston said. "We want to talk about this trip. We've been working on the arrangements. I'm going to call Jared tonight to see if he can fly us to Henderson. We reserved an SUV and have a room waiting for us.

"Sophie looked up your father's diner on Google Maps and went to a live view of the area. It looks like someone is running the diner," Houston said.

Teresa was surprised, "someone can't just take our diner. Can they?"

"No, Teresa, but someone is running it," Sophie said.

"It could be Bently. He worked with my dad in the kitchen."

"We'll go there first to take a look. Houston and I will go in. But you have to stay out of sight for now. You can stay in the car with Bully and look through the binoculars," Sophie said.

"Bully's coming?" Teresa smiled.

"Yes. He will help protect you. But if we do this, you must listen to us. You can't go off on your own. Will you agree to that?" Houston asked.

"Yes, of course. So, we are leaving Monday?" Teresa asked.

"Yes. We have the room for two weeks," Sophie said.

Houston stood, "I'll call Jared now."

"Do you think it will take that long, Miss Sophie?"

"For the probate, probably, but we can get everything in order and find an attorney to take care of it for you and then send you the funds. And we can always call Uncle Jonathan if we need help filing."

"What about my papa's killer. How do we find out if they caught him?"

"Houston and I can make inquiries. Do you want us to give over the evidence if he isn't in jail?"

"Yes, I want that man in prison."

Houston came back into the room. "Jared said he had a meeting, but Ricky has a pilot's license, and he gave him a call. He is available."

"Good. Alright, Teresa, you will need to pack for two weeks. You'll need hats, preferably ones you can put your hair up under. Also, clothes that won't bring attention to you."

"I have blue jeans and shirts and lots of ballcaps."

"Ok, Teresa. This is your last chance to back out. Are you sure you want to do this? Houston and I could go first and do reconnaissance, then bring you afterward."

"No, I need to handle this myself."

"Alright then. We will pick you up on Monday."

Teresa stood and hugged them both. "Thank you. Thank you both so much."

After Teresa left, Sophie said, "I forgot we were supposed to eat dinner at Lizzy's. I'm full."

"I know you, by seven, you'll be starving again," Houston chuckled. Sophie turned, put her hands on her hips, and gave him 'the look'. Houston adored that look, he laughed harder. Sophie was not amused.

CHAPTER EIGHT

Monday

Lizzy's brother Ricky had them in the air by nine. Sophie decided to visit with him in the cockpit.

Sophie always loved the view from a plane. It reminded her of the last line in the poem by John Gillespie Magee, Jr. 'Put out my hand, and touched the face of God.' After a bit, she spoke, "thank you for doing this, Ricky."

"No problem. Most of our business meetings don't require Liam and me to be there. Besides, I'd do anything to help Teresa and Kato. I don't know what's happening, but if she asked for your help, it must be serious."

"It is. I'm sure she'll share her story once this is over," Sophie paused. "I'm so proud of you and Liam. All those hours of playing video games paid off," she chuckled.

"Yeah, who knew," Ricky smiled.

"Houston and I bought the lot next to Lizzy's. We plan on making Austin our home base."

"Lizzy told me. She's so happy you're back," Ricky said.

Sophie looked over at him. "But not you so much?"

"Sophie, you broke my sister's heart...and mine when you left. You were my other sister. I never knew a time in my life when you weren't in it."

"I often wondered how different my life would have been. If our families hadn't all ended up at the Incirlik Air Base at the same time," Sophie said. "I can't imagine a life without you all."

"But you left. Growing up, I had no idea we weren't blood. Not that that matters. We are family in every way there is. And

Uncle Wes and his family are too, though they came in much later."

"I agree."

"No, you don't, because if you did, you could have never disappeared for nine years," Ricky chided her.

"Ricky...I'm sorry. There is no excuse for how I hurt the family. I was in a bad place, but the Lord had mercy and turned my life around. Ricky, I love you and hope you can forgive me someday. But I can't change what happened, and it's time to move forward," Sophie stopped talking but didn't move. They sat there quietly for a while. Finally, Ricky spoke.

"I'm sorry, Soph. I've been carrying this resentment around for a long time. I guess it's time to let it go."

"I hope so, Ricky. I love you and having you angry at me hurts. Does Liam feel the same way?"

"No. Liam has always been the empathetic one. He understood your pain," Ricky looked at his instruments. "We'll be landing soon. How long will you be in Henderson?"

"We are set to be gone for two weeks, but we don't know until we get into it."

"Call me when you are ready to come home. I'll come to get you. You should probably go back and buckle up now. I'll be landing this in short order."

Sophie scooted out of the co-pilot seat, kissed his cheek, and patted him on the shoulder. "Thanks, Ricky."

Henderson, Nevada.

There was an airport cart that hauled passengers, waiting for them. It took them and their luggage to the terminal to pick up their rental car.

They headed to the Marriott Residence Inn a half hour later.

Houston put the service vest on Bully, and they checked in and settled in their room on the second floor. They were on the back side of the hotel. The view out the window was of the desert. In the distance, a subdivision could be seen.

"Are we going to the diner' now?" Teresa asked.

"Yes, it's lunchtime. The diner should be busy enough that we won't stand out."

"No one will recognize me if I put my hair in the cap and wear sunglasses. I want to go in."

"Wearing sunglasses inside would be conspicuous. But I keep a pair of glasses as a disguise; they are not prescription. Let's see if it changes your look enough."

Rio's Diner was busy when they pulled up. "Teresa, you can't react to anything that happens in there. Do you understand? If you can't do that, you need to stay out here," Houston said.

"I won't, I promise."

They stepped out of the car, Bully was on leash, as required, and they stepped into the diner.

The sign said to seat yourself, so they found a booth on the far side of the building and sat. Bully laid on the floor next to Houston.

Four placemats with the state of Nevada's tourist attractions, silverware, a menu, and a glass for water were waiting for them. Houston and Sophie sat on the bench seat that allowed them to watch the diners and staff.

"Does the place look the same?" Sophie asked.

"Mostly, but we didn't have an expresso machine," Teresa responded.

A woman in a small white apron with pockets came to the table and poured water into the glasses. She had long black hair pulled back into a ponytail. Her skin was flawless with a natural tan, and wore little makeup, except she highlighted her brown eyes. She was very pretty. Sophie heard Teresa gasp.

"Good morning. Is this place always this busy?" Sophie asked.

"Yes. Is this your first visit to Henderson?"

"It is. What are your most popular dishes?"

"If you want breakfast, it's waffles or crepes. If you want lunch, it's a Rueben sandwich or chicken fried steak. Do you need more time to decide?"

"Yes, I think we do. Thank you," Sophie said.

When the waitress moved on, Houston asked. "What's going on, Teresa. You said you wouldn't react."

"That's my mother," Teresa whispered.

"Your mother?" Sophie asked. "I thought you said she disappeared years ago."

"She did."

"Well, this is a twist. Let's order," Sophie suggested.

Teresa kept her head down. Sophie could see tears trickling down her cheek as Houston gave the waitress their orders. When Teresa's mom walked away, Sophie asked Teresa if she wanted to go wait in the car.

"No, I can do this."

Their food came, and they took their time eating and lingered. They paid and went to the SUV when it began to look conspicuous. They moved it across the street and used binoculars to continue to watch. Teresa broke down in the back seat. Bully snuggled up to her, trying to comfort her.

Sophie turned around. "Are you alright, Teresa?"

"All those years, she stayed away. *Now*, she comes back. What is she doing here?"

"I don't know."

They watched as Luna Nuñez, Teresa's mother, turned the open sign around to read closed. As she did, a black SUV pulled into the parking lot, and two men stepped out.

"That's him! The detective who killed my father. Why isn't he in jail?" Teresa was angry.

Houston watched through the binoculars as Luna let them in and directed them to a booth, then locked the door behind them. One of the detectives kissed her cheek.

They watched until 'Rio's Diner' was empty and locked up.

"We lived behind the diner. My mom must be living there," Teresa said.

Houston drove down the block and turned into the alley behind Rio's Diner. They parked a safe distance away,

Teresa scooted up on the back seat to watch through the front windshield as her mother watered the flowers.

"What do we do now?" she asked.

"We go back to the room and do some research," Houston turned on the SUV and headed back to the Residence Inn.

When they walked into their hotel room, Teresa headed straight for her room. Bully followed her, but she shut the door before he could go in. He whined, so she came back and let him in.

Sophie set her purse on the desk and stood there. "We were ill-prepared for this, weren't we. We can't make that mistake again."

"No, we can't. If we could speak to someone who was around when the murders happened, we could get back on track."

"No one can know Teresa is here or we are helping her," Sophie said.

"We may have to rethink that, Sophie."

"Teresa said her dad had a friend that helped him when he was drowning in grief. He was a cook there, right? Do you think we can trust him?" Sophie asked.

"Yes, his name is Bently. She said he was a Christian, and we are going to have to trust someone," Houston answered.

"We could always get into police records on the task force. Was that because we were FBI?"

"Yes. The FBI could get access to records. But we can't start asking for favors; we just resigned," Houston said.

"Teresa said a lawyer gave them a ride to Austin."

"She is going to need a lawyer to execute the Will, anyway. If she hires him, she will have attorney-client privileges. She could talk to him about anything she wanted, and it would be confidential. He could give us insight into what has happened since," Houston said.

"That could work. His name was Burly something. But she said he was retired. I'll see if he kept his license up," Sophie said.

"You try to find the attorney. I will look up all the articles in the paper about the murders. Then I will check out the detective and Luna's miraculous reappearance."

Houston got on his laptop, and Sophie used the hotel's computer. Twenty minutes later, Sophie spoke up. "I found him, Burly Blackrock. He still lives in Henderson but has no business address or business phone. I'll call Sissy to see if she can get his home number and address."

"Good. Then come look at these clippings."

After the pleasantries were out of the way, Sophie explained to Sissy how they got caught unprepared and needed her help. When she hung up, she sat by Houston and looked at the clippings with him.

"Ok, it was obvious they had no clue what happened," Sophie said.

"Look here, Sophie. A reporter, Axel Urwin, spoke with Bently Breen the day after the murders. He was outside Rio's

Diner waiting to get inside to get his personal items." Houston read Bently's statement aloud.

"'Rio allowed the detectives to come in and eat while he closed up. I was done with my closing chores by 3:15. Rio would cook for the detective and then do the grocery inventory for the next day. He had to call it in by 4 pm if he wanted it delivered first thing in the morning. Then he would clean the grill, do the day's bookkeeping, and prepare the deposit. From what the police said, Rio must have been counting the cash drawer when he was shot. But whoever started the rumor that Rio was a criminal is lying. Rio Nuñez was a good man.'" Then the reporter said that Mr. Breen had broken down and wept. When he composed himself, he said, "'And Teresa and Kato are gone. Just gone.'"

"It looks like they tried to claim Teresa's father was a gangster. But they had no proof," Houston added. "Here is another one from three months later," Houston read aloud.

"Three months after the tragic shooting of Henderson's Detective Morry Cox. Detective Willis says he has no new information for the Henderson Tribune."

"'I have exhausted every lead in the murders.' Detective Cox's partner Detective Oscar Gilbert said. 'We worked tirelessly to locate Rio Nuñez's children Teresa, 14, and Kato, 7, who disappeared that day. We have been unable to locate them.' Their mother, Luna Nuñez, who had disappeared years earlier, was located and brought in for questioning.' Mrs. Nuñez had no information on where her children could have gone or who would have taken them. She doesn't believe they ran away. Mrs. Nuñez decided to stay in Henderson in case her children came home.

"If anyone has information on the two missing children, please call the Missing Children Hotline."

They ran across more articles, but nothing new was added.

"We know they found Teresa's mother and brought her back here. Then What? She gets close to the man who shot her husband?" Sophie was trying to make sense of it.

"Are you thinking they were in on it together? That's pretty farfetched, Soph," Houston said.

"Maybe, but we can't contact her until we have more information."

"I agree."

Sophie's cell rang. "Hello, Sissy. Have you found it already?"

"Yes. I'll text you the info. Soph, do you want me to try to get into the police files on the murders and the detective who shot them?"

"I'm going to put you on speaker. Sissy wants to know if we want her to get into the police files."

"Sissy, you could get in trouble for doing that for us," Houston said.

"You are no longer law enforcement, and I'm a private contractor. As long as I don't do it from command, it may not be exactly legal, but...."

"I don't want you doing anything that could get you in trouble," Sophie said.

"Remember, it's my job to evaluate areas where a company's security systems can be breached. I could sell the police department on letting me check their computer security," Sissy argued.

"Actually, that could work. But wait, we may need that ploy later. But can you find out where Bently Breen lives? He worked at Rio's Diner at the time," Sophie said and thanked her.

After they hung up, she said, "the more I think about it, we need Mr. Blackrock working with us. He told Teresa if she ever needed him, he would help her."

"She's had a rough day. Let's see if we can get her to eat dinner and start again in the morning."

Sophie knocked lightly on Teresa's door, there was no response, but she heard Bully scratch the door. She opened it to see that Teresa was asleep and let Bully out.

"Let her sleep a little longer. I'll take Bully for a walk."

"Ok. I'll do some more research."

Sophie leashed Bully, and they walked downstairs and out the hotel's back door. It was hot. Sophie wore a sleeveless white button-down cotton top and light blue cotton pedal pushers. When she pushed open the hotel door and stepped out, the dry heat almost sucked out her breath. It took a few seconds to adjust, and she kept to the shade behind the buildings as she walked Bully. Bully pulled her off the asphalt, so he could walk on the sand.

"Is the asphalt too hot, Bully?" She asked.

They were only half a mile from Rio's Diner, so she decided to head in that direction. Teresa's mother was outside the mobile home behind the diner, putting food on a grill. A man came up behind her, wrapped his arms around her, and kissed her cheek.

Sophie leaned against the building next door in the shade and watched. He took over the grill, and Luna went inside. He hollered something to her, Sophie couldn't quite make out, and then he turned to pick up a bowl on the table behind him. It was Detective Gilbert.

Sophie watched for a while, then decided she didn't want to be caught and returned to the hotel. Walking back into the air conditioning felt wonderful.

When she entered the room, Teresa was sitting on the couch watching television. She looked up and said, "I'm sorry. I know I didn't handle that, the way I promised."

Sophie sat down next to her. "You handled it the way anyone else would have. You're fine. It was our fault for walking into this without being properly prepared."

"So, what do we do now?" Teresa asked.

"We are going to need an attorney to execute the Will. Would you trust Burly Blackrock?"

"Mr. Blackrock? Yeah. I trust him. But I don't know where he lives."

"We have his address. Let's go out to dinner, then tomorrow we will see him," Houston said.

"There is a great Mexican restaurant not far from here. Papa would take us there sometimes, after church."

"Would anyone there recognize you?" Sophie asked.

"I don't think so, but I'll put my hair up."

"Ok, let's go," Houston said, closing his laptop.

Tuesday

They headed over to Burly's house at ten in the morning. It was in a middle-class neighborhood. The homes were brick or stucco. The roofs were either clay or terracotta tiles, enhanced asphalt shingles, or rock. Because of the watering regulations, many people turned to cacti or bushes that didn't need a lot of water and colored rock. Mr. Burly had the latter.

Mr. Blackrock had a rod iron fence around his house. It was a white brick home that looked like it had sparkles. The roof had clay tiles, and a large heating and cooling unit sat beside the garage. A newer silver F150 was sitting in the driveway.

"That's his truck. See the canopy in the back. That's where we hid before Mr. Burly found us."

"Alright, Teresa, we need to know we can trust him before we tell him what we are doing here," Houston said as he got out.

They approached the six-foot rock wall, opened a rod iron gate, and walked to the door across brick pavers. The patio had wicker furniture surrounded by concrete planters with colorful flowers.

Teresa found the doorbell and pushed it. It took a while, but the door finally opened, and an older man with longer white hair answered. His Coleville Indian heritage showed in his facial features. Mr. Blackrock was not a tall man but a fit, 5'10". He was wearing a button-down short sleeve shirt and khaki shorts that hit his knees.

"Yes, how can I help you." The man didn't seem to recognize Teresa.

"Mr. Burly, "Teresa smiled and removed her ballcap, letting her pigtails fall. It took the man a minute, but he smiled and opened the screen door between them.

"Teresa?" He hugged her. "You're alright. I've thought of you often these last three years. Is Kato with you?"

"No, Mr. Burly, these are my friends, Mr. Houston, Miss Sophie, and Bully."

"Where are my manners. Come in out of the hot sun."

"Is it alright if Bully comes in, Mr. Blackrock?" Sophie asked.

"Yes, of course, come, come."

He closed and locked the door behind them. The house was cool, the lights were off, and the shades were drawn to keep the cool of the morning in before the sun got so hot, he would have to turn on his air conditioning. The sun shone a soft light through the shades on the windows, giving plenty of light to see.

"Come sit in the kitchen. I'll get you something to drink. I have lemonade, iced tea, orange Fanta, and water."

"I'd like the orange Fanta," Teresa said.

"I'll take the lemonade, Mr. Blackrock," Sophie said.

"The same is fine," Houston said.

After Burly poured pink lemonade for his guests and one for himself over ice and Fanta for Theresa, he brought the glasses to the small kitchen table where they were seated. Then he got a bowl of water and put it down for Bully and sat down.

Burly spoke first. "I'm happy to see you, Teresa. When I returned from my lecture and you were gone, I searched for you for hours. When I came home, I heard about what happened to your father. But I don't know why you ran."

Teresa looked at Sophie. It was a risk, but Sophie nodded.

"I'm sorry we just disappeared on you, Mr. Burly. But we couldn't come back with you. I was there when my father was shot and saw who killed him. Papa told me and Kato to run before he died. So, we did."

"I would have helped you, Teresa," Burly said.

"I couldn't take the chance."

"How have you been living these past years?"

"After we left you, I found a park, and let Kato play until it got dark. I had no idea where to go. I thought we could sleep in an alley and get a hotel room the next day. We were sleeping on a bench behind a bakery when a homeless man tried to steal my duffle bag. I started pushing him away and screaming. The owner of the bakery lived upstairs and heard us. She came down and told the homeless man to leave us alone or she would never feed him again. Then she insisted we stay with her the night, and then we'd figure out what to do.

"She took us in that night, and we have been there ever since. I never told her our story or even our last names. She didn't push for answers or turn us over to child services. She saw we needed help and took us in."

"There are still many good people in this world," Burly said.

"Yes, there are. We have a whole family there now. They treat us like we are blood...we're happy."

"I'm glad, Teresa. Then why are you here?"

"I'll be eighteen this week, and I want to settle my father's estate so Kato and I can go to college, and I can take care of him. I also want to put the man who killed my father behind bars."

"I know the detective who is running the investigation. I can call him," Burly said.

Houston spoke up, "we can't do that yet, Mr. Blackrock."

"Please call me Burly. Why not?"

"Because it was the dead detective's partner that killed him and Teresa's father."

The look on Burly's face was of stunned disbelief. "No, that can't be right."

"It is. Teresa has that day's security footage from Rio's Diner. It was clearly him."

Burly put his elbows on the table and covered his face with his hands. Talking through his hands, he said, "no wonder you ran." He took his hands away from his face and said, "I know the head of Internal Affairs. He and I go fishing. We could talk to him."

"Not yet, Burly. We need to do more investigation first. But we do need a lawyer to help Teresa settle her affairs," Houston said.

"Papa left Rio's Diner to Kato and me. I want to sell it and the house, but I saw that my mother has come back and is running it. Can she do that?"

"As far as I know, your father never divorced her. Without the Will to prove otherwise, Nevada is a community property state. So yes, she can run it until we find the Will. And even then, she could contest it."

CHAPTER NINE

Teresa pulled an envelope out of the small backpack she used as a purse and handed it to him.

Burly opened it and read the Will. "Yes, this leaves everything to you and Kato. There is no stipulation to your age when you can access the funds. Now that you are eighteen, you can take control of the properties. You won't need a guardian."

"Her mother can contest the Will?" Houston asked.

"She could. She would have a case since Rio never divorced her," Burly answered. "We need to meet with her and see if she plans on doing that."

"We can't right now, Burly. She seems to be dating Detective Gilbert," Sophie said.

"What?" Teresa responded, startled.

"Last night, when I took Bully for a walk, I saw him with her outside your house. It was obvious they were more than friends," Sophie said.

"How could she," Teresa started crying. "He killed my father."

Sophie put her hand on Teresa's shoulder. "Teresa, she may have no idea what he has done. Gilbert may have ingratiated himself into her life to keep an eye on her in case you contact her. You are still a big threat to him."

"What do you want me to do?" Burly asked.

"Do you know Luna?"

"I do. The paper said the police found Rio's wife and brought her in for questioning. It went on to say she was opening up Rio's Diner again in case her children came back. I went to eat there and talked to her. I was going to tell her what I knew about you, but the Spirit of the Lord led me not to and I kept it to myself. I understand why now. I still eat there once a week to keep in touch."

"If you approach Luna about the Will, she will know you are in touch with her daughter. That means Detective Gilbert will know too. That could put you in danger. We are going to have to deal with the murders first. But we need to know you are with us if we need a lawyer," Houston said.

"Yes, of course. I'll do whatever you want," Burly said.

Houston gave Teresa a hundred-dollar bill, "Ask Mr. Blackrock if this would work as a retainer."

Teresa held out the money and said, "Mr. Burly will you be my attorney?"

"Yes. Everything we discuss is privileged. And if you wish to hire me too, Mr. Houston, our conversations would be privileged too."

Houston pulled out his wallet and paid him a five-hundred-dollar retainer. "You never know what might develop."

They sat with Burly and visited while finishing their drinks. Just before they left, Sophie asked.

"Burly, do you know Bently Breen?"

"The cook at Rio's? Yes. He is a good man. When I see him at local community events, we visit. He's a Christian. Bently was devastated when this happened.

"The police did search for you, Teresa. But when they entered the house, they saw personal items were missing, and it was determined you ran away. They still put out an Amber Alert. I never told anyone I knew what city you were in. I worried every day if I was doing the right thing," Burly lowered his head.

Teresa touched his arm, "Mr. Burly, Kato and I would be dead if you had told."

Burly looked up, shocked by the boldness of that statement.

"It's true. That detective would have killed us. I have no doubt about that," Teresa said.

Before they left, Burly noticed Bully had no protection for his feet.

"Your dog's feet can get burned on the sidewalks, even the desert. You might want to buy him foot protection at the pet store," Burly suggested.

"I didn't think about that. Thank you, Burly," Sophie said.

They bought booties for Bully at the pet store. Teresa put them on him as he wiggled.

"Now, Bully, don't you look in vogue?" Teresa chuckled. "What now?"

"We need to talk to Bently. He knows exactly what transpired after the murders. He can be our inside man. He can also let us know if he thinks your mother was somehow in on this or if she is naive to who Gilbert really is," Houston said.

"We can't talk to him at the diner. We'll wait until he goes home. Let's order lunch and take it back to the room, and after we eat, I'll take you to swim in the pool, Teresa," Sophie said.

"Oh, I never thought to bring a swimsuit."

"Houston, I saw a Fred Myers Store a few blocks from here. We can stop there for a swimsuit."

Teresa sat back in the seat and petted Bully as she considered all she learned from Mr. Burly.

Houston pulled into Bently Breen's driveway at four o'clock. There was no car in the driveway, only a Harley Davidson.

"Teresa, is that Bently's?" Houston asked.

"Yes. I don't remember him ever owning a car."

"Sophie, I'm not sure bringing her in before we know if we can trust him, is a good idea. Let's take her back to the hotel."

Sophie thought for a moment. "You're right."

Houston was getting ready to back out of the driveway when Bently opened his door.

"Too late. Stay down, Teresa. We'll leave the car running with the air conditioning and talk to him first. If it's safe, we'll come get you."

Teresa scooted down in the seat with Bully while Houston and Sophie got out before Bently came too close.

"Good afternoon. Can I help you?" Bently spoke loud enough for them to hear from his front steps.

"Are you Bently Breen?" Sophie asked, as they moved closer.

"Yes. What can I do for you?"

"May we come inside and speak with you, Mr. Breen?" Houston asked.

"Yes, but you might want to turn your car off," he said.

"Oh, we won't be long, and we don't want those leather seats to heat up again."

"If you say so," Bently furrowed his brow, questioning the wisdom of that.

Bently stepped back into his house and made room for them to enter. "Please, have a seat. Can I get you something to drink?"

"No, we're fine. Thank you," Sophie said as they sat on a retro-style dark-colored couch. Bently sat on a chair that matched close by. The house was small, with maybe two bedrooms, but it had been refinished inside. From what they could see of the kitchen, it was large and modern.

"What is it I can help you with?"

"Mr. Breen, we have been hired to look into the murder of Mr. Rio Nuñez and Detective Cox."

"Who hired you?"

"I can't divulge that. But the information we were given tells us you worked at Rio's Diner for years and were a family friend."

Bently waited to answer. He was weighing up whether he should trust them.

"I'm not sure I'm comfortable telling you anything without knowing who you are working for," he said.

"I assure you the person who hired us is only interested in getting justice for Mr. Nuñez and Detective Cox," Houston answered.

"Are you working with the police?"

"No. We are private investigators."

"Look. I loved Rio and his family. And I would do anything to help find out what happened to them. But I have had reporters show up with all sorts of stories of who they were. I'm not interested in publicity." With that, he stood up, ending the conversation.

"Alright, Mr. Breen. We are sorry to have bothered you," Houston said.

They walked back to the car and pulled out of the driveway.

"What happened?" Teresa asked as she sat back up.

"He wouldn't talk to us," Sophie said.

"He'll talk to me," Teresa said.

"Yes, he would, but we can't predict what he will do once he knows you are in town. If he tells the police or your mother, our investigation is over."

"He won't. Mr. Bently loved us. If I tell him to keep it a secret, he will."

Sophie turned in her seat, "are you willing to bet your life on it?"

Teresa looked shocked at the bluntness, but she understood. "Yes."

Houston turned at the next corner and went back to Bently's house. They all got out and headed to the door. Teresa knocked; Bently opened the door. Teresa still had her hair under the ballcap.

"I'm sorry, but I told you I would not help you," Bently said. Teresa took off her ballcap.

"Mr. Bently, it's me, Teresa."

"Teresa?" He stared at her for a moment.

"Mr. Breen, we need to get her inside," Houston insisted.

"Of course," Bently moved out of the way. He took another look at Teresa and then wrapped his arms around her. "You're alive. I was afraid you and Kato were dead. Where is Kato?"

"He's safe, Mr. Bently. But we need your help. Mr. Houston and Miss Sophie are helping me."

"Where have you been? I need to call your mother."

"No. You can't. You need to listen to us first, Mr. Breen," Houston said.

"Please. Mr. Bently, you need to hear the whole story," Teresa said.

"Alright. Sit down and tell me what's going on."

Teresa told Bently she saw the shooting and how they hitchhiked out of town but didn't give details. She never said where they went, either, but told him they had been well and happy.

"You are saying that Detective Gilbert killed his partner and your father? And you have proof of this?"

"I took my dad's laptop with the security footage."

"That's terrible news. Detective Gilbert spends time with your mother. He tells her he's trying to find you and Kato.

"Now I know it's to keep an eye on her so he will know if you show up or call her."

"I've come back to put him in jail and settle papa's estate. Papa left the diner for Kato and me. We need the money for college. But when we went to the diner, I saw that mama was running it."

"Yes, when you disappeared, they thought maybe you guys went to try to find her. The police located her working at a shelter and questioned her. They wanted her to come back to see what was missing. At the time, they thought it was a robbery. When she heard you had disappeared, she agreed to come back. She asked me to help her run the diner until you came home. I told her when she got back that Rio wanted you to have the diner. She has been saving all the profits from the business for you and Kato."

"Mr. Breen, you can't tell anyone we are here. We don't know how deep the corruption in the Henderson Police Department runs. We need to find someone we can trust."

Bently turned to Teresa, "you aren't going to see your mother?"

"No, Mr. Bently. Not now," Teresa said. Bently nodded his head and stared at the floor for a moment.

"Alright, what is it you need from me?"

"We need to know everything that happened after Teresa and Kato left."

"Someone had called in a *shots fired* call to 911. The police determined the murders happened an hour earlier. They found Detective Gilbert already at the scene. He said he had left his partner at the diner eating his meal to meet a CI that had texted him. When he returned, he found his partner and Rio dead. Everyone assumed it was him who called in the shots fired. But it wasn't, was it?"

"No. I called from a pay phone when we headed out. I'm sure Detective Gilbert came back to find the security video. He knew there were cameras," Teresa answered.

"The police contacted me immediately and wanted me to tell them everything that happened before I left. At first, they treated me like a suspect," he paused. "You know I went to prison when I was younger." Bently looked at Teresa. She nodded.

"They figured out right away I had nothing to do with it. I explained Detective Cox and Detective Gilbert came every day just as we were closing. I'd finish my chores and leave. Rio took their order, filled it, finished his closing routine, and let them be. By the time Rio put in the grocery order and prepared the day's deposit, the men were usually done.

"I knew he got as far as putting in the grocery order because the delivery came the next morning. They called me when they saw the diner was closed. Rio's body was found behind the counter in the dining room. I figured he was working on the day's deposit when it happened. Gilbert said it was likely a robbery since the money was gone."

"I took it," Teresa said. Bently nodded.

"I must say Detective Gilbert put on quite the performance. His shock and grief were convincing. I believed him. What really happened, Teresa?" Bently asked.

Teresa hesitated, then decided it was time to tell the whole story. She hadn't gone into the details with anyone. Not even Houston and Sophie.

"Margo had brought me the last load of dishes, and I had just put them through the commercial dishwasher. Margo was done and said goodbye while I was wiping down the machine. I took a tray of glasses out front and saw Detective Gilbert looking at his phone. As I headed back to the kitchen, I heard him say, 'You're working for internal affairs?' I couldn't say for sure, but I got the idea he received a text from someone telling him that. I went to the back and stood on a crate to look through the chef's window. I wanted to see the argument.

"Detective Cox stared at him. *'What?'* He said, *'are you nuts?'* Then Detective Gilbert looked at him as if he had put all the puzzle pieces together.

"*'It's true. I wondered why you were assigned to me. As a grade three detective, you should have partnered with someone from the second shift. Someone with seniority should have had the opportunity to move to the day shift. How did I not see this.'*

"Detective Cox was taken off guard. Detective Gilbert kept going at him, *'You are IA. Are you recording me?'*

"*'You're paranoid, Oscar. If you want a new partner, just say so.'*

"*'This whole time, you've been reporting back to IA. What have you told them?'* Gilbert was so angry his face was red. Cox got up to leave and tossed some money on the table, but Gilbert stood up and blocked him. Detective Gilbert got in his face and told him to hand over his phone.

"*'Get away from me,'* Detective Cox said, pushing Detective Gilbert away. At that point, my dad had come out of his office to get the cash out of the cash register. Detective Gilbert punched Detective Cox on the chin as pa walked out front. Detective Cox swung back and landed one on Detective Gilbert's cheek. Detective Cox tried to take him down to the ground when Detective Gilbert pulled his gun and shot him. I think it shocked even him by the look on his face. I'm not sure he intended to do that.

"Papa and I both gasped. His gasp must have covered mine because Gilbert turned to him and shot. I jumped off the crate and hid. I heard Gilbert run to the door, unlock it, and run out.

"Kato had been in papa's office watching cartoons when he heard the shots and came out. We knelt down by papa, blood pouring out of him. He told us to run. So we did." Teresa covered her face and cried.

Bently moved next to her. "I'm sorry you had to see that, Teresa." He put his arms around her and hugged her.

The room was quiet as she cried, and Bully went and laid his head on Teresa's lap.

When Teresa calmed down. Bently asked, "what is the plan to put Gilbert in prison?"

"We are trying to find out who we can trust in the police department," Sophie said.

"Well, Detective Willis is the lead investigator. But he hasn't produced any results after all these years, so it makes me wonder if he isn't corrupt too."

"Is there anyone you know in the Henderson Police Department that you can say for certain is not corrupt?" Houston asked.

"I know Deputy Chief Anthony Edwards; he goes to my church. I can vouch for him."

"Alright, Mr. Breen. We need to do more research before we go any further. Can you promise not to tell anyone about Teresa and what we have told you?"

Bently looked at Teresa, "you can trust me, Teresa. I won't tell a soul."

Teresa took his hand, "I trust you, Mr. Bently."

As they drove from Bently's house, Teresa asked, "what now?"

"You have the original security video that shows your father's murder, right?" Sophie asked.

"Yes, On the laptop at the hotel."

"Houston, we need to copy the footage and put the laptop somewhere safe."

"I trust Burly," Teresa said.

"I'm sure he has a safe in his house," Houston agreed.

"That's an excellent idea. Let's buy a flash drive, go back to the hotel, and download it. We'll drop the laptop off with Burly, then we need to go to Las Vegas," Sophie said.

"Las Vegas?" Houston questioned.

"I want to speak with an investigative reporter. One that knows the underbelly of the corruption in Las Vegas. They may know what's going on in Henderson or at least lead us to someone in Henderson who might know."

After dropping off the flash drive with Burly, they headed out of town.

"Where are we headed to in Las Vegas, Soph?" Houston asked as he drove.

"Head to the strip. I need to call Sissy." Sophie dialed.

"Hello, Sophie," Sissy answered.

"Hello, Sissy, is the team working yet?"

"No, they're still off. I'm doing work for a corporate client."

"Are you too busy to do a quick search for me right now and then dive into it deeper later?"

"What are we looking for?"

"Henderson is on the outskirts of Las Vegas. Everyone knows of the police corruption and organized crime in Las Vegas. But I need to get a name of a reporter who I can trust to ask questions, who might know about Henderson's corruption."

"Alright, I'll call you as soon as I have something."

"Thanks, Sissy." They hung up.

A CRY FOR JUSTICE

CHAPTER TEN

Driving through the desert only took twenty minutes to get to the outskirts of Las Vegas. Then another twenty-five minutes to get to the Las Vegas Strip, where all the major casinos were.

Even though Teresa lived a few miles from Las Vegas, she had never been there. The lights and the casinos dazzled her.

"This is so lit," Teresa said.

"Yes, figuratively and literally," Sophie said.

Sophie's cell rang, "Hello, Sissy. I'm going to put you on speaker."

"Ok. Many articles about corruption and crime in Las Vegas have been printed over the years. The problem is very few of the criminals ever made it to trial. And that includes corrupt police.

"Back in 2018, one reporter dug his teeth into a story of bribery, extortion, graft, theft, and transfer of stolen goods.

"The reporter had names, recordings, videos, and a whistleblower. He took it to the FBI because he didn't know if there was anyone, he could trust in the police department.

"The FBI moved in and arrested forty criminals, half of them police. It was a huge takedown, and most cases were pleaded out. The problem was none of the men at the top, criminal or police, were arrested. The top echelons of the illegal activities were untouchable. They had no problem letting the men under them go to jail. They shut down their illegal activities until things settled down."

"So, you're saying that the ones at the top, both police and criminal, are still running the show?" Sophie said.

"Yes. But now, they are much smarter. The reporter received an award. Three months later, he had a serious accident that almost killed him. There was no investigation of the accident, and the reporter retired."

"Wow, that sounds suspicious," Houston said.

"Goes to show, you don't mess with organized crime in Las Vegas. It was the unwritten rule in 1946, and it's still true today," Sissy said.

"Is the reporter still alive?"

"Yes, he left Las Vegas six months after the accident. He moved to Henderson. He still writes as a freelancer on websites and the local paper. His name is Axel Urwin. I'll text you his address."

"Houston, he is the one that wrote the stories you read to me."

"Your right."

"Thanks, Sissy."

After they said goodbye to Sissy. Houston said, "well, we got to see Las Vegas anyway. Do you want to eat at one of these fancy places before we go back?"

"Yeah," Teresa blurted out.

After eating at the Top of the World Restaurant, they headed back to Henderson. Teresa gave a play-by-play of her meal and the unbelievable amount of food displayed for the buffet.

"Do you think it's too late to see Axel Urwin?" Houston asked.

"I don't think so. It's not seven yet. Are we just spinning our wheels, Houston?"

"Sometimes you have to spin your wheels to get traction. We don't know who to trust or how deep the corruption goes. It could be just Detective Gilbert."

"That's not likely," Sophie commented. Houston looked over at her.

"True. What's the address?"

They arrived at Axel Urwin's address to find an average stucco home in a decent area of town. Two cars were in the driveway. He pulled in behind one of them and parked.

"Teresa, keep your hair under the cap and wear the glasses. If he is any good as a reporter, he will recognize you from the Amber Alert," Sophie said.

"Maybe we should drop her off at the hotel," Houston suggested.

"No. I want to be a part of the investigation," Teresa argued.

Houston paused and looked at his wife. She nodded. "Alright."

They exited the car and walked up to the door. Houston knocked. A woman answered the door.

"Yes, may I help you?"

"Yes, we would like to speak to Axel Urwin, please," Sophie said.

"Oh, you must be here to pay your respects. My name is Dana; I'm his daughter," the woman said and stepped aside.

"Respects?" Houston asked.

"For my mother. She passed two months ago. People still come to tell us how much she meant to them."

"No, we didn't know your mother. We apologize for bothering you," Sophie said as they turned to leave.

"Wait, please. Come in. Having company helps my father. He is out back on the patio."

"Are you sure?" Houston asked.

"Yes, and your dog is welcome too."

"Thank you," Houston said as they followed her to the covered back porch.

Axel's daughter spoke up, "Dad, you have more visitors." Axel looked up.

"Oh, I'm sorry, I don't recognize you. But my Roz knew so many people. Please sit down." Axel's voice was weak, but he was still a strapping man. His bio said he was sixty- eight, but at that moment, he looked much older. Grief will do that to you. Axel's daughter excused herself. It looked like she was packing things up.

"Mr. Urwin, my name is Houston, and this is my wife Sophie and our niece. Unfortunately, we did not know your wife. We came to talk to you about some of your articles." That seemed to stir him.

"My articles?"

"Yes, you wrote about corruption in the police department in Las Vegas."

"Yes, and it cost me. In the end, what good did it do? None of the real criminals were indicted. Just mid-level lackies and police officers."

Bully had instinctively gone to Axel and laid his head on his lap. Axel looked down and started to pet him.

Sophie was sitting closest to him and reached out her hand to touch his arm. "Fighting for what's right is always worthwhile," she said, then removed her hand.

"Mr. Urwin, my wife, and I have been hired to investigate the murder of Detective Cox and Rio Nuñez. We have run into some information that brought us to you," Houston said. Axel took a good look at his guests, stopping at Teresa. She turned her head.

"You said you were hired. Who hired you?"

"I'm sorry, I can't divulge that," Sophie said.

"You think Detective Cox was murdered by one of his own."

"Why would you say that?" Houston asked.

"You came to me. Why else would you do that."

"We do have a lead that is leaning that way. Now that you live in Henderson, we wondered if you might have investigated police corruption here. Once a reporter..."

"The last time I dug in, it nearly killed me. Maybe I learned my lesson."

"We've seen your article about the murders, Mr. Urwin. You might be freelancing, but you are still working."

Axel smiled as he looked down at Bully and stroked his coat again. "Tell me what you know."

"We have a witness to the murders that says Detective Cox's partner shot him and Rio Nuñez," Houston said.

"A witness? No one has come forward."

"Do you blame them?" Houston said.

"No, I get it. So, if you already know, why come to me?"

"The witness wants to come forward. But we have no idea who we can trust," Sophie said.

"I had stopped reporting when we first moved here. I was disillusioned and still recovering from my injuries. It took me several years of physical therapy. I had started writing again as a freelancer, not long before the murder of Detective Cox and Rio Nuñez caught my eye. I did some digging. Cox had only been a detective for less than a year. He'd never collared a crime lord or been part of any major cases that would put him ahead of more senior detectives to get on the day shift. But he was partnered with a veteran on the job for years. I couldn't find anything off with Cox, so I looked into Gilbert and saw that he lived above his means. Which on its own is not suspicious. A lot of police take second jobs.

"I had a contact in Internal Affairs who told me Gilbert's name came up, but there was no file on him. However, there were some allegations against a retired officer, Detective Philip Mason. Nothing could be proved, so he was never charged with anything. I decided to dissect his time as a detective. By all accounts, Detective Mason walked a straight line until his wife got ill. Then rumors started surfacing. I followed the trail and found a small group of officers and detectives, who also seem to live above their means."

"Did any of them have files in IA?" Houston questioned.

"No. The only complaint came against Mason. A man arrested claimed he had been paying for protection and named Mason. It was ignored of course because the man was a criminal and had no proof. This all happened years earlier so there was no one around for me to talk too. But I did put together a vivid picture of a protection racket being perpetrated by Detective Mason and his friends."

"Why didn't you turn them in or write about it?"

"My wife. You have no idea what my family went through when I published the story in Las Vegas. My wife and daughter were followed and harassed by the police. They couldn't even go to the store without being stopped and ticketed for something. When I had the accident, my wife had enough. She said either we move, or she was taking my daughter and going alone."

"Are you saying the 'accident' wasn't an accident?" Houston asked.

"Someone cut my break line. I was driving on the freeway when my brakes went out. I rear-ended a car going seventy miles an hour and rolled three times before it stopped. Fortunately, I was the only one with serious injuries. I was in the hospital for two weeks. We moved to Henderson six months later.

"When Roz found out I was digging into corruption again, she told me if I put her through that again, she would leave me. I loved my wife more than anything, so I packed up my notes and put them aside."

"Do you still have your notes?" Houston asked.

"Yes."

"Is there anyone we can trust in the Henderson Police Department, or do we need to go to the FBI?"

"I investigated Deputy Chief Anthony Edwards and head of Internal affairs, Captain Christian Desmond, myself. I was going to take my suspicions to them when my wife gave me the ultimatum. And to be fair, I didn't have the whole story, anyway. A lot of it was rumor and conjecture."

"Mr. Urwin, would you let us take your notes?" Sophie asked.

Axel looked at Teresa again. "Your Rio's daughter, aren't you? It's Teresa, right?" Teresa's eyes got big. "I looked for you when you disappeared. I knew from Margo, the waitress, and Bently that you were still at the diner when they left. I was certain you had seen the murders," he paused. "I'm sorry you had to go through that."

"Mr. Urwin. No one knows she's here. You can't tell anyone," Sophie said.

"I understand. But Teresa deserves to have justice for her father. I never heard anyone say anything bad about Rio." Axel looked around for his daughter. "My daughter lives in Boston with her family. She thinks she is taking me to live with them. But I'm not leaving. My wife and I had a good life here. I can still feel her here with me," he paused, looked up to the sky, and took a deep breath. "It's time for me to finish the work I started, and this time, if it costs me my life, so be it." He looked back at Teresa, "you deserve to have justice." He paused again, "I'm going to have a talk with my daughter. I've been putting it off. She will be upset, but it's my life. Come back tomorrow afternoon, and we will go through the notes. I will work with you on exposing Detective Gilbert."

"Mr. Urwin are you sure this is something you want to do. If you give us the notes, we can take it from there," Sophie said.

"Yes, I'm sure. It's time I got back to work. Let me see you out." Axel stood, and they headed to the door.

"We'll see you tomorrow," Houston said.

On the way to the hotel, Sophie called Sissy to do a deep dive into Detective Philip Mason. She wanted his financials, emails, social media, rumors, and media articles. Everything.

They walked past the pool at the hotel and saw no one was using it. They decided to go for a swim. Houston took Bully for a walk before he took his booties off for the night while Sophie and Teresa changed.

When he and Bully got to the pool, Sophie and Teresa were already in. Houston dove in and started doing laps. Bully ran along the side, chasing him.

Sophie and Teresa were trying to stand on their hands underwater and walk. Bully came over to watch them. They decided to have a tea party underwater, holding their breaths. Bully started barking, thinking they had been under too long, and jumped in the pool. He dived under the water and nudged under Teresa's chin to get her to come up. Teresa broke the water laughing.

"Bully, I wasn't drowning," she put her hands on Bully's face and kissed his forehead.

Houston came and helped Bully out of the water. "Come on, boy, I'll dry you off."

Sophie and Teresa pulled themselves out of the water and sat on the edge, dangling their legs in the pool. Teresa was staring at her.

Sophie looked over, "are you alright?"

"Yes. I was just noticing how beautiful you are."

"That is a nice thing to say. I think *you* are beautiful," Sophie said.

"No, I'm not pretty. Not like you."

"Teresa, most people don't see themselves the way others do. You have flawless skin, beautiful eyes, and a pretty face. But honestly, it isn't always about what you are born with.

"One of our First Ladies was considered one of the most beautiful women in the world. But if you looked at her features on their own merit, you could see her features were not flawless. But people saw how she carried herself, how she engaged with others, and her soft-spoken ways. It was the whole picture that made her beautiful."

"I get it, 'pretty is like pretty does.' Right?" Teresa said.

"I think one's graciousness and character play a role in how people see you. The scriptures talk about the 'Fruit of the Spirit,' it transforms you on the inside and outside.

"I knew a woman in the church we went to in Trenton. By the world standard, she would have been called homely. But a young woman approached me after she saw me talking to her and said, 'Isn't she beautiful? She didn't mean it figuratively. She really thought she was beautiful."

Neither spoke for a while. "Miss Sophie, why did you leave? I'd hear Sienna and Lizzy talk about 'the old days.' You were always a part of every story. But no one ever spoke of why you left," Teresa said.

"My actions hurt a lot of people I loved very much. But I was in so much pain at the time I felt the only way to get relief was to leave.

"My father and I were very close. I loved him with my whole heart. He was the one who stayed when my mother left.

"When I was in college, he collapsed in front of me and later died of a heart attack. I was devastated, as was the whole family. Duke and Lizzy stayed with me day and night when I couldn't get out of bed. They brought me back from the brink.

"My dad died a couple of weeks before Duke, and I were supposed to be married. I canceled the ceremony. There was no way I could walk down the aisle without my dad. Duke and I decided to have a private ceremony, and then when I felt better, we could do the whole big wedding thing. We already had our marriage license. To keep it small, we didn't want to tell anyone until an hour before we were supposed to meet the Pastor at the church. We had just called our families and close friends to say we needed to talk to them about something at the church and would meet them there.

"I saw a street vendor selling flowers. He had set up in a vacant lot next to a gas station. We needed gas anyway, so after I picked out flowers for my bouquet, we pulled up to the pump. Duke handed me the cash, and I headed in to pay the cashier. The sun reflected off the glass doors. I couldn't see inside. Duke felt something was wrong because other cars were at the pumps, but no one was coming in or out of the store. He moved so the reflection wasn't blinding him, and he saw a gunman holding up the store. The customers were face down on the floor. He knew if I opened the door, it would startle the gunman and he would likely shoot. Duke called my name. I reached out to grab the door handle as I turned to him. He ran and threw himself in front of me, taking me down to the concrete as the glass on the door shattered.

"I was upset with him because it hurt hitting the concrete, and I had no idea what was happening. I told him to get off of me. When he didn't respond, I looked at him; blood was everywhere. He died in my arms. The EMTs kept working on him, but he was gone. The bullet had gone through him and grazed me."

Teresa touched a thin scar on Sophie's upper arm. "Is this the scar?"

Sophie looked at it as if she forgot it was there, "Yes," she paused. "This time, there was no coming back from this. I had known Duke my whole life and loved him very much. Within a few weeks, I had lost two people who made up the most significant part of my world.

"Of course, Lizzy, CJ, and all the others were there for me. Even Duke's parents, who were in such pain of their own at the loss of their son, tried to comfort me." Sophie looked up and shuddered. "It was too much. I left and told them I was never coming back and not to look for me. I hadn't prayed about it. I didn't want to know what the Lord had to say. I dropped an iron curtain down on my past and drove away.

"But God knows all things and he knew what would happen on our next mission and he prepared me. I started having dreams of the life I left behind. Houston said I would weep and weep in my sleep and say things he couldn't understand. He was afraid to wake me. At first, I didn't remember the dreams, but eventually I remembered everything. I felt the pain of losing them all over again, but I was mature enough to handle it then."

"Wow, I got the jest of it from little things I would hear now and then. But I had no idea."

"Teresa, I don't think anyone on this earth can make it through life without some major tragedies or significant loss. Look at you, your mother disappeared, and you were with your father when he was murdered. But here you are, looking to take down the man who killed him. You took care of your brother and found a way to have a good life after all that."

Teresa nodded. "I didn't do it alone. Without Sienna and the families, I don't know what would have happened to us."

"You don't have to think about it because they did find you, or rather you found them. And you are family. As much as any one of us," Sophie said.

"If you had married Duke, you and Mr. Houston would never have met," Teresa said.

"It's hard for me to imagine now. I love Houston so much. But it goes to show, that no matter what tragedy strikes in your life. If you let him, God will take your life and make something beautiful."

Houston hollered, "you ladies ready to go upstairs?"

Sophie and Teresa smiled and got up. Houston handed them each a towel, and they gathered their things and went upstairs.

Wednesday

After breakfast, they drove to Axel Urwin's home. Houston knocked on the door. His daughter, Dana, answered. This time her demeanor was not welcoming.

Dana led them into the glass-enclosed atrium. The ceiling had three skylights, letting in lots of sunlight.

"Dad, you have company," she said. Axel was concentrating on his notes and didn't notice.

"I'll get you all something to drink," Dana said, walking away.

"Come in. I dug out the notes and articles I had assembled before my wife gave me that ultimatum. I think we might be able to piece together something that might help you," Axel said, waving them in.

Sophie whispered to Houston, "I'm going to see if Dana is alright." Houston nodded.

Sophie walked into the kitchen; Dana's back was to her. "Can I help, Dana?"

"No, you've done plenty already," Dana said bitterly.

"I'm sorry. I have no idea what you are talking about."

"I had convinced my father to live with us in Boston. Now he says he's staying here. You sparked the reporter in him again. But he needs to be with his family. Not here alone."

"I'm sorry, Dana. We had no idea. We can go. We'll tell him we changed our mind," Sophie said.

Dana turned from the counter, where she was pouring iced tea. She lowered her head. "No. I'm sorry. I was kidding myself thinking dad would leave. He'll never leave this house; mom's presence is everywhere. He loved her so much," Dana said.

"Can he take care of himself?"

"Yes, there is nothing wrong with him. He is strong as an ox; he has been as long as I've been alive. My son wants to be just like him. He's going to college this year. He wants to be an investigative journalist, like his grandpa.

"Before mom died, we talked about him attending college here. Who better to learn from than the best investigative journalist in the Southwest. He will be good company for dad. They like to fish and hike in the mountains."

"I'm sure your son will be great company for your father," Sophie said.

"Maybe, after his grandson graduate's college, dad will change his mind. But I doubt it. I just miss him." Dana went back to pouring iced tea in glasses filled with ice.

"Can I help you carry those?" Sophie asked. Dana nodded, and the conversation was over.

CHAPTER ELEVEN

They had been sorting through notes and reading articles for an hour when Sophie's cell rang. It was Sissy.

"Hello, Sissy. Can I put you on speaker? We are here with Axel Urwin, sorting through his notes on corruption in Henderson."

"If you want him to hear, that's up to you," Sissy said.

"The name you gave me to do a deep dive on, Detective Philip Mason, I'm sending it to you now by email. The file is too big to send by text. Do you want me to give you an overview?" Sissy asked.

"Yes, please."

"Detective Mason and a dozen friends joined the police academy after a short stint in college. Henderson has two newspapers. The smaller one, the Tribune, runs an article annually about the new recruits entering the Police Academy. They did a short piece on the friends joining up together. They got a quote from them about their plan to eradicate the criminal element in Henderson. They felt corruption from neighboring Las Vegas was filtering into their once cozy, safe community. Their goal was to push it back to the boundary line. After they graduated, they paired up and put in for different districts to cover the whole city. They remained best friends. They spent all their time together, even after they got married and started families. The Tribune covered police functions, including the yearly picnic. There are pictures of the group together there and at other events. The Newspapers ran articles when any of them made a big bust or got promoted. They advanced quickly, a few became detectives in three years, the now Deputy Chief Anthony Edwards made lieutenant. A couple of others were promoted to sergeant.

"They had their own private group on Facebook. All the BBQs, birthday parties, and vacations were spent together. All online for the world to see. They had been on the police force for ten years when Mason's wife became ill. The entire thing was played out on their Facebook group page. They prayed together, and dinners were brought in when she was too sick to cook. The other wives would go to appointments with her when Mason was working. The things you'd expect from a close group of friends.

"The treatment she needed was not covered by insurance because it wasn't approved by the FDA. Mason was paying for it out of pocket, and it was expensive. He blew through his savings and was getting desperate. His friends stepped up and drained all their savings to help. It was moving, but it wasn't enough.

"Mason started complaining to his friends and sometimes on his Facebook page. He was angry that the criminals they put in jail were back on the streets in no time, making all sorts of money from illegal activities. And he couldn't even pay for his wife's medicine on his police salary.

"I'm unsure what happened after that because he stopped posting on the group site. But the others posted that Mason paid back all his friends. After that, the group split. Six of them disappeared from the Facebook group at the same time as Mason.

I have theories, but I'll let you draw your own conclusions. Concerning his financials, there is one numbered account in the Bahamas I could link to him. Besides that, I saw that he went to Las Vegas four times a year. His tax returns showed small winnings at the casinos. It's about the time their lifestyle started exceeding his pay grade. I didn't check into the friends that stayed with him, but my guess is it would be a mirror image. It's also when the rumor mill started whispering his name. He retired at his twenty-year mark to get his pension and moved to Florida. The others remained on the job for a few more years. I know two are still on active duty.

"That's the jest of it. When you go through it, call me if you have any questions," Sissy offered.

"Thank you, Sissy, you are amazing, like always," Sophie said.

"Talk soon," Sissy said and hung up.

"Axel, can I print off the email on your printer?"

"Yes."

Houston found the list of recruits Sissy told them about. They spent the morning going through the email material and Axel's notes.

"Teresa, can you go through all the newspaper articles that mention any of these men," Houston turned to Axel. "Is there a whiteboard or something she can tape them to?" Houston asked.

Use the glass wall; the tape won't hurt it," Axel replied. "There is tape in that desk," Axel pointed to a desk across the room.

"Ok, Teresa, can you tape them in order on the wall."

"Sure, Mr. Houston."

"Axel, you told us you started investigating Detective Gilbert. I don't see the notes. Has anyone else run across his name in the stack of notes?" Sophie asked.

"No, not yet," Houston said.

"You won't find much. I was just getting started when I quit. And at the time, I had no reason to think Gilbert killed his partner."

"I found his name, Mis Sophie. There are articles about him in the paper." Teresa shuffled through the articles and handed her the ones that mentioned Gilbert.

"Thanks, Teresa."

Sophie read the articles and saw that he and Detective Cox were mentioned for making mid-level busts. An illegal bookmaking bust was mentioned. The reports had no hint of wrongdoing, so she set them aside.

Dana had brought sandwiches in for lunch, and they took a break so their eyes could rest.

"Axel, we need to know what Luna says about her relationship with Detective Gilbert. I don't think we can expose ourselves to her yet. Do you have any ideas?" Houston asked.

"There are two options. You can send Teresa's attorney to tell Luna he was contacted to execute the Will. But that would be showing your hand. Or I could say I'm following up on the murders and her missing children to bring the case back to the forefront."

"The latter seems like the best route. What do you think, Sophie?" Houston said.

"Yeah. I like it. Would you wear a camera and mic?"

"If you like. Nevada has a one-person consent law, so it would be legal," Axel said.

"Rio's Diner closes at three. We can watch the monitor from the hotel, it's only a few blocks away. If you wear an earpiece, we can talk to you if we want you to ask her something.

With the decision made, they decided to clean up the mess. They made piles by category and stacked them neatly to start fresh again the next day.

As Houston, Sophie, Teresa, and Bully were leaving, Dana came out of the kitchen and said goodbye. She was returning to Boston in the morning and would not likely see them again.

"Dana, I am so sorry about your mother. I know the pain of a loss like that. But your father still wants to make a difference here in Henderson. He doesn't want to be put out to pasture."

Dana nodded, she knew it was true, but she wanted to look after him. Sophie gave her a hug, and they headed back to the hotel.

Houston went through the surveillance equipment Manny had lent them and pulled out a key fob and a watch. "Sophie, which one will be less conspicuous?"

"I'd go with the key fog. Do we have an earwig?"

"Yes. We have a secure monitor too."

A knock came at the door at 3 pm. Houston answered it and let Axel in. They spent the next ten minutes talking about where to place the key fob. Houston explained the best way to sit to avoid having the earwig visible.

Finally, they discussed the information they needed from Luna and how to handle Gilbert if he showed up.

Axel headed to Luna's house. Houston, Sophie, and Teresa sat around the monitor, watching his every move. Axel drove down the alley behind the hotel that ended at the back side of the diner. He pulled over, making sure he didn't block the alley with his car, and waited.

They had agreed he should wait until he saw Luna leave the diner before approaching her.

Ten minutes later, Bently and Luna came out of the back door. Bently had two 30-gallon garbage bags and headed to the commercial garbage cans enclosed in a gate. Luna locked the back door. After closing the gate, Bently headed toward his Harley. Luna and Bently said something as they passed. Bently straddled his bike, starting the engine. Then he put on his helmet and kicked the stand as he drove off.

Luna went to where a garden hose was rolled up on a metal holder and turned it on. She laid it on the dry earth underneath her flower garden on the left side of the wide stairs and landing that led to her front door. As she waited for the water to saturate the ground, she pulled out the weeds that had sprung up. Then she moved the hose to the other side of the stairs and watered those flowers. She took the weeds to a residential garbage can on the side of the house, then turned off the hose, rolling it back on its stand.

Axel chose that moment to get out of the car and walk up to her. "Hello, Mrs. Nuñez."

Luna jumped, startled that someone had walked up on her. She put her hand to her chest, "Oh, you frightened me."

"I apologize. I didn't mean to come up so stealthily. I don't know if you remember me. I interviewed you for an article on the murder of your husband and Detective Cox. I wrote about your missing children too."

"Axel Urwin, right? I remember. I appreciated that your article focused on my missing children. A majority of the other articles were about Detective Cox. Why are you here, Mr. Urwin? She asked.

"May I come in?"

"Yes, please."

Axel followed her up the stairs and waited for her to unlock the door. She led him into the house. It was dark, to help keep it cool.

Luna turned on the air-conditioning and opened a few blinds to let light in. "Please sit. I'll get us some iced tea."

"Thank you," Axel sat down and put the key fob on the table.

"Mr. Urwin, what brings you here?" Luna asked as she pulled a pitcher of iced tea from the fridge. She took two glasses, held each under the ice dispenser in the fridge, and poured tea over them. Once she set them on the table, she took a seat.

"Please call me Axel."

"If you'll call me Luna."

Axel nodded, taking a sip of tea. "This hits the spot, thank you," he looked up at her and paused. "I know the murders have not been solved, and your children have not been located. I thought it might be time to stir things up again and get some attention brought to the lack of progress."

"I see. I appreciate that, Axel. You're right. It's been a long time since there has been any movement on the case."

"Have the police kept you in the loop?" Axel asked.

"Oscar, Detective Cox's partner, has kept in touch. He's been truly kind to me. He knows how difficult this has been."

"Luna, you left the mental institution to get off the medication. It was in one of the articles published about you when you returned. But why didn't you come home?"

Luna hung her head, "Axel, you don't understand. The medication changed me," she pointed to her head, "up here. I was on the street until I found a women's shelter that took me in. I worked for free, keeping the place clean, so they wouldn't kick me out. When an opening came up, they hired me. But I never left the shelter. I couldn't. My paranoia and anxiety kept me prisoner in my own mind. If I tried to go outside, I would have a panic attack. It was so bad at times the EMTs had to be called. I was no good to myself, let alone my family.

"When Rio was killed, the police checked the employment security department. They had them search for my social security number; that's how they found me. When they came to the shelter, the police asked me to return to Henderson. I went into a full-blown panic attack. The paramedics were called. A woman I worked with talked me down and helped me to get into the police cruiser so they could take me to Henderson.

"Under the circumstances, they took me here instead of the police station to talk to me. With Bently's help, I arranged Rio's funeral, but I couldn't go. Bently videoed it for me. So many people came and said how much they cared for him. It was quite moving. After some time, I was able to leave the house and include the diner in my safe zone."

At the hotel, Teresa was seeing and hearing all this. Tears streamed down her face. It was the first time she had heard what happened to her mother after she left.

Sophie held her. "Teresa, I don't advise it, but if you want to talk to your mother, we will go with you."

"No. Not until I know how involved she is with the man who killed my father." They went back to watching the live stream.

Axel changed the subject. "Luna, what have the police been telling you about the case?"

"Detective Willis, the lead investigator, wanted to know if the diner was a front to sell drugs. There was no way Rio was involved with drugs. Since they had no proof of the allegation, it was dropped. Then they thought it might have been a robbery. The money in the cash register was gone. But Detective Cox's gun and wallet had not been disturbed, so that led nowhere.

"Oscar thinks it was random violence. He blamed himself. He thinks when he unlocked the door to see his CI, it left an opportunity for someone to come in and kill them and take the money."

"Has Detective Gilbert ever given you pause to think maybe he knows more than he is telling you?"

"Oscar? No. He has been very forthcoming. He knows how hard this has been on me. He was devastated when he found his partner dead."

Houston turned to Sophie, "do you think we should drop the idea of letting her know that Gilbert is involved?" Sophie considered it.

"My instincts tell me Luna has nothing to do with this. But we risk her telling Oscar if she doesn't believe Axel."

"Let's see how she reacts to the idea." Houston pushed the button to speak to Axel in the earwig.

"Ask her how involved with Gilbert she is. Then drop the idea he could be involved."

Axel paused for a moment, then said, "Luna, you seem to be very fond of Detective Gilber."

"I am, he has been very kind to me," she paused. "I'm lonely here by myself. He comes over for dinner sometimes."

"Luna, I'm an investigative reporter. A few years back, I started digging into corruption in the Henderson Police Department. Oscar's name came up."

Luna was shocked, "no, you must be wrong. No way is Oscar, a corrupt police officer. He has been there for me through all of this."

Axel sat there watching Luna's mind running through the idea in her head. No doubt she was dissecting every move he's made and every questionable conversation.

"No, I don't believe it. You're wrong," Luna concluded.

Axel moved on, "when was the last time Detective Willis brought you up to date on the case?"

"I don't usually speak to him; Oscar keeps me informed of the investigation."

"I'm surprised he was allowed to work on the case since he was so close to it," Axel said.

"He's not supposed to, but his Lieutenant knows he's involved. How could he not? It was his partner that was killed."

"Did they ever locate the confidential informant?"

"The CI?" Luna looked puzzled.

"The one Gilbert said he went to go see when Cox and your husband were shot."

"Oh, I don't know."

"What did the surveillance cameras show?" Axel knew Teresa took the laptop the camera fed into.

"The laptop that stored the surveillance was taken," Luna said.

"I know there was a city-wide search for your children, but the Amber Alert was only sent out once. Do you know why?"

"No, I wasn't here yet when all that was happening. Detective Willis was convinced they ran away. When they searched the house, they found the kid's clothes and personal items missing, and other clothes discarded on the floor with dried blood on them. It wasn't like a kidnapper would have taken time to let them get their things."

"That makes sense. But why do you think Teresa and Kato would have run away?" Axel asked.

Luna turned and looked out the window toward the desert behind her house. "The only thing that makes sense is that they saw what happened, and they ran."

"But why not call the police and tell them what they saw?" Axel was trying to get her to reason this out for herself.

Luna looked at him. He could see her mind racing. "Because they knew the person who shot their father."

"You think they recognized the shooter? But why didn't the shooter kill them too?" Axel let her think that through.

"The shooter didn't know they were there, or he panicked and ran out," she reasoned.

"Yes, that makes sense. Luna, if the person who killed Rio was someone Teresa and Kato knew, why didn't they call the police and tell them?" That's when there was a breakthrough. Axel saw it in her eyes.

"Because the person who killed Rio was a cop." Luna stood up, "No, no, no. It can't be true," Luna turned and ran into the bathroom. Axel could hear her throwing up. She was going into a full-blown panic attack. Axel grabbed the key fob and stood outside the bathroom door. He spoke just loud enough for Houston to hear.

"She's having a panic attack. We can't use her to get to Oscar. This might have been a mistake."

Houston spoke in his ear, "check on her and see if she needs medical attention."

He knocked on the door. "Luna, do you need me to call paramedics?"

There was no answer. He knocked again and told her he was coming in. Luna was curled up on the floor crying. Axel knelt down beside her.

"Luna, do you need me to get you help?"

"No," she said through tears.

A knock came at the front door. "Do you want me to answer that?"

Luna pushed herself up with her arm and leaned on it, "no. It has to be Oscar, he was coming for dinner. I can't talk to him."

"What do you want me to do?"

"He knows I don't leave the property. I'm either here or at the diner. He'll go check there before he comes back," she looked up at Axel. "You think he killed them, don't you?"

"I know he did."

Luna quickly moved to the toilet and threw up again until there was nothing left to throw up. Then the dry heaves started. Axel moved out into the hall and spoke to Houston.

"Houston, she can't go to the door. What should I do?

"Tell her to stay in the bathroom. Say you will try to get rid of Oscar. You can tell him you were talking to her about doing an article on her missing children, and she had a panic attack."

Axel went back into the bathroom. "Luna, I'm going to lock this door behind me. Then I'm going to let Oscar in and tell him you had a panic attack when I started talking to you about your missing children." Axel closed the door behind him.

A few minutes later, Oscar was back, knocking again. This time he hollered through the door. "Luna, are you alright? It's me, Oscar. If you don't answer, I will come in to check on you."

Axel opened the door. Oscar was shocked to see someone other than Luna. "What are you doing here?" His words gave Axel the impression he recognized him. Axel had interviewed him when he was writing his articles about the murders.

"I came to talk to Luna about doing another article on her children. There has been no movement on the missing persons case for years. She was fine one minute, then suddenly, she ran to the bathroom and started throwing up."

Oscar pushed past Axel and went to the bathroom door. "Luna, are you alright? It's me, Oscar. Can I come in so I can check on you?"

Luna didn't answer for a long time. Finally, she said, "no, please leave me alone. I'll be fine if I just have some time to myself."

"Are you sure?" Oscar asked.

Axel would almost believe Oscar cared about her if he wasn't the man who killed her husband.

"What are you doing here, Axel. You have no right to bring up her children. She is not a stable woman."

"She must be pretty stable. She runs a restaurant," Axel rebuffed.

"She has panic attacks."

Axel changed the subject. "Detective Gilbert, what are you doing here?"

"Not that it's any of your business, but I've been keeping an eye out for her and keeping her informed of our progress."

"What progress? Nothing has been done for years on this," Axel said.

"True, the case has gone cold, but it's important to let the victim's family know that the police are still looking." Oscar moved closer to Axel. "Why don't you leave. I'll stay until Luna calms down. It takes a while sometimes."

"Let's ask her what she wants." Axel moved to the bathroom door. "Luna, do you want Detective Gilbert and me to stay to make sure you're alright?"

"No, please, both of you leave. I need to be alone."

"Luna, I don't like the idea of leaving you alone in this state," Oscar said through the door.

"Please, go, both of you."

Axel and Oscar walked to the front door. Axel turned the lock on the knob so the door would lock behind them.

"I'd like to interview you again, Detective. I plan to revive this story, so the public renews their interest in it. If the public gets involved, the police will have to reopen the case."

Oscar closed the door behind them as they stepped out onto the landing.

"Why don't you leave it alone, Axel. It only causes her more pain. You see what it does to her."

"I have one other question. Did Detective Wills ever find your CI? Axel asked, watching the detective's reaction to the idea of all this being stirred up again.

"Let sleeping dogs lie, Axel. You're just asking for trouble."

With that, they parted ways, and Axel went to his SUV.

CHAPTER TWELVE

A knock came at the door. Houston opened it and let Axel in. He handed Houston the key fob and earwig, then sat at the table.

Sophie brought him a can of Fanta Orange from the fridge.

"Axel, give me your read on Luna," Houston said.

"Luna had no idea Gilbert was involved with the murders or that he was using her to find her children. I know he believes they will call her eventually. Which leads me to the fact he is likely tapping her phone and may even have a bug in her house."

"You were in the bathroom when you told her you had proof Oscar killed them, right?" Houston asked.

Axel thought for a moment, "yes."

"Ok, assuming Oscar has a bug in the house, it is not likely there is one in the bathroom. We might be all right," Sophie said.

Teresa spoke up. "I need to go see her. She has nothing to do with this, and you said yourself she had no idea Detective Gilbert was the one that killed my father."

"Teresa, it would be a big risk. If Oscar comes back and sees you, you will be in great danger."

"I need to talk to her myself. I need some answers," Theresa insisted.

"She was still in the midst of a panic attack when I left," Axel said. We should wait until tomorrow."

"No, I need to see her."

"Luna seems very comfortable with Bently. Why don't we let him know she is having a panic attack? He may be able to calm her down," Sophie said.

Thirty minutes later, Bently pulled up alongside the SUV. Houston had parked in the alley, Bently was on his 1984 Red Harley Softail. Houston handed him a bug detector to sweep the place before they came in.

Bently went to Luna's door and knocked. When there was no response, he used his key to unlock the door. He stepped in and hollered Luna's name. No answer. He knew she often fell asleep after an episode. Bently swept the kitchen and living room. He found a listening device on a black sculpture of an American Indian Warrior. He walked down the hall and checked Kato's room. As he passed the bathroom, the door was locked. He reached above the door frame to get a long metal piece that unlocked the door. He called her name, when she didn't answer, he unlocked it. Luna was asleep on the oval throw rug on the bathroom floor. Before waking her, he swept Teresa's room and the master bedroom. There was only one more device. It was on the smoke detector in the master bedroom.

Bently knelt down next to Luna and whispered her name softly. She opened her eyes and sat up, pulling her knees to her chest, wrapping her arms around them.

"Bently, what are you doing here?"

"I came to check on you. We need to talk."

"Axel Urwin came to see me."

"I know. There are some people I need you to meet. Freshen up; I'll wait in the hall."

While Luna washed her face and brushed her teeth, Bently texted Houston to come to the back door.

When Luna stepped out of the bathroom, Bently put his finger to his lips to tell her not to say anything. He moved her to Teresa's room and asked her to sit.

"Why are we in here? You're scaring me, Bently."

"Do your breathing exercises, Luna. There are no listening devices in here."

"What?" Luna's voice went up.

"Yes, Oscar put listening devices in your home. Stay calm," Bently went to let the others in the back door.

Houston, Sophie, Axel, Teresa, and Bully stepped in. Bently pointed out the bugs. They walked down the hall to Teresa's room. Bently closed the door behind them.

"Bently, who are these people?"

He sat next to her, "I need you to stay calm."

Luna looked at him and took some deep breaths. "Please tell me what's going on."

"Luna, these people are here to help us. You know Axel," then he introduced Houston and Sophie. When he came to the young woman, Teresa took off her glasses and ballcap and waited for her mother to recognize her.

It took a moment for Luna to realize it was Teresa. She stood and moved to her slowly. "Teresa?"

"Yes, mama, it's me," then Teresa started crying. Luna wrapped her arms around her, kissing her forehead and hugging her tightly.

"Teresa, I've missed you so much. I love you. Is Kato here too?"

Teresa moved back. "No, he is safe."

"Tell me, what is going on here?"

"Mama, I hired Mr. Houston and Miss Sophie to help me put the man who killed papa in jail and to help me settle his estate."

Luna pulled Teresa over to the bed to sit down next to her. Bully lay down at Teresa's feet. Sophie sat on the desk chair, and Houston and Axel leaned against the wall.

"You have to tell me everything, Teresa."

Teresa ran her through a condensed version of what happened. She stopped before telling her mother where they were living.

"Oh, baby, I'm so sorry you went through that. But how have you survived these last three years, and where is Kato?" Luna asked.

"I'm not going to tell you that, mama."

"But he's my son. I want to see him."

"No, you left us. Kato has no idea who you are, and I won't let him come back here. It would be too traumatic for him to face this place again. Maybe in time, you could come to see him."

"Teresa, I'm his mother; you can't keep him from me."

"Yes, I can. When you didn't come home, you gave up your right to him."

Bently stepped in, "Teresa, that's not fair. Your mother was ill. It wasn't her choice to leave you. She loves you."

"No, Bently. She could have come back, but she didn't," she turned back to her mother. "You left the institution and went to a shelter; you could have just as easily called papa. He would have brought you home. We almost lost him too when he couldn't find you, but he overcame his depression and took care of us."

"Teresa, you are being too hard on her," Bently said.

"I love you, mama, but you made your choice years ago. I'm here to settle papa's estate. He left the diner to Kato and me."

"I know that," Luna said, through tears. "Bently told me. I opened it up again, so it would still be worth something when you returned. Bently and I partnered up and have been running it. We take a salary, but the profits at the end of each year have been going into a savings account for when you returned."

"We knew someday you would come back."

"Thank you. What will you do if I sell this place?"

"We've talked about that, Teresa," Bently said. "We want to buy the diner and the house from you."

"Ok. If that's what you want," Teresa said. "I have a local attorney. He can take care of that. But I'm not here just to settle the Will. I know who killed papa, and Mr. Houston and Miss Sophie are going to help me put him behind bars."

"How, Teresa? If you have proof, it was Detective Gilbert. How are you going to prove it?"

"I have the security tape from that day. It shows what happened."

"Is that why you ran? You were afraid he would kill you and Kato?" Luna asked.

"Yes, and he will if he finds out she is in town, Luna," Sophie said. "Can you keep this secret? You can't let Oscar know anything has changed. Are you able to pull that off?"

Luna looked at Bently, "I don't know. I'm not good at hiding my feelings."

"Are you going to take the security video to the police?" Bently asked.

"Yes, as soon as we decide who to trust. We don't know how many police officers are involved in this protection scheme or what other graft they have perpetrated," Houston said.

"That's true, and we aren't only exposing the officers involved but the criminals they protect. They won't want this uncovered either," Axel added.

"That's true. We are working on a plan now. Talking to you wasn't part of it, but Teresa insisted she needed to see you," Sophie said.

"Teresa, this sounds too dangerous. You need to go back to where you were. I'll help them take down the man who killed Rio and Detective Cox," Luna said. "I can't believe Oscar bugged my home," Luna dropped her head.

"No, I'm seeing this through, mama. I trust Mr. Houston and Miss Sophie to protect me." Teresa was talking when they heard Luna's phone ring in the kitchen.

"My guess, it's Oscar," Bently said.

151

"You have to answer it, or he may come over," Sophie instructed. They all moved into the kitchen. Luna put the phone on speaker when she answered it.

"Hello."

"Luna, are you alright?"

"Oscar. Yes, I'm fine now. Thank you for checking on me."

"Are you alone?"

Sophie whispered in her ear; he must have seen Bently's Harley.

"No, I called Bently to come over."

"Oh, can I come over and see for myself you are alright?"

"No, I'm fine, Oscar. I need to rest."

"Oh. All right. I'll see you tomorrow then."

"Thanks for calling," Luna hung up. She sat on the bar stool. "I can't do this, Bently." Houston waved his hand and pointed to the listening device. They moved back to Teresa's bedroom.

"I'm sorry, but I can't talk to him knowing what he has done," Luna confessed.

"I don't see another option if you want to keep Teresa safe," Sophie said.

"Oh...I can do it to keep you safe, Teresa."

"Are you dating Detective Gilbert," Sophie asked on a hunch.

Luna looked away for a moment, "not exactly. He and his new partner come in when they are on duty to eat their meal after we close. Then, once a week, he started coming back when he got off duty. He said it was to keep me up to date on the investigation. It has expanded to dinners at my place. Mostly he would bring in something from another restaurant, so I wouldn't have to cook, or we would BBQ outside."

"That explains why he feels he can intrude on your life, even make some demands," Houston said.

Luna looked at her daughter, "Teresa, I had no idea what he had done. I thought he cared about me," Luna said. Teresa didn't respond.

"Houston, may I speak with you outside, please?" Sophie said.

Houston and Sophie stepped out the back door and whispered.

"Houston, this is going to cause us complications. There is no way Luna can handle Gilbert. If she cuts him off, he is going to get suspicious. He may hurt her."

"What do you have in mind."

"We are going to have to send Teresa to stay with Burly. He will keep her safe. You and I can stay here with Luna."

"How is she going to explain this?"

"Luna can say she hired us to find her children since the police have stopped looking."

"That could work. We can't work from here with those listening devices. I have an idea how we can get rid of them."

Houston and Sophie returned to Teresa's room to tell them their new plan.

"Luna, you obviously do not feel comfortable handling Detective Gilbert alone. Sophie and I have a plan," Houston turned to Teresa. "Teresa, we need you to stay with Burly for the rest of the time we're here." Teresa started to object, but Houston put his hand up. "You will still work with us but stay with Burly in the evenings. Sophie and I will stay here with your mother. She can tell Oscar that Axel recommended she hire us to find you and Kato since the police have stopped looking."

"Oh, I see. Yes, that could work," Luna said.

"Bently, you will have to stay with her if we are out following a lead when she is off shift," Sophie said. "We can't leave any opportunity for Oscar to get to her alone."

"I'll do whatever you need," Bently said.

"Our next problem is getting these listening devices out of here," Houston said.

"I know how to get rid of the one on the statue," Bently said.

Luna looked at him and nodded. She knew what he was thinking. "Bently gave that statue to Rio. It's part of a set. Rio admired it every time he went to watch sports with Bently. One day Bently brought this one over for Rio as a gift."

"Alright, it's time for us to go. Tomorrow we will show up after the diner closes. If Oscar wants to come over, let him, and we'll get this ruse going."

Ten minutes after the others left, Bently and Luna went to the living room to remove one of the listening devices.

"Thanks for coming over, Bently."

"I'm here for you anytime, Luna. You know that."

Luna stepped over to the statue. "I'd appreciate it if you would take this. Rio loved this statue, but it belongs to you. I've been getting rid of some of Rio's things. It's a hard reminder he's gone. It needs to be reunited with its companion at your place."

"I know he left it to me in his Will, but I didn't want to take it."

"No, it belongs with you," Luna lifted it and gave it to Bently.

"Alright then. Will you be all right to work tomorrow?"

"Yes, I'll be there."

Houston dropped Axel at his car, parked in the hotel lot.

"I'll continue to work on digging up who else is in on the protection racket."

"Thanks, Axel," Sophie said.

When they got to their room, Teresa went to pack her bag. "I don't like this. I want to be with you. I shouldn't have changed our plans by insisting on seeing my mother."

"Teresa, in a way, it's a better plan. This way, we are out in the open and can move around."

"But I want to work with you," Teresa complained.

"I understand, but Burly will take good care of you, and we'll come get you when we can. Burly can work on selling Rio's Diner to Luna and Bently."

"Ok, can Bully stay with me?"

"Yes, if it's alright with Burly," Sophie said.

Houston called Burly and told him what was going on. Burly said he was happy to have Teresa anytime. They agreed to bring her over when the diner closed the next day.

Thursday

After getting Teresa and Bully settled at Burly's, Houston and Sophie headed to Luna's. As they were unloading their suitcases, Oscar showed up.

"What's going on here?" he asked.

Luna turned when she heard his voice and stepped outside. "Oh, Oscar, I'm glad you're here. I've hired Mr. and Mrs. Townsend to find Kato and Teresa. Axel recommended them."

"What? Why would you do that?" It was apparent Oscar was angry.

"Because the police consider it a cold case, and I need to have my kids back," Luna said, aggravated. "And what business is it of yours what I do."

Oscar was visibly stunned by the intensity of Luna's response.

"They will get in the way of the investigation. Private Investigators always do."

Luna put her hands on her hips. She was standing on the landing above Oscar, who was at the bottom of the steps. "What investigation, Oscar? Your department has done nothing in three years."

"That's not fair. We have worked hard on this case."

Luna took a deep breath and lowered her hands. "You're right. I know the department worked hard for months trying to solve this case. It's time for me to take my life into my own hands."

"You know nothing about these people. They could be scam artists, bilking you dry of all your money." Oscar didn't care that Houston and Sophie were standing right there.

"I appreciate your concern, but Axel knows them, and that's good enough for me."

Oscar turned to them and said. "I'm going to investigate you. If I find out you are not legitimate, I will arrest you."

"Have at it," Houston said, annoyed. They had called Sissy the night before to put up a website. They wanted it to look like it was five years old. Sissy said she'd add reviews saying how they found their loved ones. Sissy included Houston's bodyguard, and Sophie's consultant covers, to add to the illusion.

"Luna, can I speak to you privately for a moment?" Oscar asked.

"We'll put our things inside, Luna, so you can speak privately," Houston said, moving the luggage into the house.

When Oscar saw that Houston and Sophie were out of earshot, he said, "Luna, don't do this. I've been here for you, haven't I?"

"Yes, you have, and I appreciate it. But speaking with Axel yesterday reminded me I haven't done everything I can to find my children. And I want to see the man who killed my husband and your partner behind bars. If I'm ever going to get better, I need to get to the end of this."

Oscar went to take her hand, but Luna pulled it away. It surprised him. "Luna, I thought we had something."

"I may have given you the wrong impression, Oscar. It's been lonely for me since I came home. I enjoy your company and feel comfortable talking to you. I'm sorry if you thought I had romantic feelings for you. It's my fault, really. I'm sorry."

"That's not true. I know you like me."

"I do like you, Oscar. But I don't want a romantic relationship with you. I shouldn't have given you that impression. I'm sorry," she turned toward the house. He grabbed her arm.

"Luna, you will regret this."

Luna looked confused, "is that some sort of threat?"

"No, no," he removed his hand from her arm. "I just mean I have been a good friend to you. You need me."

"If I do, I'll call. Thank you for everything you've done."

Luna walked into the house and leaned against the door after she closed it. Her heart started racing, and she was hyperventilating. Luna felt a panic attack coming on. Sophie went to her.

"Luna, look at me. I want you to take slow, deep breaths and walk with me. Keep your eyes focused on something and walk."

They walked up and down the hall while Luna took deep breaths. Finally, her heart rate lowered, and she calmed down.

"I didn't think I could stand up to him."

"You did well. Now we need to get rid of the other bug. I have an idea," Houston said.

Detective Gilbert left and went back to his office. He knew this could cause him problems. He looked up Houston and Sophie Townsend on his computer and found a website. It depicted them as cape crusaders specializing in finding missing persons.

As long as they stick to looking for Luna's kids and they don't dig into my extracurriculars. I can stand a little scrutiny. If Teresa took that security tape and the Townsends found them, that could be a problem. But the chances of that are slim to none. I need that listening device more than ever, and she gave that stupid statue to Bently. I'll have to find another way to get in there.

But Luna. That surprised me. I was beginning to like her. Well, no matter. Her loss.

"Now that we are out in the open, I'm going to the police department. I am going to introduce myself to Deputy Chief Anthony Edwards. Axel vouched for the deputy chief, but I need to see for myself. Sophie, we need to check this place for bugs again," he turned to Luna. "It would be wise to change the locks and add a deadbolt to the front and back doors. We need to put an alarm on the windows too."

"You go, Houston. I'll take care of securing the house for her."

While Sophie called a locksmith and secured Luna's home, Houston headed to the Police headquarters. Deputy Chief Anthony Edwards had his office on the second floor.

Houston didn't call ahead to see if the deputy chief was available. He went through the metal detectors and asked for directions to his office. He got on an elevator and punched the button for the second floor.

When the elevator doors opened, he saw the Internal Affairs offices on the door straight ahead. He turned right, as instructed. He saw the door titled Deputy Chief of Police for the City of Henderson, Anthony Edwards.

He walked into a reception area. A woman was sitting at a desk, the desk plate said Assistant to the Deputy Chief. There wasn't room for her name after her title.

The woman looked up and smiled a pleasant smile. "Hello, may I help you?"

"Yes, I would like to speak with Deputy Chief Anthony Edwards, please."

"The assistant looked down at her computer switching from whatever she was working on to Deputy Chief Edward's appointment calendar."

"Your name, sir?"

"Houston Townsend."

"I'm sorry, sir, but I do not see you on his calendar for today."

"You're right. I do not have an appointment. But if you tell him Attorney Burly Blackrock and Axel Urwin referred me to him, he may see me."

"Mr. Townsend, I will be happy to ask, but he is very busy. It is not likely he will have time for you today. If you like, I can make you an appointment."

"No, I understand. Could you ask, just in case?

"Certainly. Can I tell the deputy chief what this is about?"

"The murder of one of your detectives," Houston said.

The look of surprise on her face left in the blink of an eye. "Yes, please have a seat."

Houston was about to sit on one of the square wooden chairs with upholstered seats and backs when the assistant returned.

"Deputy Chief Edwards will see you now."

CHAPTER THIRTEEN

Edwards stood when Houston came in and stepped out from behind his desk to reach his hand out to him. Houston shook it and thanked him for seeing him without an appointment.

"If Burly and Axel sent you, I figured it was important," Edwards said. He returned to his desk and sat, directing Houston to a seat on the other side. "What is it I can do for you, Mr. Townsend."

"Houston, please."

"Alright, let's keep it informal. Call me Anthony."

"Thank you," Houston looked behind him to make sure his assistant closed the door behind her. "Anthony, I believe I have information that could help solve the murder of one of your detectives."

"I'm listening."

"I'm afraid it's not that easy. My information exposes corruption in your ranks, and my problem is I don't know who to trust."

"You came to me, Houston. By the same token, how do I know I can trust you or your evidence."

"Fair enough. Please look up the director of the FBI in DC headquarters and call that number. You can ask him if I am to be trusted."

Anthony looked at Houston for a long minute, wondering if he would be wasting his time. He sat up, pulled his keypad closer to him and looked up the number. He dialed, and a woman answered.

"Director Cosby's office."

"Yes, ma'am, may I speak to the director?"

"May I ask your name and what this is concerning?"

"Yes. I'm Deputy Chief of Henderson, Nevada, Anthony Edwards. I have Houston Townsend in my office, and he is using your director as a character reference."

"One moment, please," the assistant put the call on hold. Anthony expected he would be on hold for a good long time, but someone picked up the line right away. Anthony sat up straighter.

"Deputy Chief Edwards, this is Director Cosby. How can I help you?"

"Yes, sir. Mr. Townsend tells me he has information that could lead to the man who murdered one of my detectives. When I questioned whether this was legit, he referenced you."

"If Mr. Townsend says he has information that will lead you to a killer. I suggest you listen to him."

"How do you know him?"

"I'm sorry, that is classified."

"Does he work for the FBI?"

"That is classified too. The only information I can divulge is that you can take what Houston Townsend tells you to the bank. Is there anything else?"

"No, I guess not. Thank you." They hung up. Edwards looked at the phone momentarily, then placed it back on its cradle. "Well, that was interesting. But he did vouch for you. Now what do you need from me before you give me the information you have."

"I need you to tell me everything you know about a retired Detective Philip Mason," Houston said.

Edwards was weighing up what to do. "Mason has been retired for years now. How could he be involved with the case you are refereeing to?" Anthony asked.

"Detective Mason started what became an underground group of corrupt officers in your police force. And I believe that led to this murder," Houston said.

Anthony rubbed his hand down his face and took a deep breath. He put his arms on his desk and leaned forward like what he was about to say was personal to him.

"Philip Mason was part of a group of twelve of us who joined the police academy. We had lofty goals of clearing Henderson of the rift raft leaching here from Las Vegas. We made a pact to apply in groups of two to each district in Henderson. We spent our off time together. When we started having our families, we spent BBQs, birthdays, and holidays together. We were closer than blood. We worked hard and did a lot of good for this city.

"When Philip's wife got sick, she needed a treatment that wasn't approved by the FDA, so it was not paid for by our insurance," Anthony went through the entire story.

"Most of the original twelve have retired now, except for me, the chief of police, and the commander of the homicide division."

"Did you ever ask him how he got the money to pay for his wife's medication?" Houston asked.

"Not back then. But a few years ago, I had an attorney come to me in confidence. He told me that his client said a group of officers extorted protection money from his client. He gave me a name. I needed to know if it had anything to do with Philip, so I went to see him in Florida.

"Philip told me everything. He said a mid-size chop shop dealer heard his wife was sick and came to him. He offered to cover her expenses if Mason ensured he didn't get closed down again.

"I'm not saying I agree with what he did. I can only hope I would have made a different decision if it were my wife. He told

163

me that he and the others started a small protection scheme. They were selective not to take on the more significant organized criminals but kept to the ma-and-pop ones. Mostly, small unlicensed gambling dens, chop shops, pawn shops that sell stolen items, and the like. It supplemented their income enough for a decent place to live and a few toys, pay for college for their kids, things like that.

"They were smart. They collected the money and gave it to Mason, who held it in safe deposit boxes. He would go to Vegas four times a year and turn it into casino chips, then distribute it to the others. They would cash them in a little at a time and even claim some winnings on their tax return.

"No one ever got wind of it. I gave Philip the name of the detective the attorney had given me and asked if he had ever been a part of his crew. He wouldn't confirm or deny."

"But you knew they were crooked and did nothing," Houston said.

"True."

"And you are turning your head again?"

"No, not this time. I called up a third-grade detective that had recently gotten promoted. Someone I felt was incorruptible and made the man his partner. But the group was too careful. They never met in public. They never flashed their cash. Six months passed, and the detective told me he thought I was wrong about his partner. Then one day, Detective Cox overheard a conversation. He told me he thought he might have something. But he was killed before he was able to tell us."

"Who was his partner?"

"Detective Oscar Gilbert."

"I know everything you told me is true. Our own investigation produced the same information."

"Do you have proof, Houston?"

"Yes, enough that we can arrest the murderer of Rio Nuñez and Detective Cox now. Or we can try to bring down Gilbert's whole crew."

"Do you have the goods to do that?"

"Not to take down his whole crew. Not yet. But we can get it with your help," Houston said.

"Why are you involved," Anthony asked.

"Teresa Nuñez hired my wife and me to help her settle her father's estate and put his murderer behind bars."

"Teresa and Kato are alive? Everyone assumed they were dead. But I thought they ran because their personal things were missing from their home."

"They are both safe and well. What do you want to do, Anthony?"

The deputy chief leaned back in his desk chair and stared at the picture of his academy graduating class.

"I want to take down the whole crew, but if the murderer gets wind, he could bolt before we arrest him if we wait."

"This has to be your decision. Because there is a good chance you could be right about that."

"Where are you staying?"

"We are staying with Luna Nuñez in the evenings. We feel she needs protection. I'll give you my number so you can call me."

"Good. I need to run this by a few people."

"I'm not sure I'm comfortable with you doing that. The more people that know, the more chance it gets out."

"I get it, but I must run it by the Chief of Police. He's one of the men I signed up with. The only other person I can vouch for completely is the head of Internal Affairs. I won't tell anyone else."

"I understand the chain of command. Call me when you decide," Houston said as he stood. Anthony entered Houston's number into his contacts.

By the time Houston returned to Luna's, the locksmith was there. Houston asked him about the windows' contact alarms, then paid the man when he was done.

"Houston, tell us about your conversation with the deputy chief," Sophie requested.

After telling her and Luna the jest of the conversation, he added, "he is going to call. I left him with the option to arrest Gilbert now or to try to take down the entire crew."

"What do you think he'll do," Luna asked.

"I'm not sure. But we have other things to deal with right now. I have an idea how to get rid of the other bug."

Luna had set her guests up in her room, and she moved to Teresa's. After dinner, a screeching beep started up. Houston had set it off, then hollered to Luna that the batteries in the smoke detectors needed to be changed. She went to get new batteries from the kitchen drawer.

While changing the one in the master bedroom, he said, "Luna, look at this."

"What is it?"

"It looks like a listening device. Do you know how it got here?"

"No."

"We should ask your detective friend to look at this. Maybe he can tell us something."

While Luna called, Houston took a picture of the device and enlarged it. He sent the serial number to Anthony Edwards to check the department's equipment and see if it was one of theirs. He added a text that it was in the smoke detector in Luna Nuñez's bedroom.

Houston planned to put a tracking device on Gilbert's car when he showed up.

"Sophie, while we keep Gilbert busy, put this under his rear bumper. This is the only way we will find the other men in his crew. These men are careful. But they have to meet sometimes, somewhere."

Twenty minutes later, Gilbert pulled up. Sophie went out the back door. Luna let Oscar in.

"Thank you for coming. I didn't know what to do."

"Let me see the device," Gilbert said.

Houston handed it to him. "Wow, you're right. It is a listening device. How did you find it?"

"I was changing the batteries in the smoke detectors," Houston said.

"Well, that was fortunate," he added.

"But I don't understand. Why would someone want to put a bug in my house?" Luna asked.

"It might have been the man who killed your husband and my partner. Maybe he thought your children might call. I better check for other devices."

Gilbert pulled out a small black bug detector and went through the house. "I don't see any other bugs, but I noticed your statue of the American Indian Warrior is missing. Did someone steal it?"

"No, it was actually a gift from Bently to Rio. I returned it to Bently; it was part of a set."

"Oh. Well, I'll see if I can track this bug by its serial number," Gilbert said.

"Thank you, Oscar. I didn't know who else to ask."

"I'm happy to help. Where is your wife, Mr. Townsend?"

"She is here somewhere," Houston said.

"I think she took the garbage out," Luna said.

"Luna, can I speak with you privately for a moment."

"Sure."

"I'll go out back, so you can speak," Houston said.

When Houston closed the door, Oscar said, "Luna, you can't trust these people. I did a background check on them. Other than a website, their background is sketchy."

"I appreciate your concern, Oscar. But I've made up my mind. I need them to find my children."

"I can take vacation time and go look for them. You don't need to pay someone," Oscar said.

"With all the resources of the police department, you haven't been able to do it. How would you do it on your own?"

"I have other ways."

"Then why haven't you used them?" Luna bit back. Oscar had no response. "Look, Oscar, I know you want to help, but they are already here. I've made up my mind."

"Alright, I'll see if I can find out who put this in your home."

"Thank you."

Luna watched as Oscar got in his car and left.

After Oscar left, Sophie and Houston came in the back door. "Alright, things are in motion. He will call for his crew and meet up with them somewhere. Gilbert needs to tell them someone is digging into their business."

"Let's get Bently over here, then Sophie and I can follow Gilbert with the tracking device."

Sophie's phone rang. "It's Teresa," Sophie answered on speaker, "hello."

"Hi, Miss Sophie. I just wanted an update."

"We put a tracker on Oscar's car. We'll follow him tonight after Bently gets here."

"I want to come. You promised me I could be a part of this," Teresa said. Sophie looked up at Houston. He nodded.

"Alright, as soon as Bently gets here, we'll pick you up."

"Thanks, Miss Sophie."

"No problem, a promise is a promise."

Bently got there before dark, and they told him what had transpired that day. Luna gave him a key to the new locks.

They picked up Teresa and Bully and followed Oscar about a quarter mile behind him, using a tracking unit. They followed him out of town.

"There isn't much out here. Only the rock quarry. Why would he go there?" Teresa asked.

"Because the desert is a perfect way to know if you are followed. There is nowhere to hide. How far ahead is it," Houston asked.

"About two miles."

"If we keep going, he is going to see us." Houston pulled to the side of the road. "Let's see if he stops up there."

"They all watched the screen while the tracker showed that he drove two miles up the road and pulled off."

"You were right, Teresa," Sophie said. "We would have been in a bad spot if you hadn't warned us."

Teresa smiled, "see, you do need me."

"Yes, we do," Sophie turned and smiled at her.

"What now?" Teresa asked.

"We passed a tavern about a quarter mile back. We can park in their lot and wait until Gilbert's crew finish their meeting and come back this way," Sophie said. "This looks like the only route back to town."

"We'll use the binoculars to get everyone's license plate number. Then we can look up who we are dealing with."

"This is really cool," Teresa said.

Other than random cars here and there, it was almost an hour before a clump of cars were heading in their direction. "Teresa, Houston and I will call out license plate numbers. Write them down as fast as you can." Sophie handed her a notebook and pen.

"Sophie, we'll leapfrog. You take the first car. I'll do the next."

When the cars got closer, Houston and Sophie started calling out numbers. Teresa wrote as fast as she could. There were eight in total.

"Now what?" Teresa asked.

"We go back to the hotel and start researching who belongs to these cars," Houston said.

"I want to come."

"Alright, you can help," Houston agreed.

Sophie called Sissy on the way to the hotel. She asked Sissy to get into the Vehicle Licensing Department in Nevada and find the names of the registered owners.

"When she calls back, we'll each take a name and look up everything we can find out about them," Sophie said.

As they walked into their hotel room, Sissy called.

"Alright, I have names to go with the plates. Do you have a pen and paper?"

Sophie hurried to the desk and pulled out the complimentary pen and paper. "Yes, go ahead."

Sissy gave them the eight names. She thanked her, and they hung up.

"Ok, let's divide the names and start looking up what we can about them. Teresa, look them up on social media. Look up their families too. You can get all sorts of information about family members there. Bully went to his bed and took a nap.

They found out that all the men were police officers. Most were detectives, and a few were patrol officers. Sophie called Sissy to have her do a deep dive into each one and their finances.

"Ok, what now?" Teresa asked.

"We'll keep an eye on the tracker and wait for Sissy to call us back," Houston replied.

"How are you doing at Burly's?" Sophie asked.

"He is a really nice man. We've been working on the contract for the sale of the diner. He was surprised I didn't want to run it myself. But there is no way I'm coming back here. When it cooled down, we worked in his garden, outback. He has watermelon and cucumbers. And he has an avocado and lemon tree too. In the morning we are going out and pick avocados off the tree and make avocado toast for breakfast."

"Houston, can we grow an avocado tree in Austin?" Sophie wondered.

"The climate is a little wetter than here but look it up. We'll see."

Teresa looked it up on her cell for her. "It says yes, but in some areas, they must be grown in pots to be moved under cover in the winter. They produce fruit year-round."

"Cool. I'd like an orange and a lemon tree, too," Sophie looked at Houston, knowing he would be the one to deal with it.

"We better go relieve Bently and get you back to Burly's,"

"You'll come get me in the morning?"

"Yes. We'll call when we head out."

It was late when Houston and Sophie went to bed. Luna had gone to bed earlier because she had to get up early for work.

Sophie and Houston started going through the financials that Sissy just sent for a couple of hours before going to bed.

Houston was startled awake. He didn't know what woke him. He laid there listening for any noise. There was none. But he couldn't rest. He got up and roamed the house, checking locks. When he got to the living room window, he saw movement outside. Two men used a Slim Jim to unlock his rented SUV and open the back hatch.

They wore black clothes and balaclava masks, but Houston recognized Gilbert's gait. He watched them place something in his car. Then they closed and locked the doors. They ran off by the east side of the diner.

Houston knew they were being set up. He woke Sophie and told her what was going on. They went outside and searched the back of the SUV. Houston opened the hatch that held the spare tire and tools. There were two-gallon size zip lock bags full of colorful designer fentanyl. Enough to put them in jail for years.

"What are we going to do, Houston?" Sophie asked.

"Remember those Honey Bucket Latrines in the alley?"

"Yeah, for the workers tearing down that old gas station."

"I'll dump the drugs in first and then the bags."

"If they bring a dog, they will still be able to detect there were drugs in here," Sophie said.

"If it was cocaine or marijuana, that would be true, but dogs that can track fentanyl are hard to come by. There is a limited number of them in the US. I doubt Henderson can afford one."

"Alright, hurry back. I'll be waiting at the back door for you."

Friday

Luna left a note for them on the kitchen table before she left for work. It said today was Teresa's birthday. She planned on making tamales and a birthday cake. She wanted to know if they felt it was safe for Teresa to come over to celebrate.

"Oh, I wish I had known, I would have gotten her a gift," Sophie said.

"You can't get her one in town. Someone may be watching and see you buy something for a young woman," Houston said.

"I'm glad her mother plans on doing something for her."

Luna was at work when three police cars pulled up to her house behind the diner. Houston opened the door, and one of the officers put him in cuffs and took him outside. Another officer did the same to Sophie.

"What's going on?" Houston asked.

"We got a tip that you are transporting drugs. We don't put up with that stuff here," the officer said.

An unmarked car pulled up, and a man Houston and Sophie recognized from his driver's license, stepped out. Sissy had sent all the crew members licenses with their financials. He was Detective Silas Bolan.

"Well, well. What have we got here? Another outsider trying to corrupt the fine citizens of our community by bringing drugs in," Bolan got in Houston's face. "We don't tolerate that here."

He was so close to Houston's face he could smell his foul breath. "I have no idea what you are talking about. My wife and I were hired by Luna Nuñez to find her children."

"We'll see about that," he turned to the police officers. "Tear that car apart. If there are drugs in there. I want them found."

While Houston and Sophie stood there, four officers tore their rental car apart. They removed the door panels, ripped out the roof liner, pulled out the radio, and anything else they could. There was nothing there to find.

Detective Bolan was getting nervous. He went directly to the spare tire well. The tire and all the tools had been taken out. There was nothing there. He moved away from everyone and made a call. When he finished the call, he ordered the officers to search inside the house.

"I want to see the warrant," Houston said. "And the one that allowed you to go through the rental car, too, for that matter."

The officers stopped at the door, not sure what to do.

"Take them to the police station," Bolan ordered.

"But we never found anything," one of the officers said.

"Just do it," Bolan ordered again.

Luna had stepped out the back door of the diner videoing the whole thing. No one noticed her. When they took Houston into custody, he nodded at Luna. She knew what to do. Luna called Burly.

CHAPTER FOURTEEN

Burly was at the police station before they brought Houston and Sophie through the Sallyport. The officers put them in separate interrogation rooms. They removed one side of the cuff and attached it to the welded bar on the metal table.

Houston had called Burly early in the morning and told him what had happened the night before. He also said there was only one man he trusted in the department: Deputy Chief Anthony Edwards. Burly called Edwards to let him know what was going on.

The deputy chief knew he couldn't interfere without giving away their connection. He asked Captain Christian Desmond to oversee it.

Detective Gilbert and Detective Bolan walked into the interview room where Houston was sitting. Bolan stood by the door, and Gilbert sat down across from him.

"I knew you were no good. What did you do with the drugs, Townsend? Who did you sell them to?"

Houston was tempted to tell him what he knew but simply said, "I believe my attorney is here. I would like to speak with him."

"We don't like strangers coming into town and getting involved with things they have no business in."

"I have no idea what you are talking about, Oscar. Did you find out who put that listening device in Luna's house?"

"I know there were drugs in your car. What did you do with them?"

"I said I want to speak with my lawyer."

Gilbert tried to stare Houston down, but Houston didn't break eye contact. Finally, Gilbert slapped his hands on the table, making a loud noise. He stood, leaned over into Houston's face, and said, "Let's see how your wife holds up."

Houston smiled, which aggravated Gilbert more.

Burly demanded to see Lieutenant Orr. The officer staffing the front desk gave him a call.

"Sir, Burly Blackstone is here. He says we arrested two of his clients. He is demanding to see them."

It took the lieutenant a few minutes to get to the front desk; he extended his hand to Burly.

"Good morning, Burly. Long time no see. I thought you retired, *again*," the lieutenant laughed. The lieutenant was a tall man with lots of hair that seemed unruly most of the time. But his uniform was always pristine, and his smile was friendly. He was known as an even-tempered man.

"I still dabble now and again. Two of my clients were arrested this morning, for drug possession. Their vehicle was searched for drugs, none were found. I want them released immediately."

"That doesn't sound like something any of my men would do. Who arrested them?"

"Detective Bolan."

"Detective Bolan did come to me this morning for a warrant to search a vehicle believed to have drugs."

"Believed to have...."

"One of his CIs called him with a tip. It's not anything we haven't done before on a tip. So, I got the warrant for him."

"Well, no drugs were found, and they were arrested anyway."

The Lieutenant looked around to see if Detective Bolan was in the bullpen. "Let me go check on this for you."

Detectives Bolan and Gilbert crossed the hall to the interrogation room where Sophie was detained.

"Mrs. Townsend, I'm sure you had nothing to do with this, but your husband has confessed to trafficking drugs."

"Detective Gilbert, that would be much more believable if drugs were in our car. I can't imagine what would make you believe we would carry drugs. You know we are here to help Luna find her children," Sophie paused, then looked Gilbert in the eye. "Unless that is, you were the one who put them there."

"That is a dangerous accusation, Mrs. Townsend," Gilbert barked.

"So, you admit there were drugs in your car?" Bolan said.

"Not unless you put them there. We certainly didn't. It's time you let me speak to my attorney. I believe he is waiting in the lobby."

"I don't know who you are, but you need to leave town if you don't want to end up in jail," Gilbert threatened.

"Is that a threat?"

"No, just good advice."

"Well, I'll ask my attorney what he thinks about it," Sophie said. The door opened before Gilbert could respond.

"Gilbert, Bolan, out here," Lieutenant Orr demanded.

The men moved to the hallway, "yes, sir."

"What's going on here, Bolan? You told me you had a CI that said drugs were in their SUV. Where are the drugs?"

"They weren't there when we searched the car, sir."

"So, why did you arrest them?"

"I know those drugs were there. They hid them somewhere else."

"And you are basing that on a call from a CI?"

"Yes, sir, he hasn't steered us wrong before."

"I want to listen to that conversation. Did it come in through the department line?"

"No, he used my cell, but I didn't think to record it."

"It is standard procedure for just this reason, Detective Bolan. I have known Burly Blackstone for many years and have never known him to represent drug dealers."

"I was following a lead, sir," Bolan said.

"Who are these people?" Orr asked.

"Houston and Sophie Townsend. They say Luna Nuñez hired them to find her children, sir."

"Can you blame her? I'm surprised it took her three years to do it. So how does that figure into them being drug dealers."

"I trusted my CI, sir," Bolan said.

"It would do you well to check out a lead before jumping in full throttle, Bolan. I'm surprised at you. Let them go."

"But, sir, I know there were drugs in the car," Gilbert said.

"How can you be so sure?"

"It's a gut feeling, sir," Gilbert said.

"Well, I suggest you take Alka Seltzer for that and let them go. Now! Detective."

"Yes, sir."

Houston, Sophie, and Burly were out the door fifteen minutes later.

Lieutenant Orr was surprised to have a message waiting for him on his desk. Captain Desmond of Internal Affairs wanted to see him ASAP. He took the stairs to the second floor and opened the door.

There was no bullpen in Internal Affairs. Each detective had their own office. There was evidence of other people in the office, muffled voices, and phones ringing, but he couldn't make out any conversations. There was a small reception area with a desk, but no receptionist, and it looked like there hadn't been one for a long time. Behind it was the head of the Internal Affairs office, Captain Christian Desmond.

The captain's door was open, and he noticed Lieutenant Orr standing in the doorway. The captain stood, moved toward him, and extended his hand. The lieutenant shook his hand and sat where directed.

When the captain was back in his seat, he looked at the lieutenant momentarily and smiled. "I believe we have never met before, Lieutenant Orr."

"Not officially, sir. But we have been at functions together."

"Well, I'm sorry we didn't have an opportunity to connect. I'd like you to tell me about an arrest in your squad today."

"Which one, sir."

"Mr. and Mrs. Townsend."

"Oh. Detective Bolan received a tip from his CI that Mr. and Mrs. Townsend had drugs in their vehicle. He asked for a warrant to search. I gave him one, and he and some patrol officers went to execute the warrant."

"Solely on the say-so of a CI?" The captain asked.

"Yes."

"Is this a registered CI? Did it come through the department line, or his private cell?"

"No. The CI is not registered, and the tip came through his private cell."

"Did he record the phone call?"

"No, sir."

"You see the problem here, Lieutenant Orr. I have received a call from the Deputy Chief to check into this. Apparently, someone sent him a video of the search."

The captain turned his computer around so the lieutenant could see it, then hit enter. He let it play clear through, then turned it off.

"Do you see any problem with this?" The captain asked.

"Yes, sir."

"Why don't you enlighten me."

"When they arrived at the home, they should have questioned them, asking what the nature of their visit was here in Henderson. Then ask if they would agree to a search of the car. If they refused, they could produce the warrant," Lieutenant Orr recited.

"And why would you speak to them first?"

"Because there is always someone watching, and to maintain a good relationship in the community, it is always best to be respectful."

"Is that what happened here?"

"No, sir. They immediately put the Townsends in cuffs, ripped their car to shreds, and arrested them."

"Can you see how this could end up in a suit?" the captain asked.

"Not really, sir. The detective had a warrant, so it wasn't an illegal search."

"Maybe in the eyes of the law, but not in public opinion. We will have to pay for the damage to the car to keep this from getting in the paper. Tourism is a good part of our local business. Many people choose to stay here when they visit Vegas to escape crime. They can drive there in twenty minutes and gamble, then come back here to be safe. But if we go around ripping visitors' cars to shreds. How do you think that will affect our local economy?"

"Not good, sir."

"This is a big problem, Lieutenant Orr. I wanted you to know that this has already reached the deputy chief's office."

"Yes, sir."

"You are dismissed."

The lieutenant sat there for a moment, not sure what to do. There was no instruction on how to fix the situation, which usually meant more trouble was coming.

After Lieutenant Orr left his office, Desmond went to speak with the deputy chief. His assistant told him he was expected and to go right in.

"Sir, I just talked with Lieutenant Orr. I do not believe he is part of Gilbert's crew."

"I agree. I checked Orr out when Gilbert's name came to my attention. He is not living above his means. But now we know Detective Bolan is part of this."

"I agree. What worries me is, if they were willing to go as far as to plant drugs on someone, how far are they willing to go. They already killed two men."

"In for a penny, in for a pound. Is that what you are saying?"

"That's what I'm afraid of, sir."

"Maybe we should call in the FBI. The Townsends have influence in DC. If they get killed, I'm afraid real trouble will rain down on us."

"Do you really want to take this out of our hands?"

"It's been three years, Christian. We have gotten nowhere with finding Detective Cox or Rio Nunez's murderer. How long do you want to wait? Until someone else is murdered?"

"No, you are right, sir. But I'd like our team to be involved. Could we negotiate that? Do you know anyone in the FBI you would be willing to work with?"

Deputy Chief Edwards thought for a moment, then looked up a number on his computer. "I know exactly who to call. But I need to speak with the chief first.

Edwards took the stairs up one flight to where the chief of police and the administration offices were. He stopped at Chief Castro's assistant's desk. Margret looked up and smiled.

"Hello, Deputy Chief. Do you have an appointment?" "No, but it's important. Can you see if he can fit me in?" She got up and headed into the office. She returned a moment later and held the door for him.

"Good afternoon, Anthony. What's on your mind?" Chief Raleigh Castro asked.

Edwards started talking before he sat down, telling him everything that had transpired in the last few days. "Sir, I am concerned that if Gilbert's crew is willing to plant drugs, they might not stop there. They already have two kills under their belt that we know of."

"Are you sure inviting in an outside agency is wise?"

"Sir, we both know this corruption has been going on for over twenty years. And nothing has been done about it. Detective Cox has been dead for three years. How long do we let this go on before we do something about it?" Edwards asked.

Castro sat for a moment thinking, tapping his pen on his desk. "But the Feds?"

"There is a connection between Director Cosby and the Townsends. When Mr. Townsend came to speak with me the other day, he asked me to call him for a reference. Director Cosby would not give me much information, saying it was classified, but he did vouch for him."

"If we do this. It will be a scandal on your and my reputations, Anthony."

Anthony smiled, "when we signed up, our goal was to clean up Henderson. We've done a respectable job, except in our own house. You know, as well as I do, that this corruption started with Mason. We turned a blind eye then, and now it's turned into the murder of one of our own. I can't live with that. If we are forced to retire after it gets in the paper. So be it."

"You said Axel Urwin is in on this. If we give him the exclusive, he may lean the article favorably toward us."

"I don't care how it's perceived. It's the right thing to do. And you know it, Raleigh."

The chief of police looked at his deputy and nodded. "You're right about one thing. We signed up to clean up Henderson and should have started with our own house. Do what you have to. What do you need from me?" Raleigh asked.

"A place to operate out of and more men we can trust," Edwards said.

"You remember that old casino the city voted to shut down four years ago, after someone was shot and killed there. The town purchased it.

"They plan to repurpose it for city use but haven't done it yet.

"They repealed the order two years later, but the casino decided to rebuild in another area of town. I'll call the mayor and tell him we need the old casino," Raleigh said.

"That should work fine," Anthony said.

"As for men and women you can trust. That will have to be your problem. You are the one that works with the rank and file."

Antony stood up. "If this is how we go out, let it be in flames," Edwards said.

"So be it," Raleigh agreed.

Quantico, Virginia

The red tape had finally ended. It was determined the new headquarters for The President's Task Force would be housed in a new wing of the FBI training center in Quantico. The team was setting up the communications network. Director Cosby was on site in case they ran into any snags.

The command center mirrored the one the task force borrowed on the Hijazi mission. They added an office similar to the one in DC in case they have another consultant on-site, like Sophie Star.

Director Cosby was given an office on the second floor for times when he needed to be there when a mission was hot. He was in there now, looking over requests from other agencies for the task force. Cosby didn't lend out the team often. He needed to keep them available for the president. His phone rang.

"Director Cosby speaking."

"Oh, I was expecting your assistant, Director Cosby."

"I'm not in my office in DC. To whom am I speaking?"

"This is Deputy Chief Anthony Edwards of the Henderson Police Department. I spoke with you the other day."

The director put down his pen and leaned back in his chair. "I remember."

"I have a situation here; I need help with."

"I'm listening."

Edwards told him everything that happened since the murder of his detective and the diner owner. He explained that he was concerned Mr. and Mrs. Townsend's life could be in danger. He said that he believed there was a crew of corrupt police that were running a protection ring in his city.

"I'm confused. What is it you want us to do? If you need help from the FBI, you can request help from offices closer than ours here in DC."

"I'm not sure who to trust. But beyond that, the Townsends have a connection to you. Am I wrong?"

"No, you are not wrong. I can't authorize our task force to go down there officially. But I could send a few of my people down there to consult with your team."

"That would be excellent, Director. How soon could they come?"

"Do you already have a task force ready to go and a place outside your stations where they can work?"

"Not yet, but I will by the time you get here. How soon can they come?" Edwards asked.

"They can be there tomorrow."

"Tomorrow?"

"Is that a problem?"

"No, Director, no problem. I'll send you the address of the safe house." *Once I have one,* he thought.

Henderson, Nevada

When the deputy chief hung up, he called Captain Desmond. He told him he had the chief of police on board, and they had the old casino to work out of.

"Now we need ten men and women we can trust," Edwards told him.

"I believe Lieutenant Orr could be one of them."

"Alright, get him up here. Between us we can figure out who else we can trust. Then we need to head down to the casino and see if we can make it work."

Burly drove Houston and Sophie to Axel's house. He had dropped Teresa there when he headed to the police station.

"Well, this certainly blew up our plans to keep the investigation under wraps," Houston said.

"Maybe it's for the best. They fired the first shot. Now we work out in the open," Sophie said.

"Yes, but how far are they willing to go to keep their money stream coming in? They already killed a fellow detective," Houston said.

"I believe that was in the heat of the moment. It wasn't planned," Burly said.

"Regardless, once you go that far, you are willing to do it again," Houston looked at Sophie. "We left the team to avoid this kind of danger."

Sophie reached up to him from the back seat and put her hand on his shoulder. "We are too far into it now to walk away and let this injustice continue. It is much harder, though, without our team."

"Yeah, we could sure use them now," Houston grumbled.

"Teresa was pretty worried about you," Burly said. "She wants to call it off and go home. Teresa doesn't want you or her mother to get killed. And she knows they are capable of doing that. She's seen that with her own eyes." Burly said.

They pulled into Axel's driveway. Teresa opened the door before they got out of the car. Bully came running out to greet them.

Sophie bent down to scratch under his ears. "Hello, Bully. Did you miss us?"

Teresa came out and hugged them. "I was so worried. Luna sent us the video of what happened."

"Yeah, it's a good thing I paid extra for the car rental's insurance," Houston said.

They all headed inside.

Axel was waiting for them at the door, "Teresa helped me make enchiladas for lunch. Let's eat before we figure out where to go from here."

No one objected. After a few bites, Sophie said, "These are delicious, Axel. Is this your wife's recipe?"

"Yes, her grandmother passed it down."

When everyone was done eating Teresa said, "we have to go home. I didn't think this through. I should have known Detective Gilbert would be willing to do anything to avoid being caught. My father is already dead. He wouldn't want me putting anyone else in danger."

"Well, you are right about one thing. We need to send you and Sophie home. I'm staying to see this through," Houston said.

Sophie looked at him with fire in her eyes, "since when do *you* send me anywhere, I don't want to go?"

"Sophie, you are pregnant, and we agreed we wouldn't put our child in danger."

"I have no problem agreeing to stay out of harm's way. But I'm not raising this baby alone. Where you go, I go."

"We have a hornet's nest stirred up for sure," Axel said.

"If you leave, I don't think the corruption will ever stop. But I understand if you don't want to endanger your lives," Burly said.

"It would be different if we had our team behind us for backup. But we are in this on our own," Houston said.

"What are we," Axel pointed to himself and Burly. "Chopped liver?" They all laughed.

"No, you guys are great, but we need men who carry guns and the authority to use them," Houston said.

"What if we go back to Deputy Chief Edwards. Maybe now that he sees how far these men are willing to go, he will bring his office to bear," Axel said.

"He is a good man," Burly said.

"Burly, he had to know this was happening in his ranks," Houston said.

"You're right. I can't defend him on that count. But I believe he will step up."

"I'm not so sure a man who is willing to 'let things be', is who we want watching our backs," Houston said. "From what you told us, he knew about this years ago and let it go on."

"True, but he deserves a chance to make things right. We know he's not involved. I say let's approach him again," Burly said.

Houston looked at Sophie, "all right. But, Teresa, you do need to go home. We can't take the chance of you getting hurt."

"No, Mr. Houston. If you stay, I stay. I'm no coward. This was my idea, and it was my father who they killed. And now my mother could be in danger. I ran when I was a kid because my dad told me to. I won't do it again."

"Without the deputy chief on our side, I'm not sure how much farther we can take it," Sophie said.

"This could be the catalyst he needs," Axel said.

"Alright, we'll give it another try," Houston agreed.

CHAPTER FIFTEEN

After lunch, the group went into the atrium to work on Axel's notes. Sophie went into the hall when her phone rang.

"Hello, Sophie."

"Hi, Sissy. Do you have more information for me on Gilbert's crew?"

"Yes, but we'll be there tomorrow. I planned on bringing the info with me."

"What do you mean you'll be here tomorrow?"

"You don't know?" Sissy asked.

"Know what?"

"The Henderson police department reached out to Director Cosby. He asked for help ferreting out the corrupt officers in his department."

"When did this happen?"

"Two hours ago. We are boarding the jet in the morning. Do you still want the information?"

"No, it can wait. I'm so glad you are coming."

"Me too. It's not the same here, without you," Sissy said.

Sophie stood at the door of the atrium. Houston saw her in his peripheral vision and looked up.

"What?" Houston asked.

"The task force is boarding a plane in the morning. They are coming here," Sophie smiled.

"How?" Houston asked.

"Deputy Chief Edwards called Director Cosby and asked for his help. He is determined to purge his department of corrupt police," Sophie said.

"What does that mean. Is that good?" Teresa asked.

"It's great, Teresa. We will have all the backup we need now," Houston told her.

"Why don't we pack things up so we can take it to wherever they have set up for a command center," Houston said.

"We still have some time. Maybe we will find something useful," Axel said.

Teresa was talking to Sophie, so Houston whispered in Axel's ear. "It's Teresa's birthday, her mom has a cake for her. Why don't you and Burly come over, too."

Deputy Chief Edwards, Captain Desmond, Lieutenant Orr, four other men and one woman they agreed on, worked through the night. They had to get the casino in good enough condition to be used as a command center.

Luckily, there was a mezzanine that was set up for casino security. Cameras were placed over every card table, roulette wheel, dice table, and slot machines.

The cameras inside would be of little use. But the cameras exposing every area outside would be helpful. The casino monitors, computers, and screens would be converted for their use.

Three officers they recruited were computer techs and set up the command center. The others put their backs into cleaning the place up.

A large garage area was in the back, used chiefly for armored truck transport of casino funds. They were able to get six cars in there, so they carpooled. Leaving spots for the consultants coming in from DC.

Saturday

Houston and Sophie were still sleeping when Luna left for the diner. She left a note saying there was a quiche in the fridge for them to heat up for breakfast.

The birthday party really boosted Teresa's morale. She hadn't said anything, but it was her eighteenth birthday and she felt bad she wasn't going to get to celebrate. But she knew what she was doing was important.

Theresa spent the night in Kato's room. She was still sleeping too.

After breakfast Houston called Axel to pick them up.

Axel picked them up and headed to his house. Houston and Sophie were waiting for instructions on where to meet the team.

Houston pulled out his cell to call a rental agency to get another car when Axel spoke up.

"Why don't you use the car I bought for Roz, it was an anniversary gift, two years ago. I haven't had the heart to sell it. Use it while you're here. A rental car would be more conspicuous, it's less likely you would be stopped in the Lexus. The windows are tinted enough it will be hard for anyone to see who's driving."

Sophie started to refuse, but Axel insisted. He tossed Houston the keys and that was the end of the discussion.

They packed up what they thought would be useful to take to the command center. Houston carried two boxes to the Lexus and thanked Axel. They went back inside and waited for a call.

A CRY FOR JUSTICE

Director Cosby sent a text to Houston. He sent the location of where the task force would be meeting and the time they would be arriving. Houston texted him back, thanking him for his help.

They wanted to leave Teresa at Burly's, on the way to meet the team, but she insisted she was part of this.

At 3 pm, Houston pulled around the back of the casino and saw that a large, motorized roll-up door was open. He pulled in and found a place to park.

Edwards saw a Lexus pull into the garage and went to meet the task force from DC. When he entered the garage, he was surprised to see Houston, Sophie, Teresa, and a dog get out of the car.

"What are you doing here, Mr. Townsend," then he noticed Teresa. "You are Rio's daughter. The one we've been searching for."

Before anyone could respond, two large, black Cadillac Escalades pulled in. The doors opened, and the passengers stepped out.

When Bully saw his friends, he got so excited his whole body wagged as he went to get attention. Fons was the first to bend down and pet him, then the others took turns. Houston and Sophie stepped over to greet them, giving hugs, handshakes, and backslaps.

Edwards had no idea what was going on. He stepped over to the group.

"Thank you for coming. I'm Deputy Chief Anthony Edwards. Who is in charge?" He asked.

The task force looked at Houston and Sophie. Edwards turned to them. "You're the head of this task force? I don't understand."

"Sophie, SAC Rodriguez, and I ran the task force. But I recently resigned, and Sophie was an independent contractor and ended her attachment."

"Well, let's get upstairs and figure out how to get this task force going."

"I'll grab our equipment," Matt said.

"We'll help," Houston said as they all grabbed large hard plastic cases. Edwards led them upstairs to the mezzanine, pushing the button to close the garage door as he went.

Sophie and Teresa each grabbed a box and Bully's things from the Lexus and followed them upstairs.

When they reached the mezzanine, the deputy chief introduced the groups to each other. Timms, Murphy, and Mathews unloaded their equipment. They worked with the techs on-site to add their own equipment to what was there and assemble a working command center.

Sissy, Teresa, and Sophie saw a window overlooking the casino floor. It had a silver sheen to it. Likely a one-way mirror that allowed security to see the action below without being seen. Even with cameras and computers, the human eye scanning the whole picture is still one of the best tools in any arsenal.

They decided to use the window as a whiteboard. They brought over the boxes of information they worked on at Axel's and added Sissy's. They taped up the pictures with the financials of each suspect under it. There was a possibility that there were others they didn't know about.

Bully walked around watching the activity looking to get attention from his friends.

The equipment was set up and the task force was waiting for instructions. Sophie looked at Fons to see if he wanted her to lay out what was going on. He nodded.

"My name is Sophie Townsend, I wanted to give you a snapshot version of what has happened so far.

"I understand how reluctant you would be to investigate one of your own. I want to give you proof this is not a witch hunt."

Sophie handed the flash drive to Special Agent Denny Timms. He pulled it up on his computer and sent it to one of the larger screens.

Teresa couldn't watch it, so she went to the window and looked out at the desert. Bully stayed by her side. There was no audio, only video.

The room was silent as they watched one of their own detectives shoot and kill his partner and Teresa's father.

When it was over no one spoke. Sergeant Sheldon Contreras broke the silence. Directing his question to the deputy chief.

"This is incriminating evidence, sir. Why haven't we arrested Gilbert?"

Deputy Chief Edwards answered. "Chain of custody. Teresa had the presence of mind to take the computer that held the security video with her, but that broke the chain of custody. Likely this could be used as supporting evidence but it's not enough to convict on its own. We need more."

Houston spoke up, "and this only incriminates Gilbert, but not the rest of the corrupt officers who are taking protection money. We would like to arrest them all.

"That's why we are here. Gilbert is already getting sloppy. He planted drugs in our car and then came to arrest us. Fortunately, I saw them being planted and got rid of them. Detective Bolan arrested us anyway."

"This FBI task force is here at my request. We have gotten nowhere with this investigation in the last three years. Captain Desmond and I agree that we should let them take the lead on this," Edwards paused to look at his officers. "Does anyone have an issue with that? If you do, please let me know now."

No one objected so he turned the floor over to SAC Rodriguez.

"Alright, Deputy Chief Edwards, our success as a task force is partly because we can anticipate each other's moves. It makes for a smooth-running operation. Sophie drafts the plan and has the sole say in any changes that happen. Houston and I run the operations," Fons turned to Houston. "You and Sophie are undercover already, right?"

"After being arrested, saying we are undercover, may be stretching it," said Houston.

"Got it. But they don't believe you are law enforcement, right?"

"Right. We told them we were private investigators, hired to find Luna Nuñez's children."

"Then let's see what Sissy and Sophie have up on the window and see if Sophie came up with a plan," Fons said.

Sophie deferred to Sissy to explain the material on the window.

"Sophie gave me eight license plate numbers. Using those, I could find the vehicle's registered owner. All the vehicles belong to police officers from different districts in Henderson. Two men are patrol officers, and one works in the evidence room. Five, including Gilbert, are detectives." Sissy pointed to the information.

"In your district, Lieutenant Orr, you have Detectives Bolan and Gilbert. And Sergeant Crawford, who works in the evidence locker."

"I know these men," Lieutenant Orr said. "They are good police. I have never had any reason to believe they were corrupt."

"The only complaint that came into Internal Affairs was on Gilbert. None of the others were even on our radar." Captain Desmond said.

"That's how they've gotten away with it all these years. They do their jobs well and keep their underground income limited," Sophie said. "That is until four years ago. From Sissy's intel, it appears that big busts from certain types of illegal activities have gone down. Now, that can be interpreted as a good thing. But when you dig into it, the crew increased their reach. They started offering protection to larger, more organized rackets."

"Successful prosecutions have gone down too. Mainly due to technical errors. One case was thrown out due to missing evidence," Sissy added.

Deputy Chief Edwards looked at Lieutenant Orr. "Have you noticed this trend in your precinct?"

"Yes, and I have friends in my position in other precincts, and they have the same information. We thought the good stats were from good policing."

"Ok, now we know why," Edwards said.

Sophie looked at Fons. She wanted to avoid stepping ahead of his authority since she and Houston were no longer part of the task force.

"Sophie, we agreed to run this like we always have. Your lead," Fons assured her.

"We want you to know everything we know and the history of the corruption in Henderson. As far back as we could go," Sophie turned to Houston. "Please brief them."

Houston explained everything they had uncovered, going clear back to Detective Philip Mason. He pointed to the window they were using as a whiteboard, where the pictures were up. "As far as we know all of Mason's crew have retired. These are the men we believe are involved now. There may be more. It is our job to shut them down." He handed the floor back to Sophie.

"Our first objective will be to track these men's daily activities. Agent Timms, do we have the equipment to keep track of all these men simultaneously."

"Yes, ma'am."

"Good, now Deputy Chief Edwards..."

"Let's keep this simple; chief is fine," he said.

"Thank you, Chief. We can't have seven or eight of your men disappear from work. Let's explain away one tech as being on vacation. We could use one of the patrol officers here. He could call in sick. The other one will have to be on duty, which will help us keep an eye on our bad actors. Lieutenant Dickerson, if you're at work, you can come and go as you like. Chief, you, Lieutenant Orr, and Captain Desmond can say you're in meetings. Is that acceptable, Chief?

"Yes. Lieutenant Orr, please make those arrangements."

"Yes, Sir."

"It goes without saying that no one outside this room can know anything about this task force. Unfortunately, that will include your family. If you have an issue with that, it would be best to let us know now," Sophie looked around. No one moved. "Ok. Major Murphy, I see you brought two drones with you,"

"Yes, ma'am."

"We know they met at the rock quarry east of town. There is only one way in and out. That allows them the confidence to know if anyone is following them. That's where your drones can help. We have no guarantee they will use it again. On the other hand, they have no reason to believe the place is compromised. I'm hoping it is their safe spot. Can you check it out and see if you can get a drone there without them seeing it?"

"I can do that. I'll need someone to take me there."

"I'll go with you, Major," Sergeant Julia Stone said.

"Good. Take my personal car. It's not flashy," the chief handed him the keys.

"The next problem is getting tracking devices on the vehicles," Sophie said.

Sergeant Sheldon Contreras spoke up. "If they use police force vehicles, we can use the GPS systems to track them. If they use their own vehicles and are new enough to have GPS, we can get theirs too, if we can get the VINs. But the other vehicles will need to have physical trackers placed on them."

"Thank you, Sergeant. Will you please put that into action," Sophie turned to Sissy. "Can you find the VIN numbers on their personal cars and determine which ones we need to get trackers on?"

"No problem."

"Sir," Sophie spoke to Captain Desmond. "Sissy has the financials of all those we know are involved. Will you work with Agent Timms to determine an idea of how much money each man is getting from this racket? We know Philip Mason was making at least one hundred thousand a year."

"Yes, ma'am." Desmond and Timms moved to the window to grab the financials. Then moved to one of the tables in the back of the room, taking laptops with them.

While everyone was busy, Teresa put on Bully's booties, and she and Sophie took Bully out for a walk. Then they got in the Lexus to pick up dinner. Teresa opened and closed the garage door so Sophie could drive out. Then she joined her.

"What shall we bring the crew back for dinner?" Sophie asked Teresa.

"Kentucky Fried Chicken will travel well and hold up," Teresa said.

"I forgot you are a schooled restauranteur," she smiled. "Ok, Kentucky Fried it is."

When they returned from their food run, Major Murphy and Sergeant Stone were waiting for the garage door to open. They pulled in behind them and parked.

Major Murphy waited for Sophie to get out of the car.

"I'll take the food up," Teresa said. Sergeant Stone helped her carry the boxes of takeout.

"What did you find out?" Sophie asked.

"It's a perfect place for clandestine meetings. You can see where they had set up an area to sit together and talk. I would have to get the drone in position before they came. There is no way they wouldn't see it otherwise."

"Is there a place close enough to see and hear everything?" Sophie asked.

"Yes, I can spray paint the small drone to blend into the rocks." He lifted a can of spray paint. "We picked it up on the way back."

"Excellent, Flynn. Now how do we ensure you get it there before them?"

"If Henderson is like most cities in America, I'm sure teens go out at night to drink and climb up on the rocks. So, I can't put it there ahead of time. We are only fifteen minutes from the quarry. With some notice, I can park in the bar parking lot a couple of miles west of it. I can fly the drone in from there before they show up. If not, I will have to land it on the top of the quarry rocks. It's not ideal.

"Ok, we'll see how things develop," she paused. "Before we found out you were coming, we realized how lucky we were to have had the team watching our backs. It's much harder without backup you can trust."

"I can say it's not the same team without you. I know people move on, but..." he looked up at her. "We all accomplished so much together. And I know someday Fons will want to join your agency. Change is hard."

"Yes, it is. Let's tell the team what you found and get some food before it's all gone. It's not Carol's, but it's not bad."

After they ate, Major Murphy told them what he had found at the quarry. Then Edwards sent one of his techs, Sergeant Navarro, his patrol officer, Officer Byrd, and Lieutenant Dickerson, from internal affairs, back to work with burner phones and trackers. Officer Byrd and Lieutenant Dickerson would be available if they needed to put a tracker on one of the cars.

Sissy announced what she found. Four of Gilbert's crew had disabled their GPS, so they needed to get trackers on the cars.

"We can have Sergeant Navarro find out where they are assigned for the day. Lieutenant Dickerson and Officer Byrd can find a way to put a device on their vehicles. I'll let them know," Lieutenant Orr said.

Sophie looked at the pictures of the other officers in Gilbert's crew. She went through them.

"Five of the crew are detectives, including Gilbert. Gilroy, Kapadia, Bolan, and Rostova. Sergeant Crawford works in the evidence locker, convenient for their protection scheme. They can make evidence disappear. There are two patrol officers, Solis, and Zhang. We need to be sure there aren't any others.

"Captain Desmond, your internal affairs. Is there anyone not on our list that you opened a file on or heard rumors about?"

"No other files, but there are some rumors. I'll write the names down."

"Please give them to Sissy. She can do a deep dive into their financials. Teresa can look into their social media accounts."

There would have been a day when Sophie would have wondered how these officers justified taking an oath to protect and serve while taking protection money from the criminals. But not anymore. She knew the answer. When someone knows to do good and chooses not to, it sears their conscience. Without a Godly conscience, there is no limit to the evil man would do. One just needed to read the paper or watch the news to prove it.

Teresa came over, bringing Sophie out of her musings.

"Miss Sophie, are you alright?"

"Yes, I was just wondering why these men chose to live a double life."

"Are we really going to be able to put them all behind bars?"

"I hope so. I don't want you, Kato, or your mother to ever have to worry about your safety."

Sissy gave Orr the list of cars that needed trackers. He called Sergeant Navarro. "Sarge, can you get a location on the cars belonging to Kapadia, Solis, Rostova, and Zhang."

"Give me one second," there was a pause. "Got it. Solis is patrolling in the third district commercial area. Zhang is parked at Denny's, and Kapadia is at the sight of a home invasion; he gave Orr the address. Hold on...Rostova's car is in the parking lot of his assigned police station."

"Thanks, Sarge."

Lieutenant Orr decided it would not be suspicious for Dickerson to go to that Denny's, and he could go to Rostova's assigned station's parking lot and not be seen. Officer Byrd could show up at the house invasion. It's in his district, and he could also put a tracker on Solis' car when he called in a 10-7b for a break." He texted the orders to the men.

An hour later, Sophie got word that all the vehicles were now able to be tracked. She turned to Matt.

"Alright, Agent Mathews, do we have a lock on all the GPS signals?" Sophie asked.

"On the screen now, ma'am."

Sophie looked at the two screens he pointed to. Eash was segmented into four boxes. Each showed a segment of the streets in the city with a dot moving or stationery. In the top left corner of each box was the name of the man it was tracking.

"Look, Houston, Gilbert is at Luna's. Bently's there with her, right?"

"Yes, I called him before we came here. I'll text him and see what's going on."

Houston texted Bently: **What is Gilbert doing there?**

Bently: **Trying to convince Luna to fire you and hire him to find the kids. Again.**

Houston: **What is she saying?**

Bently: **She said, 'Why would I have to hire you. It's your job. Why haven't you already done it?'**

Houston: **Good for her. Can you stay until we get there later tonight?**

Bently: **Yes.**

At seven, Agent Timms got everyone's attention. "Look, the cars are all headed in the same direction."

"Major, can you get a drone to the quarry before they arrive?" Houston asked.

"I'll sure try," Major Murphy had sprayed the drone outback then put it in the garage to dry. He headed to the door.

"I'll go with you," Sergeant Stone said as she ran to catch up."

"Send us a feed," Houston hollered after them.

A CRY FOR JUSTICE

CHAPTER SIXTEEN

Fifteen minutes later, the screen showed all the dots converging on the quarry. There was still no feed from Murphy's drone.

"How much time before the crew makes it to the quarry, Sergeant Contreras?" Sophie asked.

"Five to seven minutes at the most."

They all watched, looking for the feed to come up before the cars made it there. The dots kept getting closer and closer.

"I've got it," Timms yelled as the feed from the drone came up on the screen.

The team watched as one vehicle after another drove into the parking area at the quarry. The picture was as clear as if you were standing there watching. A group of teen boys were there drinking beer and smoking.

When Gilbert and his team stepped out of their cars, they told the boys they would arrest them if they didn't clean up their mess and get out of there fast. The kids grabbed their stuff and scrambled.

The group sat in a circle on logs in front of the fire the boys had already lit. Bolan found a case of beer the boys had left behind and passed them around.

"Planting those drugs was a stupid move, Gilbert. Now there is all sorts of attention on the missing kids and Cox's murder," Kapadia said.

"I agree with Kapadia. You should have just left them alone. If we couldn't find those kids, the Townsends weren't going to either," Crawford said.

205

"Well, hindsight is 20/20, isn't it," Bolan said.

"Now you've given us no choice. If they start digging into Cox's murder and find something, we'll have no choice but to kill them," Zhang said.

"No, we never agreed on murder. If that is where this is going, I'm out." Rostova said adamantly.

"We understood that Cox was a spur of the moment decision. You had no choice once you got the text saying he was working for Internal Affairs. But killing the Townsends would bring too much attention to Henderson. I heard they have connections in DC," Solis said.

"How would you know that?" Bolan asked.

"Townsend went to introduce himself to Deputy Chief Edwards. I'm dating his assistant. She listened in on the intercom."

Houston turned to Edwards, looking for an explanation.

"She has only been with me a few months. My last assistant worked with me for years, but she retired. I'll have to watch what I say until this is over. I don't dare fire her now."

"You're right. We won't be meeting there anyway, now that we have this place," Houston said.

Their attention went back to the feed. "I'm done," Rostova stood. "You can keep my share. I'm not going to jail. I never wanted to be a corrupt cop. When you approached me, I couldn't see the harm in protecting mid-level chop shops and pawn shops selling stolen goods. But now, you've signed us up to protect drug dealers and pimps. I can't stomach it," Rostova turned to walk away.

"You're not going anywhere, Rostova," Gilbert said.

Rostova turned around and got in Gilbert's face, "how are you going to stop me?" Then turned around to leave again.

Gilbert pulled his gun. Bolan stood and said, "Gilbert, put that away."

"No, he will snitch on us. When we joined, we agreed no one quits, and no one turns state's evidence if we get caught; he is a loose end."

"PUT IT AWAY, GILBERT!" Bolan said again.

Rostova had turned back when he heard Gilbert had pulled his gun. "I'm not going to turn on anyone here. I just want out."

Gilbert lowered his gun. The minute Bolan turned away from him, he lifted it again and shot.

Sophie gasped. "We need to intervene."

"No, he didn't shoot him. He shot at his feet," Edwards said.

Gilbert yelled at Rostova, who stopped but didn't turn. "Just know this if you say anything to anyone. I'll put the next one in your head."

Rostova got in his car and left.

"Anyone else wanting to walk away?" Bolan asked.

"Not me. I've become accustomed to a comfortable lifestyle. But if you kill anyone else, you better put one in my head too. Because I will turn you in myself. Am I clear, Gilbert? You need to reign yourself in," Gilroy had moved into Gilbert's space. He was three inches taller and fifty pounds of pure muscle bigger than Gilbert. Gilbert didn't flinch.

Gilroy and the others calmed down and sat. "I don't think Rostova will talk," Zhang said. "His wife is pregnant; it's made him overly cautious."

"Let's move on. We came here to distribute this quarter's earnings." Gilbert went to his SUV and pulled a duffle bag out from the back.

He took out eight bundles of cash, each one would fill a shoe box, and handed one to each man.

"What do we do with Rostova's portion," Bolan asked.

Gilbert pulled a pocket knife out and cut the plastic wrap that held it together. "Let's see, $50,000 divided by seven is just under seventy-two hundred. I'll take the shortfall." Gilbert counted out seven thousand two hundred and handed it to each man. Leaving himself sixty-eight hundred."

"How are they laundering that much money. It's over two hundred thousand a year for each one," Desmond asked.

"They have to keep it in safe deposit boxes or home safes," Sissy said.

"True, but it's unusable until they explain how they came into it. They have to launder it somewhere. We need to know," Sophie insisted.

"She's right. If they went anywhere and bought big-ticket items in cash, it would bring too much attention," Fons agreed.

They all watched as the men in the quarry dispersed.

"Gilbert is a loose cannon. We need to get him off the streets before he kills someone else," Orr said.

"Chief, do we want to offer Rostova immunity to give us enough information to shut them down?" Dickerson suggested.

"He could tell us how they wash their money and the businesses they protect," Lieutenant Orr agreed.

"We need corroborating evidence first. The chief of police won't let us move solely on the word of an informant."

"Alright, Matt and I will start searching for how they are laundering their money," Sissy said.

"Fons, where are you and the team staying?" Sophie asked.

"Ms. Deasun set us up at a Hyatt about a mile down the road."

"Is that the woman who replaced Cosby's assistant, Cassi," Sophie asked.

"Yes, he doesn't like change," Fons chuckled. Sophie smiled; she knew that was true.

Teresa came up and said, "Bully needs to go out again, Miss Sophie. I'll take him."

"Thank you, but you can't go by yourself."

"I'll walk with her," Agent Timms volunteered. "I could use some fresh air."

The wind had kicked up and Teresa could see small dirt devils swirling around in little bursts in the distance. Teresa let Bully off leash once they were out back. She and Denny leaned against the building while Bully did his business. It was dusk and the air was cooling down. When Bully was done, he started chasing lizards.

"Have you known Miss Sophie a long time?" Teresa asked.

"For several years, yes. I worked with Miss Star when she took down the larges... Let's just say it was a successful mission."

"Miss Star?"

"That is her maiden name. She used it while working with the task force."

"Was she really the boss of all those people?"

"Sophie, Houston, and Fons ran the task force. That is true."

"Miss Sophie must be really smart."

"Sophie is a brilliant strategist. The best any of us have ever worked with. But that's not what makes her so valuable. It's the compassion she has. Sophie always tried to work things out to ensure no one was injured or died on either side."

"Is that possible?" Teresa asked.

"No, we have had losses on both sides...she took it hard when it happened. Mis Star tends to blame herself if someone gets hurt. It's been a real privilege to have been able to work with her."

Bully must have scared away all the little critters because he came over and sat in the shade panting.

"I guess it's time to go in," Teresa said, bending down and ruffling Bully's coat.

"I think I want to be like her," Teresa said.

"That is a commendable goal, but she would tell you she would want you to be better than her. She'd want you to pray and find God's plan for you. God's plans are always greater than our plans for ourselves."

"Are you a Christian?"

"Yes, largely because of the example of Houston and Sophie."

"It's so cool that they get to work together."

"It is, but this job is dangerous, and he almost lost her more than once. That's why Houston resigned. He didn't want his wife and future children to be in harm's way."

Teresa hung her head, "sometimes trouble comes no matter how far removed from it you are."

"You're talking about the loss of your father?" Timms asked.

"Yes, he was just standing there in his own restaurant, and he was gunned down. He should have been safe," Teresa said, tears crawling down her cheeks.

"I'm sorry that you lost your father. Putting Gilbert away won't bring him back, but you'll know you did what you could to give him justice. Was he a Christian?"

"Yes."

"Then you know he is with Jesus and happy. I know that won't take away the pain now. But in time, knowing that and knowing you will see him again someday, will mean everything to you."

Teresa nodded as they headed back in.

It was coming up on 9 pm, and all the targets were at their residences. Sissy spoke up, "we need these guys' tax returns. They can't use this cash outright unless they claim at least some of it on their income tax."

"Chief, how do you want to handle this?" Fons asked.

"I know several judges. I can get a subpoena for the records, but news like that can get out."

"What about a judge in a different county?" Desmond asked.

"Fons, do you think Director Cosby would subpoena them for us in DC?" Sophie asked.

"Maybe. We are dealing with corruption in a police department. That does fall in our jurisdiction," Fons said.

"Give him a call. Then let's call it a night," Sophie said.

"It's too late in DC. I'll call him in the morning," Fons said.

"I think we should keep an eye on these guys 24/7," Sergeant Stone suggested.

"I agree," Timms said.

"We can do three-hour shifts through the night," Murphy said.

"I'm used to staying up late; I'll take the graveyard shift," Matt said.

"All right, Sergeant Stone, please set up a schedule," Fons said.

"And include Dickerson, Navarro, and Byrd on the rotation for the duration," Deputy Chief Edmonds said.

"Let's meet back here at 8 am," Houston suggested.

Fons stopped Houston and Sophie on the way out. "Do you guys want to have a late meal together?" Fons asked.

"Yeah, sure, why don't you come to Luna's. I got a text saying she has left over tamales waiting for us. I'll text to see if there is room for one more."

"I don't want to impose."

"Luna isn't like that. She likes feeding people. And she will likely still be up since tomorrow is Sunday and they have the day off," Sophie said.

Teresa heard, "can I come?"

Sophie looked at Houston. Houston looked at the monitors. "Gilbert is home for the night. I think it will be fine."

"Everyone headed out."

Bently was still at Luna's, so he stayed to eat with them. The group had a good time. It felt good to relax for a few hours.

Bently took Teresa to Burly's on his way home. She loved being able to ride on a motorcycle. Bully stayed with Sophie and Luna headed to bed,

Houston, Sophie, and Fons had a second helping of Tiramisu and a cup of coffee.

"This is quite the first job for your new detective agency," Fons joked.

"For sure," Houston agreed.

"Have you found a storefront yet?" Fons asked.

"We haven't had an opportunity. As soon as we get back, we'll start looking," Houston said.

There was a pause in the conversation while they finished their dessert. Sophie refilled their cups with coffee.

"Carol and I have been talking. The people renting my home have shown interest in purchasing it. With that, Carol's income, and our savings, we've made a decision." He looked up from his empty bowl of dessert and continued. "If your offer is still open for a partnership, we will have enough to pay our equity portion. And still have enough to put a pretty hefty down payment on a home and be able to live for six months."

"Are you saying you would move down here before we had a stable income for the agency?" Sophie asked.

"Yes. We've been praying about it and decided some risks are worth taking. I loved working with the task force, but it was because we were all working together. Now it's just another job. Living in your apartment upstairs has been great, but it's lonely now. We miss you guys."

"Fons, are you sure? We have no idea how long it will take to get enough clients to give ourselves a decent salary," Houston said.

"It's worth the risk to us."

"I won't take a salary until you two have yours first," Sophie said.

"No, Sophie, what you put into the business is equal to ours," Fons objected.

"Fons, what Houston brings home will be sufficient for both of us."

Houston smiled and stood, extending his hand, "welcome aboard, partner." They shook hands that ended in a hug. Sophie welcomed him to the company with a hug, too.

After they sat down again, Fons said, "you know Matt and Sissy would move down and work with us as soon as we need them full-time."

"That would be perfect. There are no better computer forensic specialists than those two," Sophie said.

"I'll call Carol when I get to the hotel. She wanted to know as soon as we discussed it," Fons got up to go.

Bully's ears turned toward the door; he got up and went to the window. He started barking, as a text came in from Sergeant Stone.

You have a visitor. Gilbert.

Houston opened the door, and Bully tore out, chasing him. Houston and Fons followed. They saw taillights on a vehicle as they reached the diner's parking lot. Bully was chasing it.

Houston whistled to bring him back. Bully stopped but kept looking at the car. Houston hollered for him to come. It broke Bully's concentration, and he ran back.

"He wasn't here for long. What do you think, Fons?" Houston asked.

"We need to check our cars for trackers and contraband."

As they returned to the house, they saw Sophie outside checking the cars with a device that detected frequency transmissions. While she did that, they looked in the SUVs for contraband. Another text came in.

Sergeant Stone: **He's back home.**

Houston saw he had missed an earlier text from Sergeant Stone saying that Gilbert was on the move heading in their direction.

The device Sophie was using detected two trackers, one on each SUV.

"What shall we do with them?" Fons asked.

"There is a truck stop down the street. Put yours on an 18-wheeler. Gilbert will track it heading up the freeway, and think you left town. The range on this device is twenty miles. I'll take this one and attach it under the front steps. He'll think we're here all day until he catches on," Houston said.

"Sounds good to me. I'll see you in the morning, partners," Fons smiled.

Fons left, and Houston saw Sophie texting someone. "Who are you texting at this hour?" He asked.

"Carol. I'm welcoming her as a partner. I told her to act surprised when Fons calls her," Sophie smiled.

"Fons wanted to tell her."

"Too bad, she's my friend," Sophie laughed.

Sunday

Houston, Sophie, and Teresa went with Burly to an early service at his church. Houston dropped Burly at his house after breakfast at the Waffle House.

Teresa, Bully, Houston, and Sophie headed to the casino. They were the last ones there. Dickerson and Navarro were off today. Byrd was there for an update before he went to work. Fons was catching everyone up.

"Last night, Sergeant Stone gave us a heads up that Gilbert was outside Luna's. We found trackers on my and Houston's vehicles. I put mine on an 18-wheeler heading out of town. The other one is attached to the front porch of Luna's home."

"I called Director Cosby early this morning. He is contacting a judge to get subpoenas so we can look at the crew's income tax forms for the last six years," Fons brought everyone up to speed.

"When will we get them," Sissy asked.

"We should have the subpoenas by the end of the day," Fons said.

"Have you found anything questionable on the list of possible other suspects, Captain Desmond gave you?" Sophie asked Sissy.

I went through all the financials I could find. I didn't see anything out of order. Teresa didn't find anything suspicious on social media either."

"That's good. Let's hope it stays that way. We don't need more bad actors in this story," Sophie said.

"What do you think of bringing Rostova in to question him?" Edwards asked.

"Chief, that will be helpful after we have other evidence. Bringing him in now may be premature," Sophie said. He nodded in agreement.

"What is the plan for today?" Lieutenant Orr asked.

"We need to track them and see if they lead us to some of their clients. It will be helpful for the prosecution when they go to trial," Sophie said. "We also need to have someone go into the evidence room to find out where the drugs Gilbert placed in our SUV came from."

"Lieutenant Dickerson could find a case that would give him a reason to be in the evidence room," Captain Desmond said.

"Good." Sophie turned to Dickerson. Will Crawford be on duty?" Sophie asked.

"He should be off today. If he's there I'll wait until he's at lunch," Dickerson said.

Sissy got the team's attention, "I have found a business license showing that Crawford, Solis, and Zhang are partners in a security company. That could be how they are laundering their money. I'll verify their tax records when the subpoenas come in."

"That would make sense. Can you see if any of these men are regulars at the Vegas casinos? That's how Mason's group laundered their money," Captain Desmond said.

"I'll do that," Matt responded.

"Ok, anyone else with an idea of how they could be laundering money?" Fons asked. It was a long time before anyone answered.

Sergeant Contreras spoke up. "Following up on Mrs. Corban-Mathew's revelation about laundering money through a business. I looked up relatives of the other men in the crew. Kapadia has a brother who owns a trucking company close to bankruptcy four years ago. Then out of nowhere, an infusion of money gave it a second wind. That would be an ideal place to launder money."

"Good catch, Sergeant Contreras," Houston said.

Sophie took one of the black erasable pens and wrote on the window under the pictures of their targets. She marked under each one how they were laundering their money.

"Assuming we are right, Gilbert filters his through a Vegas casino. That leaves Bolan, Rostova, and Gilroy. We need to dig into their lives. Find out who they are linked to," Sophie suggested.

Timms spoke up. "Ms. Star, I have Bolan, Crawford, and Gilbert converging at the Omelet House off North Boulder Hwy. It appears this is one of their days off."

"Major Murphy, do you have anything in your arsenal sensitive enough to pick them up from several tables away?" Sophie asked.

"Yes."

"Alright, head out and get what you can."

"Yes, ma'am."

"He needs a cover. If he's alone, he'll bring too much attention to himself," Edwards suggested.

"You're right. Sissy, can you go with him?" Sophie asked.

"Sure."

Murphy grabbed something out of a black box and ran out. Sissy followed.

"I'll close the garage door behind you," Teresa said, and she and Bully followed them downstairs.

The Major and Sissy pulled into the Omelet House ten minutes later. The sign said to seat yourself, so after they spotted Gilbert and his men, they sat across from them, one back. Flynn sat so he could see them. He had picked up a newspaper from a machine on the way in and took out a section. He placed the directional mic and camera underneath. Facing it in their target's direction.

Sissy and Flynn had earwigs and could hear the conversation. The men kept their voices low. Their meal had come, and they weren't saying much.

"I don't trust Rostova. If he talks, we all go down," Gilbert broke the silence.

"Shut up, Gilbert. We are not going to discuss getting rid of him. Who's to say who you will take out next. Rostova will not talk. If he does, he will end up in jail right next to us," Crawford said.

"Maybe it's time to retire our business dealings. If the Townsends are connected to the DC FBI, they must be on to us," Bolan added.

"Right, and the crooks we protect will just let us walk away. Are you nuts? They can blackmail us into doing it for free. No, we might as well get paid for it," Gilbert snarked.

"He has a point, Bolan. The men we protect won't let us walk away," Crawford said.

"We could bust them one by one over time. We were careful to only work with the top man in each organization. If he gets caught in the crossfire, that's not on us," Gilbert said.

The food Sissy and Flynn ordered came. They tried not to look at their targets and kept their conversation going sporadically.

Gilbert drank his iced tea and swallowed a bite of his omelet. "We need to close the Cox murder case."

"How? Do you plan to turn yourself in?" Crawford said sarcastically.

"No, we need a patsy. As long as Rio's daughter is never found, there will be no one to prove otherwise."

"Who are you going to frame?" Bolan asked.

"I don't know yet. But he'll be found with the gun that shot Rio and Cox. That's all the evidence they would need to convict him. Better yet, if he's dead, there will be no reason to investigate at all."

"That's pretty cold, even for you," Crawford said.

"It's either me or someone else. I vote for someone else. It's a good thing I kept the gun."

That was the last of their conversation. The waitress left the bill and took the empty plates. Bolan, Crawford, and Gilbert paid their bills at the cash register and went on their way.

While they finished their meal, Flynn called command.

"Did you get that?

"Yes," Timms responded. "We have it all recorded. Video and audio."

"Great, we'll be back shortly."

"Now that you filled your belly. How about you bring us some food?" Timms prodded.

"What do you want?"

"Five pizzas ought to do it. Make sure one is pepperoni and olive."

"Don't you think it's a little early for pizza?" Flynn teased.

"Don't even joke about that," Timms said. Flynn laughed.

CHAPTER SEVENTEEN

A pparently, Flynn was the only one that thought it was too early to eat pizza because the five boxes were empty in record time. Bully managed to get scraps from his friends.

"I wish I could say I was surprised Gilbert is willing to sacrifice someone else for his crimes. We'll have to keep an eye on him. He has no problem framing someone posthumously," Lieutenant Orr said.

"I agree, tracking him is not enough. We couldn't stop him from killing someone from here," Sophie said.

"Captain Desmond, who can you trust that is good enough not to get spotted?" Edwards asked.

"Gilbert knows everyone in his own precinct, but Officer Byrd is from another station. If he used his car and wore civilian clothes, he could do it," Desmond suggested.

"Ok, Sergeant Stone, call him in. We'll need to have someone he can trade off with."

"I can do it," Timms said. "I'll need an inconspicuous car."

"It can't come from impound, and it can't be a rental," Sophie said.

"Chief Castro's brother-in-law owns a car dealership. I'm sure he can provide us with a used vehicle," Edwards said. "I'll call him now." Edwards moved to a corner to speak with the Chief.

An hour later, Timms and Byrd had decided that one would follow, and one would run parallel, then they would trade off.

It was four in the afternoon when the subpoenas came in. Sissy and Matt pulled tax records of their targets off the IRS site and were going through them.

Matt said, "we were right about Crawford, Solis, and Zhang. They have an LLC and file a 1065 form with their income tax."

Sophie put a checkmark on the window under each name, showing it was verified. "I have to believe you are right about Kapadia running money through his brother's trucking company too. His brother probably gets a cut to help his business."

"Matt, have you found out if Gilbert runs his money through a casino?" Sophie asked.

"I'm still working on that," Matt said.

"We still don't know how Gilroy, Rostova, and Bolan hide their money," Fons commented.

"Working on it," Sergeant Contreras said.

Houston, Sophie, Fons, Edwards, and Desmond were discussing if the new recording would be enough to bring in the crew.

"Gilbert confessed he killed Cox. Even if he denies it. We have the security footage to back it up," Houston paused. "We need that gun. Once he goes to trial, we want rock solid evidence. The group talking about their rackets is good but not enough on its own. Though the video of them splitting the money is pretty convincing," Houston said.

"Do you want to take the chance and pick them up now or do we want to see what else we can get?" Sophie asked Edwards.

"I think the DA would prosecute the crew on what we have. But I don't think it's a slam dunk for the murders yet," Edwards said.

"We still have the issue of the chain of custody on the security footage, even though it can be forensically proven that it was not doctored. It's still an issue," Desmond said.

"So, we keep going? Are we agreed?" Sophie asked.

"I'd really like to catch them taking money for protection. If we can," Edwards said.

"I agree with Houston, we need that gun," Fons said.

Sissy spoke up. "I know where Gilroy launders his money."

The group moved over to the large screen where Sissy put up a Will and a statement from a trust account. "Gilroy's father passed away ten years ago. Gilroy was eighteen at the time; he had just graduated high school. His father had set up a trust for college. His only asset was a home he owned. But the Will said when it was sold, it was to go into a trust for college. He would get the balance when he turned twenty-five.

"I don't know what Gilroy had on the attorney who was the trustee, or if he offered him money. But it looks like Gilroy gives the attorney his share of the illegal fund, and he deposits it in the trust account. Then the attorney distributes it to Gilroy in $8,000 increments each month. The attorney reports the year's interest from the trust on his income tax, and Gilroy pays taxes on that amount."

"Wow, that is clever. No one will look at that as long as it is reported and the interest portion is paid," Lieutenant Orr said.

"Now, we only need to know how Rostova and Bolan do it," Contreras said.

"Sophie, in order to get pictures of one of the crew taking protection money we first are going to have to know who pays them or follow them. Tracking them won't do it," Fons said.

"I agree, but Sophie and I are compromised. Gilbert knows who we are, and so does Bolan," Houston said.

"You can't follow them, but you could follow Solis or Zhang. As patrol officers, they are free to go all over their district. Same with Detective Gilroy and Detective Kapadia," Fons said.

"Sophie and I can follow Solis. I don't think he was around when we got arrested," Houston said.

"I can follow Detective Gilroy," Fons said.

"Byrd and Timms are following Gilbert," Captain Desmond said.

"Captain Desmond, do we have anyone else we can trust?" Edwards asked.

"I don't think we should bring anyone else in," Sophie said. "Let's follow who we can for now. Our only problem is getting close enough to take pictures without getting caught."

"How do we narrow this down? It would help if we knew who was paying them. That way if one of the others is heading in that direction, we could redirect someone," Fons suggested.

"I can pull up the names of known chop shops and pawn shops that have been on the police watch list," Lieutenant Orr said.

Lieutenant Orr got on a computer and brought up every suspected chop shop and questionable pawn shop. We have probably a dozen underground gambling dens, but we can't locate them."

"Gambling is legal in Nevada. What is the need to do it underground?" Teresa asked.

"If you have a criminal record, you can't get a license to open a gambling establishment. Not only that, but some gamblers like to play with big stakes. Gambling dens have card games with no limits. Casinos are required by law to have limits," Lieutenant Orr explained.

"Then why aren't they shut down?" Teresa asked.

"They tend to move around. But once in a while, we'll catch up with one."

"My guess is Gilbert's crew gets the most protection money from those dens. We need to get intel and locate one," Sophie said. "And I know just the man that can find that out for us," Sophie looked at Houston.

"Axel Urwin," Houston said. "We need to bring him in on this.

"Axel Urwin is a retired investigative reporter. How can he help?" Desmond asked.

"He's been investigating police corruption for years. I'm sure he still has contacts. And before you brought in the FBI, he was helping us find Gilbert's crew," Houston said.

"I know him, and his reputation is stellar. I don't have a problem bringing him on board if you think he can help," Captain Desmond said.

"I know him too. He is an honest man," Edwards said.

Matt spoke up before Houston, Sophie, and Teresa left to speak to Axel. "I've confirmed that Gilbert claims gambling winnings on his tax return. It isn't nearly what he makes, but if anyone asks questions about a purchase, he can claim he used his gambling winnings."

"Good work. Keep digging into Bolan and Rostova," Houston said as they headed out the door."

Axel was happy to see his friends again. It had been a few days.

"I'm glad you came by. I was worried about you," Axel bent down to pet bully.

"We should have told you Teresa was staying with Burly. If you ever need to get ahold of us, you have our cell numbers. Call anytime," Sophie said.

"What have you found out," Axel asked.

"We'll fill you in, but I need to remind you, you can't write about this or breathe a word to anyone until this is over," Houston said.

"I understand the need to keep a lid on this."

Houston filled him in on the names of Gilbert's crew and how they were laundering their protection money.

"I have to say, that's clever. It's amazing how your team was able to track that down. Do you have enough to arrest them now?"

"On the crew, maybe. It's mostly supporting evidence, but we want to make the case rock solid, so we are going to keep working. We don't have the gun that killed Detective Cox, yet," Sophie said. "Though he admitted he has it."

"What about the security tape?" Axel asked.

Teresa answered, "Deputy Chief Edwards thinks a good lawyer could get it tossed out because of the chain of custody issues." She looked at Sophie, "is that right? Chain of custody?"

"Yes. A forensic tech would be able to prove it wasn't doctored, but it's still iffy," Sophie said. "We need the gun. We have a lead on it. But we came here to get your help on something else. Being an investigative reporter, did you ever do a story on underground gambling dens in Henderson?"

"Yes, not long after I moved here. I became acquainted with a man that ran a gambling den from a large, converted RV. He kept the game moving, so the police wouldn't catch him. I explained that I wanted to do a story about underground gambling. He agreed to talk as long as I didn't mention his RV or where I got the information.

"I wrote the story. It made the front page and was picked up by AP and Reuters. Several of the gambling houses were raided by police after that, but I have no illusion others didn't take their place."

"We need pictures of Gilbert's crew taking money from one of the clients they are protecting. My guess is that gambling dens would pay quite a bit for that kind of protection," Houston said.

"Yes, they would. Can you find your source again? If he could give us the location of one den, we could put a camera up to watch the place."

"I have no doubt my source would talk to me again. I kept my promise and put many of his competitors out of business. But he died four years ago. I'm sure someone else took over his business, but I don't know who...however, I know where he lived and his old route. I could see if the RV is still at his house. The person may have bought his house too. It's worth a shot. I can approach him there."

"Axel, no. That would put you in danger. I can't let that happen," Sophie said.

"I'm an investigative reporter. It's more than what I do. It's who I am. I want to do this," Axel insisted.

Houston looked over at Sophie; she shrugged. "Alright, Axel, but I'm going with you. I won't follow you inside, but you'll have to wear a wire, so I know if you are in danger."

"I'm alright with you coming with me. But I won't wear a wire, Houston. If I tell this man, it is off the record, it has to be off the record. I can't have the police shutting him down. It doesn't work that way."

Houston was going to argue with him, but Axel was right. If he gives the man his word, he can't go back on it.

"I could get the police to agree," Houston said.

"No, it's too risky." That ended the conversation.

"Alright, what time do you want to go?" Houston asked.

"The previous owner only worked four days a week, and he started his runs at 4 pm. It would be better to catch him before he goes on the road."

"I'm sure he sleeps in. That RV runs until four in the morning. So, I say noon."

"Ok," Houston said.

"Can you stay for dinner?" Axel asked. They hadn't planned to do that, but Sophie could see he was lonely and proud of his cooking.

"Of course, Axel, we'd love to. What are you offering?" Sophie asked.

"I made empanadas," Axel said with a big smile.

Monday

Houston picked up Axel at noon.

"I'm excited to be back in the saddle again," Axel said as they got in the Lexus.

"Don't push too hard. Sophie will kill me if you get hurt. I'll be outside. You'll have to find a way to let me know if you need me," Houston said.

"I'll be alright."

Axel gave directions to a nice middle-class neighborhood. They stopped at a house in the middle of the block.

"This is it? Where is the RV?" Houston asked.

"In an oversized garage out back. It runs two six-seat card tables. My source vetted all the players and limited the number of drinks they could have. That way, no one could come back to him saying he let them lose all their money when they were drunk.

"He used two drivers; they switched off. They drove out of the city limits and kept the RV rolling through the night. The clients pay a hefty flat fee for the ride, and they get to keep their winnings. He catered dinner and snacks throughout the night. Pure card playing, no showgirls, no drunkenness. It's for serious players with money to burn.

At least that's how Milo, my source ran it."

"Alright, I'll be right out here."

Axel could hear kids playing in the backyard when he approached the front door. He knocked. Axel saw a glint of recognition on the young man's face when he answered the door. But he was sure he had never met him before.

"Hello?"

"Hello, my name is Axel Urwin. I am looking for the man that took over the RV from Milo Oxley."

The young man looked around. He saw Houston sitting in the car. "Who is that?"

"A friend."

"Are you wired?"

"No, I'm not law enforcement; I'm a reporter."

"I know who you are. Come in," the young man moved so Axel could come in. A woman came into the entry. "This is Axel Urwin, sweetheart. We'll talk in my office." The woman nodded and went out to watch her children in the backyard.

Walking into his office, he finally introduced himself. "I'm Milo's son, Brax. He told me about you. He said you kept your word to him. My dad followed your column from then on. He said you were a man of integrity."

"I didn't know Milo had a son."

"I lived with my mother in Sparks. But I spent summers with my father, and he came every week to spend time with me. He supported me, and he and my mom got along. She just couldn't abide what he did for a living."

"But you still took over your father's business?"

"My mother died a few years before dad. I moved here when she did."

"Are you worried about getting arrested?"

"It concerns me, but I take all the same precautions my father did. And I don't plan to do this forever. My wife and I agreed that we would save all of the RV's earnings and live on our day jobs. We are both CPAs. I work that job on the days I don't run the RV. We plan to retire to Sparks and buy a nice house. We'll have enough money to enjoy life and put our kids through college," he paused. "What are you doing here, Axel?"

"I'm here because I'm trying to help a young girl get justice for her father's death. In doing that, I've come across a group of corrupt police. I know they have a protection racket going, among other things. I doubt they would have approached you since you run off the radar. But I was hoping you could direct me to any gambling houses that might be paying protection money."

"I do hear things. But who are you trying to take down, the dens or the corrupt police?"

"Brax, one might end up taking down the other. But it won't touch you. Ending the corruption in Henderson's police is good for everyone. They went too far when they killed a detective and a hard-working diner owner. They crossed a line; they can't come back from."

"Are you talking about the owner of Rio's Diner? My dad and I ate there twice a week in the summers. Rio and my dad were friends. He had two young kids that disappeared. My dad was one of the volunteers looking for them."

"She is the one who is asking for justice."

"Wow, she must be an adult now."

"Teresa is eighteen," Axel said.

"Ok, I'll help, but you have to give me the promise you gave my father."

"Done."

"There are three stationary houses that didn't have a choice but to pay. I can give you their names and the addresses of those shops. I know they pay weekly. They get a text from a burner phone to meet at a certain GPS location. It's usually somewhere in the desert, so they can see if they are followed."

"Do you know how much they pay each week or who they pay?"

"I know they pay $5,000 a week, but I don't know who they hand it to." Brax grabbed a piece of paper from the printer behind him and wrote down the names and addresses. "Turning in my competitors seems wrong, but putting Rio's killer behind bars is the right thing to do."

"I understand, Brax. Thank you." They stood. Brax handed him the paper and walked Axel to the door.

Back in the car, Axel handed Houston the paper Brax gave him. "He knew of three gambling dens that are paying protection. They pay $5,000 a week. A text with GPS coordinates comes from a burner phone for the money exchange."

Houston took Axel home. He promised Axel would get the inside story to publish as soon as the operation was over.

"You'll come back to see me?"

"Yes, Axel, we'll come to see you. I know Teresa will want to say goodbye before we go."

"She isn't going to stay here with her mother?" Axel asked.

"No, she plans to return to where she came from."

Houston handed the paper with the location of the gambling dens to Matt. He put the spots on a city map up on a screen.

"It helps to know the locations and how they pay for protection. But it doesn't get us a way to take pictures of the money changing hands," Deputy Chief Edwards said.

"Major, can one of your drones help?" Houston asked.

"There are a lot of ifs to that answer. If we know one of them is heading to a meet, if we can get there before the exchange is over, and if we can do it without the drone being seen," the Major paused. "You said the meets are somewhere in the desert so that they can see if anyone is following. That makes it difficult, too."

"How high does a drone have to be to not be seen?" Lieutenant Orr asked.

"One of the drones I brought has an invisible coat. Meaning it will reflect whatever color is around it. For instance, it will reflect the sky or the desert and has a stealth mode. I would fly it about a couple hundred feet above and to the side of the target."

"Can we get video and audio from that height?" Edwards asked.

"Yes, on that drone, but I prefer to get closer. If there is cover, like a cactus or tumbleweed, I could land it and walk it closer. But for that, I need time."

"Well, it's all we have. So, let's get these guys covered and see what happens," Fons said.

The task force followed who they were assigned and tracked the GPS on the other crew members until midnight. They took turns staffing the command center through the night.

Tuesday

Solis and Zhang were off. Houston and Sophie still needed to follow Solis. When he was settled at home for the night, Houston took Sophie to Luna's so Bently could go home. Then he went back to keep an eye on Solis until midnight.

"Sophie, I know Teresa said she would never come back here or bring Kato back. But they are my children. I know Teresa is eighteen, but Kato is still a minor. I could insist he comes back here," Luna said as they sat drinking coffee.

"You do have rights, Luna. But is it best for him? He doesn't know you. He has friends and people he considers family where he is. He would have to start over again. And you are still not well. He would be isolated in this house with you. You couldn't take him to the zoo or even for a walk.

"Wouldn't it be better to work on your recovery first? You still have issues you need to overcome. Then you could come to where he is and see what he wants to do. At least that way, you can make a connection with him. It may be possible he would be willing to come out for a few weeks in the summer. And eventually, he might want to come back."

Luna lowered her head, and tears trickled down her cheeks. "It's true. I never bonded with him. I had a severe case of postpartum depression. A chemical imbalance that got worse with every medication they gave me."

"That wasn't your fault. It wasn't your fault, doctors made it worse, either. But you could have come here instead of the shelter when you left the medical facility. You could have recovered here with your family."

"I know that is how Teresa looks at it. But at the time, I wasn't in a place to come home and take care of a family. I wish I had made a different choice, but I can't go back and undo the past."

A text came in from Timms: **It looks like Oscar may be headed your way.**

Sophie read the text and asked Luna, "are you expecting Oscar?"

"No, but he is used to dropping by whenever he wants," Luna said.

"Not to worry. If he shows up, we have men following him. They resumed their conversation.

"I can't tell you what to do, Luna. Kato is your son, but I can tell you he is a wonderful young man with many people who love him."

Sophie heard a car pull up outside. She peeked out the window.

"He doesn't think anyone is with you." After the city agreed to pay for the damage, the rental company came and hauled off the SUV.

"What should I do?" Luna asked.

"Invite him in. But you can't let on that you know what he's done," Sophie knew that Byrd and Timms were outside if they needed help.

CHAPTER EIGHTEEN

O scar knocked on the door. Luna answered.

"Oscar, what are you doing here?" Luna asked.

"You never used to mind me stopping by," Oscar said with a smile.

"Come in," Luna opened the door wider.

"Oh," Oscar said, startled, when he saw Sophie.

"Good evening, Detective."

"Mrs. Townsend, I didn't expect to see you here."

Sophie texted Houston and told him Oscar was at Luna's house. She would let him know what was said.

"Luna, I wanted to update you."

"Great, would you like something to drink?" Luna offered.

"Yes, I'd love some of your sweet tea," Oscar said, dripping in charm.

"Come in the kitchen and have a seat."

Sophie stayed in the living room. The way the house was designed, you could hear everything said in the kitchen with little effort. She also felt he would reveal more if she weren't around.

Luna placed a glass of tea before him and sat down. "What news? Did you find out who put a listening device in my home?"

"Um, no. Not yet. But I have a lead on who may have killed Rio and my partner."

"Really?" Luna was doing an excellent job, pretending to believe him.

"Yes, I got a tip that a mentally ill homeless man who has other incidents of violence had come in to rob the place. Cox tried to stop him, but the man had a gun and shot Cox before he could pull his gun from its holster, then he killed Rio. He was the one that took the money out of the cash register."

"After all these years, you get this tip now?" Luna asked.

"I know, it's crazy, huh. But when it happened, we put out a reward for any information leading to an arrest. The reward is still active."

"Have you located him?"

"Not yet, but I know some places he hangs out. I'm going to start looking for him tomorrow."

"That is good news. Thank you for coming over to tell me. Have you heard anything about my kids?"

"Not yet, but after I get the man that killed my partner, I'll take some time off and look for them."

"No need to do that. I have the Townsends searching for them."

"I don't know how; they've never left Henderson," Oscar snarked.

"They have contacts all over the US. They have people looking."

"Well, I'll be glad when they are gone. I used to like coming to see you."

"Oscar, we talked about that. I am not interested in having a relationship with anyone at this point. I still need to work on myself. I appreciate that you have kept me informed all these years. But that's all there is to our friendship."

Oscar reached out to take her hand. It took everything she had not to recoil. But he needed to think nothing had changed.

"Actually, Luna, I like you. And though you are saying there was no chemistry between us. I know that's not so. And I know you feel it too."

"I'm sorry if I gave you that impression. But I don't have feelings for you."

Oscar pulled back his hand. "The Townsends have poisoned you against me for some reason."

"No, Oscar. I can see how you got the impression I was interested in romance. But I was lonely. I liked talking to you. But it was never more than that. I'm sorry."

Sophie moved to another spot in the living room where she could hear better, but still be hidden from Oscar. She began to wonder if Oscar had real feelings for Luna. She was a very attractive woman and had a trim but feminine figure. Knowing Oscar's type, he probably liked the idea she was still fragile, and he could control her. Sophie knew that kind firsthand from Nikko, a boyfriend who nearly beat her to death.

But something else he said caught her attention. He was going after a homeless man to frame him for the murder of Rio and Detective Cox. He was going to retrieve the gun and kill the homeless man he was targeting, intending to plant the gun on him.

Sophie heard two chairs scrape on the floor. She moved further into the living room before Luna walked Oscar to the door.

"I'll let you know as soon as I've captured the killer, Luna."

"Thank you, Oscar; I'll wait to hear from you."

When the door closed, Sophie called Houston and put the call on speaker.

"Sophie, what was Oscar doing there?" Houston asked.

"You're on speaker, Houston. He came to tell Luna that he was close to catching her husband's killer. Houston, we can't lose him. Are you close?"

"I'm still at Solis' house, but Timms or Byrd are there. I'll call and make sure they don't lose him."

Houston called back right away.

"Yeah, they said he just turned left on Clementine." I'll be there shortly to get you."

Sophie ran out the door when she saw lights in the driveway. She turned to Luna. "Lock this door, and don't open it to anyone." Sophie hopped in with Houston to follow Oscar.

"What did he say, Sophie?"

"Oscar said he knew who killed Rio and was looking for him. That it was a homeless man who came to rob the place. Detective Cox tried to stop him, but the man shot first and then shot Rio. Supposedly taking the money out of the cash register before he left."

"He needs the murders solved. He knows we are connected to the DC FBI office."

"Yes, and he really has feelings for Luna. He thinks if he solves her husband's murder, he will be her hero."

"Wow, I didn't see that coming," Houston said.

"You have your camera, right?

"In the back seat," Houston said.

"Sophie, call Fons; he's still watching Gilroy. Tell him what's going on," Houston said. Sophie made the call.

"Fons. Houston and I are behind Byrd following Gilbert. Timms must be on another road. Gilbert has stayed on Clementine, but we'll have to back off if he goes down an alley or some dead end."

"Where are you now?" Fons asked.

"We are passing the Taco Bell."

"Murphy is staffing the command center right now. Do we need the drone?" Fons asked.

"Put him on notice and call Deputy Chief Edwards. If things get dicey tonight, he needs to be in on it."

Fons called Murphy and told him we might need him to put a drone up.

"I can have the drone in the air in five to six minutes," Murphy said.

"Alright, I'm almost caught up with Houston. I'm going to call Edwards next," Fons said.

"Ok, I'm getting the drone ready now," Murphy said.

"Gilbert is turning on Hwy 582, heading toward the desert. The road heading out there is pretty bare of any other cars. We're going to have to stay quite a way behind,"

"Ok, I'll conference in Murphy, Byrd, and Timms. I'm right behind you, Houston." Fons added the other men to the call.

"We just past the El Torito Café," Byrd said.

"Where is Gilbert going?" Murphy broke in.

"He is turning again onto Hwy 93," Timms said.

"No, he passed the intersection. He's getting off the highway onto Nevada State Drive. Now he is on Conestoga Way," Houston said.

"Oh, this doesn't look good. Do you think Gilbert is going to the casino?" Byrd asked.

"He just turned onto Dawson Ave. There is nowhere else he could be going. Murphy, you need to turn all the lights off in the casino," Houston continued. "He is almost to the frontage road where Dawson Ave turns sharp left to the old casino. He must be after the gun."

"Ok, we need to get a video of him getting the gun. Do you have a night vision camera with you, Major?" Sophie asked.

"Yes, ma'am. I'll watch the casinos outside cameras to see what door he comes in. I hope he doesn't come into the garage. My SUV is in there."

"Alright, we can't follow him any further. He is turning toward the casino." Fons pulled into an empty lot behind Houston. "We're parked on a side street in case you need us."

Sophie spoke up, "Sergeant Byrd, will you text Deputy Chief Edwards to pull over? He was heading to command. Can you see us from where you are?"

"Yes, ma'am."

Fons got out of the car and went to the back of the SUV, where he kept the gear, the team brought from DC. He pulled out three bulletproof vests and handed two to Houston, who handed one to Sophie. Fons put his on and got back into his SUV.

Murphy watched as the camera showed Gilbert driving into the front parking lot of the casino. He headed to the main door, flashlight in hand, and got a key from under a rock not far from the door. Gilbert unlocked the door and turned on the flashlight.

Murphy hurried downstairs; he needed to be closer. He followed Gilbert's flashlight and videoed his movements. Gilbert walked over to a picture on the wall and took it down, revealing a hole. On a cross board between two, two by fours was something wrapped in a red mechanics rag. He needed Gilbert to unwrap the gun so he could get it on video. Luckily, he did. Murphy got the shot, big as day.

Gilbert put the picture back up and headed back to his car, putting the key back and turning off his flashlight.

"Major, tell me you got it on video," Houston said.

"I did."

"Good job. But now we need to see if Gilbert is going after the homeless man tonight or going home."

"I'll get the drone on him."

"Great. We'll fall behind so he doesn't pick up the tail."

"Will you let the deputy chief know he can continue to the command center," Sophie asked Sergeant Byrd.

"If Gilbert goes home. I can keep the drone on him through the night. If he's going after a fall guy, we need to stop him before he kills somebody," Murphy said.

"Yeah. Let's see where Gilbert is going," Fons said.

They followed Gilbert for fifteen minutes while he headed back to town.

"It looks like he's headed home. He lives in that area," Murphy said, watching the drone footage.

"We'll keep following," Houston said.

"The deputy chief just walked in, Miss Star," Murphy said.

"I need to fill him in. Murphy, will you put your cell on speaker?"

"Yes, ma'am."

"Chief, we've been following Gilbert. He went to Luna Nuñez's home tonight. He said he got a tip on who shot her husband and his partner. We knew he had to get the gun from where he stashed it to frame someone, so Houston and I joined Timms and Byrd and followed him. The gun was stashed at the casino."

"You're kidding. He hid it at our command center?" The chief asked.

"Yes, sir. Major Murphy had enough time to shut down all the lights. Fortunately, he didn't go through the garage. He entered the front door with a key hidden under a rock. He took a

A CRY FOR JUSTICE

picture off the wall, and behind it was a hole where he had stashed the gun. Murphy got it all on his night vision camera."

"Excellent."

"Chief, do you want us to stop him now and arrest him? It's your town that will be affected if Gilbert kills somebody to frame him."

"Are you certain he plans on killing someone?" Edwards asked.

"Yes, we are confident. Gilbert plans to kill a homeless man and plant the gun. Then he can use the gun as proof he was the murderer. There is no other way it will work. The man has to be dead, or he would deny it.

"Our question is, do you want to pick up Gilbert now, or try to catch him kidnapping the homeless man?" Sophie asked.

Houston broke in, "My concern is he may say he received a tip that led him to the gun if we pick him up now."

"I agree. But if Gilbert gets to that homeless man before we do..." Edwards said.

"I know, sir. It will be on you," Houston acknowledged.

"What is the opinion of your team?" Edwards asked.

"There on this conference call, sir," Murphy told him.

"Can you add Captain Desmond to the call?" Edwards asked Murphy.

"Yes, sir." It took a minute to get Captain Desmond on the line. The deputy chief had Sophie replay what happened tonight for Desmond's sake.

Captain Desmond spoke, "sir, Mr. Townsend is right. All Gilbert has to say is that he got a tip and retrieved the gun. Even if he didn't use department protocol in retrieving it, we couldn't convince a jury he killed his partner. We already know the diner's security footage is only good as supporting evidence. And if we get the wrong judge, it could even be thrown out because of the chain of custody issues. If we don't catch him in the act, a jury may not believe he is a cold-blooded killer. Even with Teresa's testimony, there are shrinks out there that will say that an eyewitness's testimony is not reliable. The defense will certainly put a psychologist on the stand that will confirm that opinion. A DA may not want to move on it until we have more."

"What do the rest of you think," Edwards asked.

"He is right, Deputy Chief. We need to wait," Major Murphy said. Fons, Byrd, and Timms agreed. Sophie did not like taking a risk with a man's life.

"Make sure you're wearing vests. Gilbert will have nothing to lose if he is cornered," Desmond said. Where is he now? Is he heading home?"

"It looks that way. But I see on the map the city has a small dog park a couple of miles in the same direction. A lot of homeless camps are on city property," Byrd said.

"Alright, let's stay connected," Edwards said.

As they got closer to Gilbert's house, they were convinced he was headed home. He started to pull into his driveway. The tail cars didn't follow him onto his street because they would have been spotted, but the drone followed him. Murphy called out what the drone was seeing.

"He is almost at his house. Wait, he's stopped at the curb. He's not going home. He is headed to that park. I'm sure of it. Go down the next street; it parallels his road. We have to get to that park before him."

Sophie turned to Houston. "We can't get this wrong. I couldn't live with the fact we let an innocent man get killed."

"I know, Sophie," Houston agreed.

Houston got to the end of the street. Gilbert would have to turn left in front of them to get to that park. He turned right.

"Deputy Chief Edward, where are the homeless encampments in your city? He's not going to the one by his house."

"We have three that the city cleans up after—all city parks around town. We designated the southwest portion, of Roadrunner Park, past Fox Chase Street for the homeless. And Paradise Park on McLeod Drive also has a portioned set aside."

"We need to head to Roadrunner Park first," Sophie said.

When Captain Desmond walked into command, Edwards turned to him and ordered, "Captain, call the rest of the team. Take them off whatever they are doing and give them directions to meet up with SAC Rodriguez," he paused. "And, Major, can you connect them all on this line?"

"Yes, sir."

The Major used the drone to give the team a play-by-play of Gilbert's every move.

"I think he is heading to Roadrunner Park," Murphy said. "We have everyone conferenced in now. Matt and Sissy are in command with me, along with Captain Desmond, and Chief Deputy Edwards. Everyone else has been read in and is headed to Roadrunner Park, Ms. Star," Murphy said.

"Matt, can you send us a live feed of the park? We need to see if there are places to hide," Sophie explained.

They traveled another ten minutes in the direction of Roadrunner Park.

"He is on So. Racetrack Rd. He's pulling into the Casino parking lot. Maybe he is just there to gamble." Byrd remarked.

"Maybe, but the park is within walking distance. I don't think that is a coincidence," Timms said.

"Ok, everyone, park in the back of the Casino parking lot. Murphy, let us know if he is going inside," Fons said.

"Will do."

"Do you think he's there to gamble?" Fons asked Houston and Sophie.

"I don't know, but the drone can't follow him in to see what he is doing," Houston said.

"But I can tap into the casino's internal security cameras," Sissy jumped into the conversation.

"Won't you need a warrant for that? Is it legal?" Sophie asked.

"Do you want to ask that question?" Sissy answered.

Sophie knew the deputy chief was listening. He didn't object, so Sophie answered.

"No. If Gilbert goes inside, we need to track him."

As the rest of the team parked around the casino, Houston and Fons parked closer to Roadrunner Park. The drone followed Gilbert to the casino door; then Sissy brought up the feed from the casino's security system. She sent it out to everyone's cells. They all watched Gilbert walk through the casino and out the back door.

"What's he doing?" Murphy asked. The video from inside the casino went dark on everyone cells, as Sissy disconnected from their security.

"He must be making sure he isn't followed. The Roadrunner Park is within walking distance," Fons said.

"Wait. There is a man outside smoking. He is looking at Gilbert. It would be best if a couple of you went over there. He doesn't look like a homeless man, but who knows," Edwards said.

The drone was in stealth mode, so Murphy landed it behind the dumpster that was close by. It had a perfect view of the two men.

"Ok, team, Fons and I will watch them. I don't think Gilbert will kill a man behind the casino. It's too visible; anyone could step out to smoke.

"I need the rest of you to head to the park and stay out of sight. This may not have anything to do with our case," Houston said.

Houston asked Sophie to wait in the car, and he and Fons hurried to the back of the casino. They spotted Gilbert talking to a young man smoking a cigarette. They could see the young man was wearing a vest and a name tag from where they stood. He was a casino worker.

"Murphy, we need to hear the conversation; patch us into the drone." Fons requested.

"Doing it as we speak."

"Hey there, Ivan," Gilbert said.

"What do you want, Oscar? I only have a ten-minute break."

"Hey, watch your tone with me. I want you to remember something in case I need you to testify for me in court."

"I don't do court," Ivan said.

Oscar grabbed the young man's lapel and pulled him close. "You listen to me. I own you. You should be in jail for selling opioids, but you're not. You have a good job, freedom, and extra cash from me. So, don't tell me what you will or won't do."

"Alright, already. Back off. What is it you want me to remember?"

"Two days ago, you were out here smoking. You saw two homeless guys about twenty feet from you, talking loud enough for you to hear. One of them said that a detective was asking about Magic. The other guy said, do they know he killed that detective? Then the first guy said he didn't think so. He just said he was looking for him."

"There is no way I'm going to remember all that," Ivan said.

"Yes, you will. Then you say you called me and gave me the guy's name. Magic."

"Are you going to pin something on that poor guy? Man, you are supposed to be the police. Not a goombah," Ivan said.

Oscar slugged the kid in the face, and the kid fell to the ground. He put his hand to his lip. It was bleeding. He took out a handkerchief from his pocket.

"Why'd you do that? It hurt. How am I supposed to explain this?"

"I don't care. You listen to me. Just do what I told you."

The young man got up and went back into the casino. Gilbert headed to the park on foot.

"Sissy, we need to see where each of the team is. Can you put up a grid and send it to our cells."

Sissy assigned each man a color with an initial and sent it to the team.

"Team, it looks like Gilbert is walking the outside perimeter of the encampment."

"Lieutenant Orr, does Detective Gilbert know this man?" Sophie asked.

"Yes, he is a repeat offender. He spent at least ten of his fifty years in jail. Generally, in short spurts, for theft, and on occasion assault."

"Does he have mental issues?" She asked.

"Yes, he had been diagnosed as a paranoid schizophrenic. He has medication, but he only takes it when he is in jail."

"That's why Gilbert is targeting this guy. The charge of assault and mental illness will make it look like he had no choice but to protect himself."

Murphy broke in, "Gilbert has stopped at the back of a tent. Are you seeing this?"

"I'm switching to the live drone feed you sent us now," Fons said.

"He's slicing the back of the tent," Houston said.

"He is checking to see if Magic is in there," Contreras added.

"Ok. I need the team to move closer to that location without being scene." Houston headed toward Magic's tent like the others.

"I will land the drone behind him far enough away that he doesn't see it. Then I'll walk it up closer so we can get a good look at what he is doing."

CHAPTER NINETEEN

Gilbert waited patiently for over an hour for Magic to turn in for the night. When he did, Gilbert stuck his head into the tent through the rip and pointed the gun at him.

"I need you to come with me, Magic."

"Whoa, whoa, what's this about? I ain't done nothin' detective."

"I said move," Gilbert kept his voice low but menacing.

Magic stepped out of the back of his tent and stood. The full moon shone off his bald head. They may have been a match in height, but Magic was easily thirty pounds heavier and more muscular. But the gun was the great equalizer. Magic complied.

Murphy lifted the drone from the ground and followed from behind.

"What's this all about? I'm telling you, I ain't done nothin'."

"Remember that detective and the diner owner that got shot three years ago?"

"Yeah."

"You shouldn't have killed them," Gilbert said.

Magic stopped and turned toward Gilbert, "no. No way I killed Rio. He set out a bag of food for me every day at three o'clock. He even left me a large cup of Coke with ice. I liked him. Why would I kill him?"

"Well, here's the thing, cameras in the area show you were in the vicinity. You couldn't help yourself; you wanted the money in the cash register."

"No. I'm bein' straight with ya. I didn' do it," Magic yelled at him.

"Keep your voice down. The problem is I'm the only one who knows that, Magic. And since you are going to resist arrest. I will have to shoot you, and mine is the only story anyone will hear. Now turn around and keep walking."

"What is he going to do? Walk him to his car and drive him somewhere quiet?" Contreras asked.

"No, that makes no sense. He would be seen on the casino cameras," Timms said.

"If he shoots that gun out here it will bring a lot of attention," Fons said.

"What do you think, Sophie," Matt asked.

"He has to make it look like he was arresting Magic, and he resisted. He's going to say that he heard Magic was at the encampment and came to arrest him. The casino cameras are exactly what he wants. He wants the cameras to show Magic attacking him."

"But he needs Magic's cooperation for that," Houston said.

"You can see Oscar hasn't put cuffs on him and keeps provoking him. Magic will figure his only choice to live would be to fight. Oscar wants him to make a move. He has him under control with his hand tightly around Magic's arm, right now. He will loosen his grip when he is ready for Magic to try to get away. That is why Oscar told Magic he was going to kill him.," Sophie said.

"I get it. Gilbert parked in the back of the lot on purpose to be in view of the cameras but far enough away not to catch everything clearly. He'll make sure the camera is at his back where it can't get the whole story. He'll shoot Magic with his service weapon, then put the gun that killed his partner in Magic's dead hand. That is devious," Lieutenant Dickerson said.

"It's Machiavellian," Lieutenant Orr said.

"I do believe Gilbert *is* a psychopath," Sophie said.

"Alright, team, I need you to find a way to converge on Gilbert's car without being seen," Fons instructed.

Sophie was switching back and forth between watching the drone footage on her phone and keeping an eye on the grid that showed everyone's locations.

"Deputy Chief Edwards, I don't feel we can take the chance of letting them get too close to Gilbert's car. My gut tells me he will leave room for Magic to fight him before he puts him in the car. We need to take him down before that," Sophie said.

"I agree, Mrs. Townsend."

"Team, take him down when he gets twenty feet from his car," Sophie instructed.

"Copy that," the team echoed.

Sophie could see Houston and Fons walking parallel to Gilbert. They were on the edge of the parking lot, past where the lights could reach.

Contreras, Orr, and Stone ran down the alley ahead of them to get on the other side of Gilbert's car. Timms, Byrd, Dickerson, and Navarro hid behind vehicles in the parking lot one aisle over.

"Houston, you give the order," Fons said.

"Ok, men, he is still about fifty yards out. Let's stand by for now," Houston said.

The team had their guns unholstered and ready.

Houston could feel his heart racing in his chest. He knew this was risky. But this was the job. Even though he no longer worked for the task force. He would do his part to keep his team safe. Houston's grandfather was a WWII vet. He told him more than once. The soldiers in the foxholes weren't fighting for some vague ideology politicians spew out from their safe homes, away from the front lines. They fight for love of country and the men and women next to them in the foxhole. He understood that.

Sophie was praying that their plan would play out without any casualties. She switched to the drone feed again. The men were holding their positions. She saw Gilbert was close to the twenty-foot mark.

"Team, when he reaches the mark, Fons and I will step out of the shadows and have our guns on Gilbert. That will be your signal to reveal yourselves. He may surrender if he knows he's outgunned. The best scenario is that he gives up without a fight," Houston said.

The team waited for Houston's cue. There was silence from the command center. When Gilbert hit the mark, Houston and Fons revealed themselves.

"DETECTIVE GILBERT, DROP THE GUN AND MOVE AWAY FROM MAGIC. GET DOWN ON YOUR KNEES WITH YOUR FINGERS INTERLACED BEHIND YOUR HEAD," Houston hollered.

"What do you think you're doing, Townsend. You are interfering with a legal arrest..." Magic butted in on Gilbert's lies.

"No, man, it ain't true. He's going to kill me. He's trying to frame..."

Gilbert hit him in the head with the butt of his service weapon, but Magic didn't go down.

"Look around you, Gilbert. We know it was you who killed your partner and Rio. We have it on the security tape," Fons said.

Gilbert looked around and saw all the men pointing their guns at him.

"Lieutenant Orr, you know me. I'm one of you. I got a tip Magic was the one who shot my partner, and he admits he was at the diner that day..."

"To get the food..." Magic tried to explain.

"Shut up, Magic. No one believes you. I'm glad you are here. You can help me get him into cuffs and take him downtown. The chief will give us all medals for capturing a cop killer."

"Gilbert, we have video of you getting the gun from behind the picture at the abandoned casino," Byrd said.

Gilbert knew they had him. He had to find a way to get out of this. He had plenty of money to live well in a tropical paradise.

Gilbert put Magic in a chokehold and put the gun to his head. "Move out of the way, or I'll kill him."

Houston stepped forward, "what's the point, Oscar? You can't get away from all of us. Put the gun down."

"I know the regulations. You have to back off if a civilian's life is in danger. So, BACK OFF!"

What are you going to do? You can't get him in the car without exposing yourself. You don't want to die, and neither does anyone else here," Navarro said.

Gilbert knew that was true. He needed to get back over to the encampment. Letting off some rounds would get all the homeless out of their tents, and he could get lost in the crowd.

"Back up. I don't want to kill any of you, but I will. A cop doesn't stand a chance in jail," Gilbert tried to keep Magic in front of him. He started walking backward toward the darkness.

"We can't let you go, Oscar. DROP THE GUN," Lieutenant Orr yelled.

"BACK OFF, OR I WILL KILL HIM! You know the rules." Gilbert kept walking backward. He had a long way to go. He didn't know if he could keep control of Magic that long. He noticed cars parked not far from the homeless camp. He headed that way.

Sophie was watching the feed and saw Gilbert backing up toward the encampment. She locked the door, grabbed the keys from the ignition, and scooted down in her seat. If she got out and tried to run, it would add to the chaos, and Gilbert might get startled and shoot her.

The men were still following him. He'd have to make them take cover so he could get in one of the cars. He was getting close to a Lexus. The windows were tinted, so he didn't see anyone at first. He tried the driver's door, but it was locked. As he continued backing up, something caught his eye through the windshield. There was someone inside. He pointed the gun at her face. "Unlock the door."

"That's Axel's Lexus, Fons. Sophie's in there. We can't let him take her." Houston and Fons started running toward Gilbert.

Sophie knew she had no choice. The glass wasn't bulletproof. She unlocked the door.

Gilbert saw how close Houston and the others were getting. He shot at Houston first and missed. Then shot at Dickerson and hit him in the leg. Dickerson went down. Gilbert shot a few more times and then opened the door.

"Where are the keys? Put them in the ignition and start the car, or I will shoot your husband, and I won't miss this time."

Sophie reached over, put the key in the ignition, and started the car. Houston was running full out now, trying to get to Gilbert.

Gilbert shot and hit Houston in the chest. The bullet knocked him off his feet. Fons kept running. He knew Houston had a vest on, and he couldn't let Gilbert take Sophie hostage. The others were too far away.

Gilbert shot at Fons. Fons instinctively ducked. It gave Gilbert time to let go of Magic and get in the Lexus. He put his left hand on the steering wheel with the gun pointing at Sophie. Using his other hand, he put the car in drive, and stomped on the gas, burning rubber. He drove the car into the desert behind the encampment with his lights off. Fons kept running after the car, but he was too far behind.

Even though Fons knew everyone saw what happened. He still said it out loud. "Gilbert got away in the Townsends Lexus with Sophie in it."

Timms ran over to Houston to make sure he was alright. He made sure the bullet didn't go through the Kevlar, then helped him up. Houston was in pain but ran beside Timms to get to Fons.

"We're going after them, Deputy Chief Edwards. Call dispatch and have the State police shut down the roads crossing into Arizona. Make sure they know he has a hostage," Houston headed to Fons' car while Fons got in the driver's seat.

Houston looked over at him, "Fons..."

"I know. We'll get her back," Fons said as he started the engine and headed into the desert.

By the time all the men got in their vehicles, Gilbert had a two-minute lead on them.

The sand Gilbert's car dusted up made it impossible for the cars behind him to see. They had to stay far enough behind for the sand to settle. On the other hand, Gilbert couldn't see if anyone was behind him.

"Please tell me your drone is still on him," Houston said.

"It is. Check your feed. Gilbert is driving without lights, but if I keep the drone above him, I can turn on a red light for you to follow. He won't be able to see it."

"There's the red-light, Fons," Houston pointed. "If he can drive without lights, so can we. We don't want him to know we are on him. Does everyone have eyes on the drone," Houston asked.

Everyone acknowledged they had a visual on it.

Sissy broke in, "I've locked into the GPS on the Lexus. Between the drone and the GPS, we won't lose him."

"Thank you, Sissy," Houston said. "Who got hit?"

"Dickerson, sir," Officer Stone said.

"Is he on the way to the hospital?" Houston asked.

"No, sir, he's in the car with me. He refuses to go to the hospital until we get Mrs. Townsend back."

"Lieutenant Dickerson, are you on the line?"

"Yes, sir."

"You need to go to the hospital and get that wound taken care of."

"But, sir, we need all hands on deck."

Houston softened his voice, "you've done your part, Lieutenant. Get your leg taken care of."

"Yes, sir."

"Sergeant Stone, stay with him until someone from his family comes. Then head back to command."

"Yes, sir," Stone said, then turned the car around, heading for the nearest hospital.

Sophie had to figure out how to get out of this car, she considered jumping, but he was going fifty miles per hour. Even landing in the desert instead of asphalt, she could do real damage. She was tempted to keep her seat belt unbuckled in case an opportunity arose. But the way he was driving, they could end up in an accident. Gilbert was losing it, becoming unstable. He was mumbling to himself. Sophie carefully pulled her phone out from where she slid it under her leg when Gilbert got in. She lowered the volume and turned off the screen light so Gilbert couldn't hear her dialing Houston. She was confident the drone was following them. Sophie needed them to be able to listen to the conversation in the car, in case Gilbert gave a clue to where he was headed.

Houston saw Sophie's name come up on his cell screen. He told the group he was dropping off the conference call and clicked over to Sophie.

Houston didn't speak; just listened. He knew she would try to get messages to him about Gilbert's plans. If she did, they could try to get to the location ahead of them. He put her on speaker so Fons could hear.

"Oscar, what are you doing?" Sophie asked.

"Shut up. This is all your fault. No one would have ever figured out I killed Cox and Nuñez until you came to town and stirred everything up. You turned Luna against me."

Sophie stayed quiet for a while, hoping Gilbert would calm down. When Oscar almost hit a cactus, she spoke up.

"Why don't you get on the road? How do you even know where you are going."

Oscar nodded toward car lights on a road parallel to where they were. "As long as I can see the highway, I know where I am."

"Where are we going, Oscar? Do you even have a plan?" Sophie asked again.

Oscar knew it was over, there was no reason to keep his secret any longer. "When I got the text that my partner was working for Internal Affairs. I knew it was only time before they found out some of us had a little business on the side. I hoped to make it to 20 years like Philip Mason. He retired and disappeared to Florida without ever being on IA's radar.

"I've been working on an escape plan since that day at the diner. I spent my vacations in the Bahamas. I deposited my money in a numbered account while I was there. Not all of it, the rest I would take to the casinos and claim some winning, so the IRS wouldn't start digging into my income."

"Are you following your plan now?" Sophie asked.

"Yeah, I have a safe house in the mountains. We'll stay there for a while. The police will assume I left the area. After a few days, they will take down the roadblocks. I'll move to the second stage of my plan."

"Agent Mathews, you know Mrs. Townsend. Can she keep her head about her while being held hostage?" Deputy Chief Edwards asked.

"Miss Star was in a much worse situation, when I met her. She knows what she is doing. Sophie has an inner strength that carries her through the worst of times."

"Captain Desmond, make sure the roadblocks are up at the border," Fons said.

"Yes, sir, and Mrs. Corban-Mathews is searching for properties in the mountains. He must have a new identity stashed away. It will take her forever to find the property until we have it."

Fons' cell was on speaker, so Houston could hear the team. "Timms, do you have ears?"

"Yes, Houston, I'm here."

"Go back and tear apart Gilbert's car; maybe we can find something. Chief, he'll need a warrant."

"Yes, sir." Timms turned around and headed back to the casino.

"Chief, we need someone to search Gilbert's house. He must have a safe," Houston said.

Edwards turned to Captain Desmond. "Christian, you go."

"Yes, sir. Lieutenant Orr, meet me at Gilbert's house," Desmond said. Lieutenant Orr made a big 'U' turn in the desert and headed back to town.

"I'll have a digital warrant for the house and the car by the time you arrive. I'll call the evidence technicians; they can meet you at the house. We can't take any chances evidence can be thrown out," Desmond said.

Captain Desmond and Lieutenant Orr arrived at Detective Gilbert's two-story colonial home in an upper-class neighborhood. The evidence techs were waiting outside for them.

"Sergeant Arias, thanks for getting here so fast," Desmond said.

"Deputy Chief Edwards said it was urgent."

"It is. We'll need to break in, but let's do as little damage as possible," Desmond said.

"Yes, sir, we have a Halligan bar."

Once the door was opened, Desmond told the sergeant he and Orr would take Gilbert's office.

"We are mainly looking for a safe. It could be in the floor or on a wall. We need anything you find with a name other than Oscar Gilbert," Desmond explained.

"Call out, if you or your men find anything," Desmond said.

Oscar's office was on the main floor. Contrary to what they do in TV police dramas, they did not throw things around, making a mess. Doing that ran the risk of missing something important. Desmond went through Oscar's desk while Orr hunted for a safe or a hidden compartment and checked the bookshelf.

"If we do find a safe, we will have to wait for *our guy* to open it. I'm going to call him and have him head this way," Desmond decided.

"Good call," Orr agreed.

The team had been following Detective Gilbert for forty-five minutes now. Gilbert drove onto the highway about twenty minutes earlier. The team staggered their entry onto the road behind him. Houston was a quarter mile behind him and turned his lights on. The car behind him kept them off and the next car turned them on, going back and forth. They didn't want Gilbert to look in his rear-view mirror and see a caravan following him.

"You are on your own, Mrs. Townsend. I've lost your husband. You weren't as important to him as you thought."

"How much longer are we on the road? I need to go to the bathroom. You know I'm pregnant, right?"

"You're going to have to hold it. We're still a couple of hours away from my cabin."

"Now that you have lost your tail, you no longer need me. Why don't you drop me off on the side of the road? That way, I could never tell anyone where your cabin is."

"Nice try, Sophie, but I'll keep you until the next stage of my plan is in play."

"Then you'll let me go?"

"Sure, I'm not a murderer. I would never have killed Rio if he hadn't seen me kill my partner. I felt bad about that."

"You didn't seem to mind killing Magic. That was your plan, right?" Sophie asked.

"Magic is a menace to the community. I would have been doing a public service," Oscar said.

"You don't get to make those determinations."

Gilbert didn't answer. He was looking at something behind him. Sophie turned to see what he was looking at.

"That's strange," he said.

"What?" Sophie asked.

"There are a few cars behind us. They seem to be keeping pace. Travelers usually go faster than the speed limit on this road. I'm surprised one of them hasn't passed me yet."

"Maybe they don't want to get a ticket."

"Maybe, we do put speed traps on this road occasionally."
"Do you think it's the police?"
"No way. They would have chased me down by now."

A CRY FOR JUSTICE

CHAPTER TWENTY

The team decided to switch out the lead car randomly, thinking the difference in the car's front lights would look natural.

"Matt, Sissy, have you found the cabin?" Houston asked.

"No, there are cabins all over the mountains. I'm going through the tax roll to get names. Matt is checking their background to make sure who they are. It's a slow process. We need Captain Desmond to find something at Gilbert's house," Sissy said.

"Timms, what have you found in Gilbert's car?" Houston asked.

"Nothing that will help us, but he does have a stash of cocaine. I'll put it in an evidence bag and catch up with you."

"No. Go back to command. Stay there. We might need you for something else," Houston said.

"Will do."

"Should we take him down now? I'm not sure taking him down at the cabin will be safer," Fons said.

"The only way we could take him down now is to have a high-speed chase. That's too risky, Fons," Houston said.

"Not necessarily. We could have the State Patrol put out a spike strip."

"Gilbert could lose control of the car. We can't take any chances with Sophie in that car."

Navarro broke in, "what if the State Patrol moves the roadblock closer to our location. Once no cars are coming from the other direction, our team could pull up on both sides of him. He'd have nowhere to go."

"I understand, but Gilbert could blast through the roadblock or bypass it through the desert, and he would know we were following him. The safest thing for us to do is follow him to where he's going," Houston said, turning to Fons. "Sophie's pregnant. I won't take any chances. I want him out of the car when we take him down."

"Ok, I get it. I'm not sure how much safer it's going to be. He'll have her as a hostage inside his cabin," Fons said.

"Not if we take him into custody before he gets inside."

The other team members didn't give their opinions. It was Houston's wife at risk. It had to be his decision.

"Alright, Houston, it's your call," Fons let the subject drop.

Captain Desmond and Lieutenant Orr found nothing in Gilbert's office. Desmond had gone through his computer but found nothing that led him to an alias. They headed to his bedroom.

"Captain Desmond, we have something," Sergeant Arias hollered from the garage. The two men rushed to his voice.

"What do you have?" Desmond asked.

"The safe. It's drilled into the cement floor. Gilbert had a stack of large plastic containers covering it."

"Has our safe cracker gotten here yet?" Orr asked.

"I'm here," he heard from the living room.

"We're in the garage, Rocha," Orr hollered.

Rocha was arrested for attempted robbery of a jewelry store five years ago. His partner disarmed the security system, not realizing the store had redundant alarms.

Rocha was an expert safe cracker. He could crack any safe anywhere. The Chief of Police asked the DA to make a deal with

Rocha. He wanted to use him to open safes for the police department. The *would-be* thieves were arrested before they even breached the jewelry store door. The DA gave them each a year in a minimum-security prison on the condition Rocha worked for the police when they needed him. Rocha agreed, and when he got out of prison, he found a good job as a consultant for a company that built safes.

"What do we have here?" Rocha asked, walking to the floor safe. He checked it out and opened his bag of tools. He had it open in three minutes.

"Thanks, Rocha, now step back. We are racing against time."

"If that's all you need from me, I'll go. I left my girlfriend at the movies," Rocha said.

"Yeah, you're done," Orr said while Desmond pulled everything out of the safe."

"Do you want us to keep looking," Sergeant Arias asked.

"Yes, we need anything that is incriminating," Desmond said.

"Copy that."

Desmond set the contents of the safe on the plastic boxes that once hid it. They went through every item. He found insurance policies, ten thousand dollars cash, and two flash drives, along with other papers.

"Go check these out on Gilbert's computer," Desmond ordered, handing Orr the flash drives. Lieutenant Orr hurried out of the garage.

Desmond was still sorting through papers when he came across a receipt from a passport agency in Las Vegas. It was a receipt in the name of Jaxon Maddox.

"There is no way you can leave the country, Oscar. Your name will be flagged at every form of transit," Sophie said.

"You think I'm stupid? I know that. I have a new identity."

"But you didn't have time to go back and get it."

"I figured if I got caught, that would be the case. I stored a *go bag* at the cabin. Your friends will be searching my house, but there isn't a trace of my new identity there. Sorry to disappoint," Oscar looked over at Sophie and laughed.

Sophie was watching the road signs. US Hwy 93 split into US Hwy 95 outside of Boulder City. But Gilbert stayed on 93. They were pretty close to the Arizona border. She saw the sign that the border was twenty miles ahead. She knew there would be a roadblock.

Gilbert got off the highway two miles before the border, turned off his lights, and got on a dirt road. The road went a mile into the desert and then crossed the border.

Sophie figured the road must be used by drug traffickers. She had no idea when they crossed the border since the desert looked the same. He drove two more miles on the dirt road, then made his way back to the highway and turned his lights back on.

Captain Desmond headed to Gilbert's office. "I got it. A receipt in Gilbert's alias," he told Orr, then repeated it for command.

"Deputy Chief, I have it. His alias is Jaxon Maddox."

"Copy that. Mrs. Coban-Mathews is searching now," Edwards responded.

Captain Desmond took a picture of the receipt and handed it to Sergeant Arias. Chief Edwards told them to head back to the casino command center.

"Found it," Sissy hollered. "He is heading to Kingsman, Arizona. The cabin doesn't have an address, but I have GPS coordinates."

"How is he going to get over the border. You have all roads into Arizona blocked, right?" Mathews asked.

"The State Patrol is handling it," Edwards said.

Houston broke in, "He just got off the highway. He is running with his lights off through the desert to bypass the roadblock. Timms, I need you to get on a helicopter and get to that GPS location before they get there."

Timms asked Deputy Chief Edwards, "can you get us a chopper?"

"Yes, I'll call it in. Give me ten minutes," Edwards was already on the phone. "Land in the old casino parking lot," he told them.

"We are going to need a few more men, Houston," Timms said.

"I'll go with you," Matt said.

"Captain Desmond and Lieutenant Orr should be back soon. They'll go with you," Edwards said.

Sergeant Stone was walking into command and heard what was happening. "I'll go with them."

"Good. When you get there, wait for Gilbert alongside the house. We can't let him get her inside. We should be right behind him," Houston directed.

The team agreed not to get off the highway to follow Gilbert in the desert. They knew they wouldn't lose them because the drone was still following. They called the State Patrol to tell them Gilbert had bypassed the roadblock. They asked them to remove it, so they could come through without slowing down.

The team passed the roadblock without incident. Houston was getting physically ill from worry. This wasn't the first time he had been in this situation where people he loved were in harm's way. He came to the same conclusion every time. Their lives were in the hands of Jesus, and only He controlled the outcome.

When Gilbert got back on the highway, Sophie asked, "How much longer? I told you I need to go to the bathroom."

"We'll take a turn here in fifteen minutes. Then another half hour and we'll be at the cabin.

Houston began to pour his heart out to the Lord. He shared his fears and acknowledged his need for Jesus. Houston told Him how he trusted Him to take care of his wife. He prayed that Jesus would cover Sophie and the team with His blood. And that no harm would come to his unborn child.

Though they knew they were on an open line, Fons started praying with his best friend and partner. He could hear Timms' voice added to the prayers. One other voice came on the line. Fons didn't recognize it but welcomed it. Other than the prayers, the rest of the team remained silent out of respect.

Lieutenant Orr was raised by educators. Everyone in his family were Professors. He chose another path. His family did not approve. His parents had tenure at the University of Nevada in Reno. His sister and brothers worked for the University of Nevada in Las Vegas.

Whenever guests mentioned religion, his parents had no problem telling them exactly what they thought. Explicitly, that the Bible was just another history book with misinformation. They said no way Jesus was born of a virgin. 'Religion is for the weak-minded and those that can't manage their own lives,' he heard more than once.

Lieutenant Orr had started to read the Bible once. He loved the stories in the Old Testament. But to him, that was all they were, stories no different than any other book of fiction. But the men he heard praying were not weak-minded or afraid to face life. These men lived their lives with their eyes wide open. Houston was a man's man, a warrior in a battle, and mentally astute. Same with Special Agent Timms and SAC Rodriguez. He had never met a true believer before. And Sophie was brilliant, maybe even a genius as a strategist. And from the stories the task force told him, she was a warrior in her own right.

Houston didn't know how long he prayed when the Holy Spirit gave him peace. He changed his prayers from intersession to praise. When the Spirit of the Lord lifted, he quieted.

When Sissy heard the prayers end, she spoke up. "Gilbert just turned off Highway 93; he is now on Interstate 40, heading towards Kingsman."

"Thanks, Sissy. How far behind them are we?"

"Maybe four minutes. The helicopter came for Timms, Matt, Sergeant Stone, Captain Desmond, and Lieutenant Orr."

"Can they get there before Gilbert?" Fons asked.

"Yes, they think so, and they will approach from behind the cabin."

"Keep us up to date," Houston said.

"The team is still connected," Sissy said.

"Anyone have word on Dickerson?" Houston asked.

"Not yet. Sergeant Stone said he was in surgery when his wife and mother came, so she left. I'll let the team know," Edwards said.

Sophie hadn't spoken for the last half hour. Gilbert turned off Interstate 40 a few minutes earlier. He turned again on CR 20. The mountain road had no signage and was winding through the mountains, making the going slow. Clouds covered the moon, making it too dark outside to see anything.

"How much further, Oscar?"

"You are worse than a little kid. We are still fifteen minutes out."

Sophie knew she couldn't let him take her into the house. Once inside, it would become a fortress. With a hostage, the team would be restrained in their response.

Sophie started to devise a plan. She knew the team was following them but likely would only get there after he took her into the house. It was dark enough outside that if she ran fast enough into the darkness, she could hide until Houston came.

There was no safe place to land the helicopter, so the men lowered their gear down with ropes. Then fast roped down the twenty-five feet to the ground.

Agent Timms waved the helicopter off, and the men grabbed their gear. They double-timed it to the cabin one mile east of where they landed.

"Command, we are on the ground and heading to the cabin," Timms reported.

"Deputy Chief, we are going to need a warrant to search the cabin after we have Detective Gilbert in custody," Captain Desmond said.

"You'll have it," Edwards replied.

"How do we want to do this?" Lieutenant Orr asked Timms.

"We can't let Gilbert take Sophie into the cabin. He'd be able to hold us off for hours or even days. He knows we can't put the hostage in the line of fire.

"Houston asked that we stay hidden on the side of the house. Gilbert will be relaxed and unguarded when he arrives. He has no idea we know where his cabin is. When he gets out of the car, we need to be as close to him as possible before we make our presence known," Timms suggested.

"That's a sound plan." The others agreed.

Gilbert turned onto an overgrown dirt path. Unless you knew it was there, you wouldn't happen upon it. About a mile down the driveway, a log cabin appeared. No light or signs of life were seen.

"Is this your cabin?" Sophie asked.

"Yeah. I've only been here a couple of times to bring what I needed to leave the country."

"You knew this day would come?"

"No. I thought I'd be able to retire. But you know the old adage from Robert Burns' poem. 'The best laid schemes of mice and men often go awry.' I figured I better be prepared." Gilbert turned off the engine and put the keys in his pocket. "Alright. I'll come around and get you. Don't get any idea about running. There are mountain lions out here and coyotes. Besides, there are no other cabins for miles. You would get so lost that no one would ever find you."

Sophie knew Houston wasn't far behind. If she did run, she wouldn't have to go far. Just far enough, he couldn't see her. She felt a check in her spirit not to do it. She decided to listen.

Agent Timms and Matt were on the left side of the house, Desmond, Stone, and Orr on the right. They saw the lights from Gilbert's car coming.

"Let's let him get far enough away from the car that he can't jump in and drive off," Agent Timms said.

"Copy that."

Gilbert opened the car door; the dome light came on. Sophie's face came into view. She looked unharmed.

Houston and Fons reached the path to the cabin. Fons pulled off the trail as far as he could, and they walked the rest of the way. The rest of the team did the same, just behind them.

Detective Gilbert was at the front of the car. He took two more steps before the men stepped into the car's headlights and into view.

"GILBERT, STOP RIGHT THERE AND PUT YOUR HANDS IN THE AIR!" Agent Timms yelled. The team moved closer to Gilbert.

Sophie locked the door so Gilbert couldn't get back in.

Gilbert was shocked. He looked like a deer in the headlights. He was not expecting this.

"How did..."

"GET YOUR HANDs IN THE AIR. WE WILL NOT TELL YOU AGAIN," Lieutenant Orr yelled.

No, no. He didn't have a move. His gun was in the back of his belt, but he would get shot if he reached for it. He needed to get Sophie in the line of fire. He started moving slowly to the passenger's side of the car."

"STOP!"

"You can't shoot me with my arms up. I don't have a weapon," Gilbert lied. The men followed Gilbert's move.

Houston and Fons could hear the exchange. They needed to get behind Gilbert without being seen.

"Timms, Fons and I are going to sneak up behind him."

"Copy that."

Gilbert kept moving closer to the passenger door.

"STOP MOVING!" Desmond yelled.

"I'm no threat to you. You can't shoot me."

Timms could see Houston and Fons out of the corner of his eye. He made no movement to give them away.

Contreras, Byrd, and Navarro were circling around the perimeter. They needed to get closer before Gilbert made a move.

"Maybe not, but I have no problem shooting you in the leg and taking the heat," Timms said. "NOW STOP MOVING!"

Gilbert stopped moving, not sure if the threat was real. "I won't go to jail. You'll have to kill me, and you have no cause."

Houston was less than ten feet behind Gilbert before he heard him. Gilbert turned and pulled his gun from behind him. Houston ran headlong into him, tackling him to the ground, before he could get a shot off. They were struggling. Houston was trying to get the weapon from Gilbert. Fons grabbed the hand with the gun and wrenched it until he gave it up.

Houston and Fons were able to bring Gilbert under submission. Sergeant Contreras had a pair of handcuffs and tossed them to Fons to restrain him.

Once Gilbert was in custody, Sophie unlocked the door. Houston opened it to help her out.

"Are you alright, sweetheart?"

"I knew you were coming for me, Houston," she kissed him as he held her tight. "My prince charming," she chuckled in his ear.

"Always, princess."

"Now you have to stop hugging me so tight. I wasn't kidding. I have to go to the bathroom, really bad."

He loosened his hold on her, but before he let her go, he put his hand on her stomach, "how's our baby?"

"Our baby is fine, but his mother won't be if I don't get to a bathroom." She patted his hand on her stomach.

"We can't enter the cabin until the warrant comes," Houston said.

"Agent Timms, I need to use the bathroom now," Sophie hollered.

"Let me see if the digital warrant came through," Timms checked his text."

"I don't...wait, it just came through."

Houston and Sophie headed to the cabin. The lock on the door was flimsy, so Houston leaned hard into it, and it opened. He found a light switch and then helped her find the bathroom.

Chief Castro contacted the Arizona Sherriff's Department. He needed to inform them they apprehended a felon in their jurisdiction. Since Gilbert committed a felony and the Nevada Police crossed the border in a fresh pursuit. They didn't need extradition papers or consent. But it was common courtesy, and they would likely need to work with the Sherriff's Department again.

Captain Desmond called for the return of the helicopter to pick up Gilbert. It had returned to command to pick up evidence techs. They needed to get Gilbert processed and put behind bars. Houston wanted Sophie to return on the helicopter to Henderson, but she refused.

The task force would return after the scene was processed.

The men searched the cabin and were still amped up from the chase. They were running on adrenaline from the arrest of the man who murdered Detective Cox. Houston stayed close to Sophie to ensure she was as *fine* as she said.

"I need to call Teresa and Luna to let them know we caught Oscar Gilbert."

"I saw a wicker loveseat on the front porch. It's too noisy in here," Houston said, following her outside. Fons called his name, and after Sophie was seated, he went back inside. Sophie called Teresa first.

"Miss Sophie, where are you guys. I couldn't reach anyone. Mom said you ran out of there after Detective Gilbert visited her. Mr. Burly and I have been praying for you. We had no idea what was going on."

"The prayers were needed, Teresa. She was right, after Gilbert left, Houston, and I followed him. Right now, I'm in a cabin in the mountains outside of Kingsman, Arizona."

"What? How did you get there?"

"The short version is we caught Gilbert red-handed. He planned to kill a homeless man and plant the gun that killed your father on him. He led us on a chase to where we are now. But we got him, Teresa, with enough evidence to put him away for life." Sophie heard Teresa take a big breath. She started crying.

"You got him?" She asked through her tears.

"Yes. He is in custody."

"No one got hurt?"

"Lieutenant Dickerson was shot in the leg, but he is at the hospital getting taken care of."

"Miss Sophie, I don't know how to thank you and Mr. Houston..."

"No need. Getting justice for your father was the right thing to do. Can you call your mother and let her know Gilbert is in custody? And tell Burly, Axel, and Bently too."

"Yes, I'll do it right away. You're coming back here tonight, right?"

"Yes, but we will likely stay in our room at the hotel tonight. It will be late when we get back. It's safe to stay at your mom's tonight if you like."

"Yeah, I might do that."

"Is Bully alright?"

"He is, but he must have sensed something was wrong because he's been sitting by the door whining."

"Will you put the phone on speaker, so I can speak to him?" Sophie heard her call Bully. She put the phone on speaker.

"Sophie is on the line, Bully." Bully's ears perked up.

"Bully, you are a good boy. Take care of Theresa, ok?" Sophie said. She heard Bully bark.

"He's so excited he's wagging his whole body," Teresa's attention went to Bully. She put the phone on her chair, got down in front of Bully, and started scratching under his ears. "Yes, you are such a good boy." Bully began to lick her face. Sophie heard her say, "He's fine now, Miss Sophie. We'll see you tomorrow." The phone disconnected.

Sophie took a deep breath, and tears fell. The stress of the night finally caught up with her.

CHAPTER TWENTY-ONE

Fons led Houston into the main bedroom in the cabin and showed him what they found. In the bedroom was a small pile of clothes and shoes. They stepped around it to the empty closet and found an open trap door. Lined up next to it was a large pile of money, a passport, a driver's license, and credit cards in a plastic zip bag along with some keys.

"These look like keys to a car and a boat," Houston said.

Navarro and Contreras started going through the papers. Among them were names of overseas banks and account numbers. They found a title to a Silver Star 48 liveaboard, located in a storage facility in Corpus Christi, Texas.

"He must have planned on holding up here until the roadblocks were gone, then driving to Texas to get his boat and take off to places unknown," Contreras told the other men.

"That's what it looks like," Fons agreed.

"How did you find the stash, Sergeant Navarro?" Houston asked.

"When I was searching under the clothes, bent over, my cell fell out of my pocket. When it landed on the trap, it sounded hollow. That's when I cleared the closet and searched for a way to open it. There wasn't anything to grab, so I started pressing in different spots, and it popped open."

"So, dumb luck?" Fons said as they all laughed.

"Sophie has to see this," Houston said and headed outside. He saw her crying and sat beside her on the outdoor loveseat.

"What's the matter, sweetheart?" He asked as he held her.

Sophie laid her head on his shoulder. "The stress of tonight is catching up to me, Houston. I'm fine. I thought we were done with this sort of thing when we left the task force."

"I did too. Do you think it was a mistake to agree to help Teresa?" Houston asked.

Sophie didn't answer for a moment, "no. It was the right thing to do. We'll have to accept that even as private investigators, we may end up in situations like this." She lifted her head to look at him. "Are we sure it's what we want to do?"

"Tonight, is not the night to ask me that, but if you don't want to, I'm ok with that. I want you to be happy and be safe." Houston said as he wiped away tears from her cheeks. "As soon as the techs come and fingerprint the Lexus, I'll get you home."

"I'm going to stay out here a while," Sophie said.

"Sergeant Navarro found a trap door in Gilbert's closet. It had his papers, cash, and keys to a boat. Do you want to see it?"

"I don't think so, sweetheart. I want to sit here for a while. I like how the cool breeze of the mountain air feels on my face."

Houston went back inside. Fons noticed Sophie wasn't with him.

"Where's Sophie?"

"She's processing. Sophie's a strong woman, but being a hostage takes a toll."

"For sure. Once we close down the command center and do our action reports, it's likely that we'll be called back to DC. When are you heading back to Austin?" Fons asked.

"I'm going to leave that up to Sophie. I want her to be totally rested before we leave. As soon as the Lexus is released, I'll take her to the hotel."

Lieutenant Orr approached Houston and asked if he could speak to him privately. They stepped outside and walked toward the Lexus.

"How can I help you, Lieutenant?" Houston asked.

"I was raised by an atheist. My parents and my siblings are all educators. They don't believe in God and believe the Bible is a book filled with fables intermingled with some historical events. I fell into that pattern too, but somewhere deep inside, I wondered."

"We are all born with an instinct to search for God, he is our creator, and the one created always searches for its creator. But unfortunately, like yourself, life can crush that desire."

"Yeah, I can see that. But today when I heard you praying. That was real, I'm certain of it. It stirred something inside me. You have something I don't have. My folks always told us religion was for the weak-minded who couldn't face life head on. But you guys are not how they describe," Orr said.

"I had the advantage of being raised in a Christian home. It never crossed my mind that God didn't exist. But I did struggle with my faith when I became a DEA agent. I didn't take the time to stay in communion with God and found myself leaning on my own understanding. I may have stayed in that state had I not seen someone else dependent on God for her very life. She made me realize how important it is to recognize that we can't go through this life on our own. But 'through Christ' we can do all things,' as the scripture says."

"Are you talking about Sophie?"

"Yes."

"But how do you know that God is real, Houston. I mean, really know," Lieutenant Orr asked.

"To start with, you take it by faith. You start reading the Bible, and He will make himself real to you. The Bible says,

'And the Word was made flesh.'" It's saying that the Bible became alive in the form of Jesus. And even though we believe by faith, you will feel him in the flesh."

"I want to believe. I don't know how."

"First, you have to believe that Jesus is the Son of God and that he shed his blood on the cross to pay for our sins. We all have sinned, and when sin is in our lives, we lose connection to God, because God cannot look upon sin. The only way to reconnect with our Father is through the blood of Christ. Christ died to give us life. When we become born again, God sees us through the cleansing blood of his son. His blood makes us spotless in God's eyes. We first have to believe, and then we have to repent of our sins and give our lives over to Him. It's simple. You could do it right here."

"Now?" Orr asked.

"Yes. If you are ready."

"I don't know that I am yet."

"That's alright. When you're ready, you know how to repent of your sins and ask Jesus into your life. If you do, please let me know. I'll be praying for you."

Before Lieutenant Orr could respond, they heard the helicopter coming with the evidence techs. Houston needed to talk to them. He wanted them to search and print the Lexus first so he could take Sophie home.

"Cameron, do you have a Bible?"

"I have a small New Testament, somewhere."

"I'll get you one when we get back. Start by reading the Word. It will talk to your Spirit. If you have any more questions, call me, you have my number."

The helicopter found a place to land a mile down the road. Sergeant Stone, Captain Desmond, and Sergeant Byrd drove

Gilbert to meet it. Captain Desmond and Sergeant Stone took custody of Gilbert and escorted him back to Henderson to process his arrest. Byrd drove the evidence techs back to the cabin.

It was one in the morning when Houston pulled into the Marriott Residence. Sophie fell asleep almost immediately after they left the cabin. She woke up when he opened her door.

"I'm sorry I wasn't more company on the long drive home," Sophie said.

"I'm glad you were able to sleep. You had a hard night."

When they got to their room, they headed straight for bed. But Houston couldn't sleep. He left the task force so Sophie wouldn't be in this position again. Maybe being private investigators isn't the right move for them. But what would they do? Neither of them needed to work. They had plenty of money to live comfortably for the rest of their lives. But could they live without a purpose? He wasn't sure. He needed to talk to the Lord about it. The Lord's opinion was the only one that mattered.

Houston got out of bed and went into the living room. He knelt down using the couch as his altar and prayed. He needed guidance. He wanted to have a purpose in his life; they both did. But he wasn't sure anymore what that purpose was.

Houston prayed for over an hour before falling asleep, kneeling on the floor with his head on the couch cushion. He hadn't gotten an answer.

Wednesday

When Sophie woke up in the morning, she saw that Houston was out of bed. She headed to the bathroom, then went to look for him. She saw him asleep on his knees. Sophie went to him, sat on the couch, and whispered.

"Love, you need to wake up," she ran her hand down his cheek.

Houston opened his eyes, "good morning, sweetheart. I must have fallen asleep."

"What had you so troubled you had to pray in the middle of the night?"

"I'm wondering if being private investigators is the right move for us. We left the task force so you wouldn't be in harm's way, and here we are, out of the frying pan, into the fire," Houston said. Sophie chuckled.

"While you were praying, I had a dream."

"What was it?"

"You and I were walking in a beautiful garden. We were so happy. You carried our little girl on your shoulders as she held onto your head. She was laughing."

"We're having a girl?" Houston asked with a huge smile on his face.

"I don't know for sure. But in the dream, our baby was a girl. Anyway, we were so happy. As we walked, I could hear these voices crying out to us. 'Why won't you look for us? We're missing.' It was disturbing. I ignored the voices, and we kept walking. Then I heard a voice say, 'What you do unto these little ones, you do unto me.'

"I wasn't sure what that meant, then I heard another cry. 'Why won't you come to find me? I'm lost'. That's when I realized they were missing persons, calling out for help.

"I know you are concerned for me. And after last night, I wasn't sure I wanted to go through that again. But, Houston, who are we if we aren't willing to put ourselves at risk to save others? Can we live so selfish a life?" Sophie asked.

Houston didn't say anything for a long time. He knew what he prayed last night. He needed to know for sure what direction to go. Now he knew. He still wasn't sure he could live with the idea that his wife's life could be in danger again. But he asked for the Lord's will. How could he turn away from the answer?

Houston tried to get up from the floor, but his legs were asleep. He couldn't stand, so he scooted onto the couch next to Sophie.

"I want you to tell me exactly what you are saying," Houston said.

"I'm saying we were on the right path, becoming private investigators specializing in missing persons. If some danger comes along with it, then we will have to do what we always do. Put our lives in the Lord's hands. He knows the number of hairs on our heads. Who better to trust."

"Then it's settled," Houston said.

"I agree." They sat silently for a while, then Houston said, "Lieutenant Orr asked me about being a Christian last night."

"He did? How did that come about?"

"He heard Fons, Timms, and me praying. We were still on an open line. We heard another voice praying, but I didn't recognize it. Cameron said he was raised in an atheist family but often wondered if God existed.

"I walked him through the road to salvation. He said he wasn't ready to turn his life to Christ yet. I encouraged him to read the Bible and if he changed his mind someday to let me know."

"It never fails. When we are in a major battle, Jesus always finds a way to use it to lead someone to him. I hope he makes the right decision," Sophie said.

"Me too. We need to get dressed and head to the casino. We have after-action reports to do for Deputy Chief Edwards, and I want to help tear down command. But first, I need to stop somewhere and get a Bible for Cameron."

"I'll make breakfast," Sophie said.

"No, you get ready. It takes you longer. I'll make pancakes."

Sophie kissed him on the cheek. "Thank you, darling."

Houston and Sophie were heading to pick up Teresa and Bully. She was going to call her to see if she was staying with her mom when her cell rang.

"Sophie, Teresa stayed with me last night. She said you arrested Oscar. Is that true?"

"Yes, Luna, we caught him trying to frame a homeless man for the murders. We have everything on tape. He won't be getting out of this."

Luna was quiet for a moment. "Thank you."

"The team took him down, but I'll relay the message."

"Bently, Teresa, and I want to put on a special dinner for the task force tonight at the diner. Please let everyone know they are welcome and their wives or girlfriends."

"That's very thoughtful, Luna. I'll pass it on. What time?"

"Six would work for us," Luna said.

"Will you ask Teresa if she wants to come to the command center with us?"

Sophie could hear her ask Teresa. "Teresa said she would stay and help me at the restaurant today."

"Ok. We'll stop and pick up Bully when we head out," Sophie said.

Everyone else was already at the casino command center when they arrived. After the team made sure Sophie was all right, they passed on the latest news.

"Chief Castro and Deputy Chief Edwards had us arrest the Gilbert's crew last night. They feared the news of Gilbert's arrest would leak, and the men would run," Captain Desmond told them.

"Are you charging them with murder?" Sophie asked.

"Yes. Even though the others didn't agree to the murders. They are culpable because they perpetrated a felony leading to Rio's and Detective Cox's death," Deputy Chief Edwards explained."

"Sir, Axel Urwin was critical in helping to solve this. He should get the inside scoop on how it developed for his article."

"I agree, Houston. I'll tell my men they can feel free to talk to him."

"Thank you, sir. But no one can mention the task force from DC was even here. Their names can't be mentioned," Houston said.

"Director Cosby told me the task force team was classified. Can they talk about you and your wife?" The deputy chief asked.

"Yes, we no longer are a part of the task force."

Sophie got everyone's attention. "Luna, Bently, and Teresa would like to invite you all to dinner at Rio's Diner tonight at six. They said your families were welcome, too.

Houston helped the task force pack up all their equipment and carry it to the vehicles. He spoke to Fons as he shut the back of one of the SUVs.

"Fons, you guys will stay for the dinner, right?"

"After briefing Director Cosby, I told him we would leave tomorrow. He was fine with that. Are you still going to pursue the detective agency?"

"I spent the night praying about it. When Gilbert took Sophie, I could only think of getting her back or die trying. Fons, I'm not ashamed to say how scared I was. We quit the task force for just this reason."

"Does that mean you've changed your mind?"

"I was leaning that way, but this morning Sophie told me she had a dream. She said we were walking in a garden and heard voices crying out to us. 'Why won't you look for us? We're missing.' Then the Lord said, 'What you do unto these little ones, you do unto me.'

"The Spirit of the Lord in me gave confirmation. It was my answer. So, long story short, yes, we are going forward."

As they headed back up to the mezzanine, Lieutenant Orr brought down police equipment. "Houston, do you have a minute to talk to me?"

"Sure," he said, then turned to Fons. "I'll meet you back upstairs." Fons nodded and took the stairs two at a time.

"Houston, I wanted to tell you I couldn't sleep last night after we spoke. When I got home, I searched for the New Testament Bible I had and read it for hours.

"What I read became real to me. Like you said, it was a living Word. My eyes were opened, and the words penetrated my soul. I knew it was true. All of it.

"I knelt and asked Jesus to forgive my sins and to cover me with his cleansing blood. Then I said I knew he was the Son of God and that he died for my sins and rose again and now is with the Father, making a place for us to be with Him forever."

Houston grabbed Lieutenant Orr and gave him a big hug. "I'm so happy for you. That moment will change your life forever. You will never be the same. Get ahold of Burly. He goes to a great church."

"Thanks, Houston."

"Wait a minute." Houston opened his car door and pulled out a bag. "Sophie and I wanted you to have this," he handed it to Cameron.

Cameron opened the bag and pulled out a box. In it was a new marron color, leather Bible. He looked up at Houston. His eyes watered, "thank you, Houston."

"You're welcome, Cameron," they hugged again and returned to work.

As Houston headed back upstairs, he thought about his burden to pray last night. Maybe it was for more than his own future. He laughed to himself; *that's just like Jesus, to turn near tragedy into triumph.* He couldn't wait to tell Sophie.

One whole section of the diner was full. Sergeants Stone and Contreras were on the second shift but got permission to take a two-hour lunch.

Axel published part of the story of the capture of Detective Gilbert and the corrupt officers taking protection money. It wasn't the whole story. He needed to talk to the rest of the men involved with taking them down. He wanted to know how they felt about arresting one of their own. His piece this morning mentioned there would be more to come.

Teresa helped her mom serve the guests while Bently cooked ribs and chicken on the BBQ out back.

The chatter was loud, and laughter and banter could be heard throughout the evening. Bully made the rounds to get his share of attention and scraps.

Teresa stood to speak.

"My mother, my brother Kato, and I, can't begin to thank you for getting justice for my father. We loved him so much. His death changed our lives forever. Only by God's grace did we land in the open arms of people who love us. My brother and I are now safe to live our lives in the open. Thank you all."

As the others visited over dessert and coffee, Burly, Bently, Luna, and Teresa sat in a booth signing the paperwork on the sale. Luna had already transferred the two hundred thousand to Teresa's account. The balance of two hundred thousand would be paid in yearly increments. After signing over Rio's Diner to her mother and Bently, Luna asked.

"Teresa, won't you please stay? I love you. I want you with me." Burly and Bently left so they could have a private conversation.

Teresa reached for her mother's hand. "Mama, I love you too, but I have to go back. Kato needs me, and I have a life there too. I don't think Kato will ever come back here."

"Will you tell him about me?" Luna was crying.

"Yes, of course, mama. And I'll ask him if he wants to visit. But I don't think he will," she paused. "Mama, try to get well, then you can visit us. He can get to know you."

"Will you ask him if he will talk to me on the phone?" Luna asked.

"Yes, we can Facetime."

"Thank you. I love you so much," Luna got up to hug her daughter.

"I love you too, mama. Get better," Teresa held her mom and cried.

No one wanted to leave. Most had never been on a task force like this and had bonded over it. Sophie heard Burly and Axel talk about having breakfast at the diner in the morning. She hoped they would form a close friendship. They were both widowers and needed companionship.

Finally, all the local police, Burly, and Axel left. Fons and the task force stayed a while to visit Houston and Sophie.

It was always hard to say goodbye to such good friends.

Teresa decided to spend the night with her mother again, so Houston, Sophie, and Bully went to their hotel room.

A CRY FOR JUSTICE

CHAPTER TWENTY-TWO

Thursday

Houston and Sophie met their friends at Rio's Diner for breakfast. Burly and Axel were already there. Bently was cooking, and they all ate breakfast together.

As Sophie sat down, she said, "I love breakfast." Houston laughed. "What?" Sophie asked, staring at him.

"Sweetheart, you love breakfast, lunch, a mid-day snack, dinner, and a late snack," Houston laughed. Sophie gave him *the look* the task force had seen many times in the old command center. They all laughed.

Teresa asked Houston if telling her mom where they were living was safe.

"Teresa, you are no longer in any danger. You can tell whoever you want," Houston replied.

Before Burly and Axel left, Teresa wanted to thank them.

"Burly, you helped us without asking questions on the worst day of our lives. Kato and I will always owe you a debt. And Axel, without your help, I don't know how we would have been able to put papa's killer in jail. Thank you."

Teresa stayed and helped her mom at the diner. Houston and Sophie went to see their friends off at the executive airport. An FBI jet was landing to pick them up.

Everyone repeated their goodbyes. It was hard knowing they would likely never see some of them again. Bully got his fair share of goodbyes, too. As the others carried the equipment to the jet, Fons stayed behind to speak with Houston.

"Houston, get busy finding a place for our detective agency. Carol and I want to come as soon as you call for us."

"I will, partner. We don't want to do this without you." They hugged, and Fons picked up his duffle and a large hard-cover equipment case and headed to the jet.

Houston, Sophie, and Bully watched the jet taxi and get airborne before leaving. They decided to go to Police headquarters to see Deputy Chief Edwards.

They didn't have an appointment, but when the new assistant told him they were there, he came out to greet them.

"Come in. Please have a seat. We've been busy cleaning up after Gilbert and his crew."

"I see you replaced your assistant," Houston said.

"I fired her this morning, Margret sent down a replacement an hour ago."

"What's going to happen to Rostova? He did walk away from them," Houston asked.

"Too little, too late. The DA did offer him a lesser sentence if he gave us the names of the businesses that paid them protection. I haven't heard yet if he took the deal."

"Will they all get life?" Sophie asked.

"Not likely, even though we charged them with murder. The others weren't present when Gilbert murdered Detective Cox and Rio Nuñez. They had no foreknowledge or the opportunity to stop him. But they will get at least 15 to 25 for racketeering. I can live with that. What I couldn't live with was the two unsolved murders, one being a fellow officer, and the corruption in our ranks.

"I don't know that we would have ever gotten to the bottom of this without you. We owe you a debt."

"You don't owe us anything. We were glad to help. If you ever have a missing persons case. You can always call on us."

"Will do. Are you leaving today?"

"Yes, we need to get back to Austin."

"Teresa isn't staying?"

"No, it's too painful for her. I can't imagine seeing your father shot in front of you and kneeling in his blood as you watched him die," Sophie said.

"Yeah, I can't imagine that either."

After a moment of silence, Houston and Sophie stood and said their goodbyes.

They made one more stop at Axel's house.

"Come in, come in. I'm working on my articles in the atrium. Do you want something to drink?" Axel offered, then bent down to ruffle Bully's ears. "I'll get some water for Bully."

"No, we just wanted to return your Lexus and say goodbye. I'm sorry there are so many miles on it. I had it washed and detailed and filled the gas tank."

"That wasn't necessary but appreciated."

"I read your articles, Axel. It's excellent reporting," Houston said.

"AP and Reuters have picked it up. It's gone national. I still have three more articles in the works. One of them is about you guys," Axel said.

"You're the one who deserves the attention, Axel. You got us started on the right path," Sophie added.

"From what I've been told by the rest of the task force, you were the brave one, being taken by Gilbert," Axel said.

"If you are ever in Austin, call us. You have our number. We want you to stay with us," Sophie said.

"Is that where Teresa and her brother live too?"

"Yes."

"I'll want to do a follow-up story someday. People will be wondering what happened to them."

"Luna and Bently purchased the diner from Teresa. They aren't changing the name," Sophie said.

"Good, I like eating there. Burly and I plan to have breakfast there together, often. We're going fishing this weekend," Axel lowered his head. He was going to miss them. "Let me give you a ride back to your hotel."

"Thanks, Axel, for everything," Sophie said.

When they called Ricky that morning, he said he would arrive by three that afternoon. It was coming up on two. Houston called for a taxi. They stopped at Luna's to pick up Teresa.

It was hard to watch Luna saying goodbye to her daughter. She cried as Teresa got in the taxi. Teresa was in tears too.

On the plane, Sophie went to speak with Ricky in the cockpit. He asked if Teresa had found what she was looking for.

"She found justice for her father. That was what she wanted. But it was a little more complicated than that. I think after Teresa explains everything to Kato, she plans on telling her story at the next BBQ.

"But I will tell you she saw her father murdered by a police detective, who also shot his partner in her father's diner."

"What? That's horrible," Ricky said, glancing over to her.

"Her father told her to run with his dying breath. She grabbed what she could, taking the security video that showed the murder and she and Kato hid in the back of a truck with a canopy. Luckily the man who found them in the back of his pickup was a good man. He told them he would take care of them. He was an attorney from Henderson, he was traveling, doing lectures at law schools. Austin was his last stop. Teresa knew they couldn't go back with him, so while he was gone, they left.

"You know the rest. Sienna found them on the bench behind her bakery."

"I feel so bad that they had to go through that."

"I think now that she feels she did right by her father she can start to put it behind her. The diner was left to her in his Will. When we got there, we found that her mother had come back, and she was running it. Teresa sold it to her and the man who had helped her father run it. She will have college money for them both with enough left over to help them get a good start in life."

Ricky sat quietly for a while absorbing the information. Then he said, "Uncle Jared is renting a yacht again so we can see the 4th of July fireworks on the water. He might be bringing a girlfriend to the BBQ Sunday."

"What? I don't remember Uncle Jared ever dating."

"Oh, he always dated, but he never found someone he wanted to introduce the family too. The one time he did Aunt Anna knew the woman and told Uncle Jared she was married. Apparently, the couple had been separated for a few weeks before Uncle Jared met her. He was angry. You know he would never date a married woman. That was the last time we ever saw her."

"How come we never knew any of this when we were kids?" Sophie asked.

"He's always been pretty private about his personal life."

"Yeah, but I can't believe we had no idea," They both laughed.

"Your coming, right?" Ricky asked.

"Of course. Wouldn't miss it," she paused. "Who are you bringing?"

Ricky hesitated, "you probably won't remember her, but I invited a girl to come to Jared's to swim with us the summer before seventh grade."

Sophie had to think about it, "yeah, a pretty girl with thick dark brown hair she wore in pigtails. I remember you had a crush on her."

"No, I didn't"

Sophie laughed, "yes you did. Did you date her in high school?"

"No. Her father got a promotion and they moved to Dallas before the school year started. But I ran into her when I was at the courthouse to file some paperwork. She was waiting there too. I took a number and looked around for an empty seat and recognized her. I sat next to her. I invited her to come with us on the forth."

"That's awesome. What's her name?"

"Deanna," Ricky said. "Now you are up to date on the gossip," Ricky smiled.

Teresa heard Sophie laughing with Ricky. She moved to the seat across the aisle from Houston.

"Uncle Houston... Is it alright if I call you that?"

"It will make me very happy if you think of me that way."

"What should I tell Kato?"

Houston thought about it for a few seconds. "I think he deserves the truth. Don't you? You don't have to tell him every detail, but he should know."

"Bently thinks I was too hard on my mother, but she left us, and Kato doesn't know mama at all."

"I can't imagine how hard that was for you, but everyone has a right to know their mother. Your mother never bonded with Kato. But your father did, and they had a real father son relationship. But you were the female he bonded to. You were there to hold him when he got hurt. You rocked him to sleep when he cried, hugged him, played with him. His bond with you was formed as a comforter, and protector. The role a mother generally has. That will likely never change. It may take some time for him to accept her. But Luna does love him, and he should know that. Even if he acts like it doesn't matter. Knowing his mother didn't just abandon him is going to make a difference in his life."

"I guess so. I believe she loves him. What happened to her wasn't her fault. But it will take me time to forgive her for not coming back."

"Forgiveness will come. Just make sure you do your best to give a positive picture of your mother to Kato. He needs her, even if he doesn't know it yet."

"Thank you, Uncle Houston. That makes sense."

In just three hours, Ricky was driving them all home. Now it was time for Teresa to explain to Kato everything that happened.

FROM THE AUTHOR

Thank you for reading 'A CRY FOR JUSTICE'. I like the new characters in this book. The good and the bad.
I always try to show that people are complicated. Including the bad guys. Usually, one can find some moral compas in everyone, even in an antagonist.
I would say, though, that Oscar Gilbert might be an exception to that rule, as I could not find many redeeming qualities in him. But good or bad, without repentance no man will see God.

If you enjoyed the book, please write a review. I'd love to hear your comments.

Thank you. An remember if you tell others, you are a Christian, be sure to live the life that makes them believe it.

L.J.

BOOKS IN THE SOPHIE STAR SERIES

Dangerous Obsession
Unintended Consequences
Flesh Peddlers
Seize on the High Seas
A Cry for Justice.

Sophies Story

The One Who Stayed
The Promise
Sophie's Table
The Best of Friends
The Guardians
Broken

www.ingramcontent.com/pod-product-compliance
Lightning Source LLC
Chambersburg PA
CBHW030648260626
47157CB00007B/2546